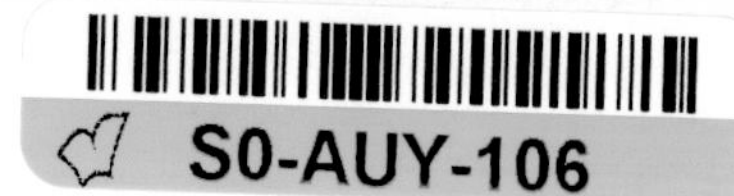

Praise for Vivian Arend's *Diamond Dust*

"Arend proves once again that no matter the genre, she's a master."

~ *Lauren Dane,* New York Times *bestselling author*

"Fights, power struggles and romance are intertwined into an entertaining story that revolves around a non-shifting human! [...] I found myself totally involved with the story and I really had no desire for it to end. Now, to wait for the next one...or find the previous ones which I haven't read!"

~ *Night Owl Reviews*

"I had a lot of fun reading this book. It was extremely well written, and the dialogue was warm and witty. I found myself smiling more and more as I read along."

~ *Long and Short Reviews*

"Where for me to begin? How about with a general statement of how much I enjoyed this book. It's hard to believe, but for me this paranormal series just keeps getting better with each new release."

~ *Literary Nymphs*

Look for these titles by *Vivian Arend*

Now Available:

Baby, Be Mine

Granite Lake Wolves
Wolf Signs
Wolf Flight
Wolf Games
Wolf Tracks
Wolf Line
Wolf Nip

Forces of Nature
Tidal Wave
Whirlpool

Turner Twins
Turn It On
Turn It Up

Pacific Passion
Stormchild
Stormy Seduction
Silent Storm

Bandicoot Cove
Paradise Found
Exotic Indulgence

Six Pack Ranch
Rocky Mountain Heat
Rocky Mountain Haven
Rocky Mountain Desire
Rocky Mountain Angel
Rocky Mountain Rebel
Rocky Mountain Freedom

Xtreme Adventures
Falling, Freestyle
Rising, Freestyle

Takhini Wolves
Black Gold
Silver Mine
Diamond Dust

Print Collections
Under the Northern Lights
Under the Midnight Sun
Under an Endless Sky
Breaking Waves
Storm Swept
Freestyle
Tropical Desires

Diamond Dust

Vivian Arend

Samhain Publishing, Ltd.
11821 Mason Montgomery Road, 4B
Cincinnati, OH 45249
www.samhainpublishing.com

Diamond Dust

Print ISBN: 978-1-61921-951-9
Digital ISBN: 978-1-61921-556-6

Editing by Anne Scott
Cover by Angela Waters

First Samhain Publishing, Ltd. electronic publication: August 2013
First Samhain Publishing, Ltd. print publication: May 2014

Dedication

Because they demanded bears: Lillie Applegarth, Fatin Soufan, Ericka Brooks. May you always have a grumpy, furry, hot-tempered hero with a heart of gold (and a pocket full of diamonds) at your beck and call.

Hey, we can dream, right?

Part One

Life is a fiddler, and we all must dance.
From gloom where mocks that will-o'-wisp,
Free-will I heard a voice cry: "Say, give us a chance."

Chance! Oh, there is no chance!
The scene is set,
Up with the curtain!
Man, the marionette,
Resumes his part.

"Quatrains"—Robert Service

Interlude

On the other side of the ornate sanctuary doors, voices murmured. The low tones of pipe-organ music lent an air of anticipation to the setting. Caroline Bradley took a deep breath to calm her nerves and the rich scent of roses swirled upward from the bouquet in her hand to fill her senses.

One of life's mysteries. How did a fully human woman, who just happened to know about the shifters living in Whitehorse, end up in this predicament?

Just lucky, I guess.

Caroline laughed at her own joke as she regarded her companion in limbo, the Takhini Alpha. Evan Stone wore a sharply tailored black tux and a crisp white shirt that only emphasized his dark good looks. There was no way to stop her heart from skipping a beat. Wolf genes were damn sexy in the first place. Add in that GQ outfit and the lazy smile twisting his lips, and she was liable to end up a sloppy puddle of melted butter if she wasn't careful.

"You look gorgeous." Evan tugged one of the spirals of blonde hair falling artistically from her temple. "And bonus, a little less like you're going to puke than you did five minutes ago."

Her stomach gave a warning twinge. "You're such a soothing fellow."

He tucked his fingers under her chin and lifted until there was nowhere for her to look but into his beautiful dark gaze. His thumb caressed her cheek. A gesture he'd made many times over the past months that connected them so intimately. So caringly.

Caroline cupped his hand to her face, the familiar touch reassuring and right. "You sure about this?"

"Are you?"

Good grief, as sure as she could be. "Evan, I'm wearing a bloody wedding dress. I've got flowers in my hair and the most uncomfortable bit of elastic around my thigh masquerading as a garter belt. There are over a thousand people on the other side of that door, and in two minutes we're supposed to march down that aisle and..."

"...and simply make official what we already knew." He leaned in and pressed his warm lips to her forehead, passing over his unwavering confidence. "I'll be with you every step of the way, holding your hand."

She turned her face and nuzzled his palm before tugging his hand away. "You're going to make things crazy, getting your scent all over me."

"Hey, what could happen, a fight to the death on a mountain hillside or something? I don't think so." His raised brow made her smile. As the head of the Takhini pack, having Evan on her side had been more wonderful than anything she'd remembered. Until now—

The world was about to change for good.

The doors opened a crack and the music swelled.

"Shit." The word snuck out even as she straightened her spine.

Evan snorted as he pulled her veil forward then helped her

face the doors, the expansive train of her dress flaring behind her like a semiobedient dragon tail. “Smile. You’d think we were walking toward a firing squad.”

“I could arrange that.”

“Of course you could, but you don’t have to. There’s no need for any more fighting.” Evan shook a finger at her. “Because of you. I’m so proud.”

They stared at each other, and Caroline’s lips curled into a real smile this time. “Damn right, you are.”

Evan laughed, the sound ringing full and clear as they faced the gathering. People turned in expectation as they passed, Evan supporting her fingers over his arm as they marched in time with the processional. He petted her gently. “You are, as always, incredible. One step at a time, you can do this.”

One step at a time. Caroline clutched him tighter.

The pews were filled, leaving standing room only along the edges of the sanctuary. Turned toward them was a sea of faces. Pack members and visiting bears all mixed in with locals, most humans totally unaware they were seated next to a man or woman who in their spare time loved to go furry and run through the Yukon wilderness.

Good people, all of them. She was doing this for them. So Mr. Jacks over there, who didn’t know he was flirting with a lynx shifter, wouldn’t have to find out. So the bloodshed that had threatened her pack and her city would stop—she was doing this because it was right for more people than her alone.

Evan paused three feet short of the stairs that rose to where the actual ceremony was to take place. He twisted her to face him, lifted her veil and cleared his throat. “I know it’s not proper, but screw it. For old times’ sake. You’re one in a million, Caroline. Thanks for being a part of my life.”

He leaned in and kissed her. For real. Never slipped her any tongue, though, which was good, because the involuntary reaction to *Evan* and *tongue* wasn't the kind of thing she wanted to deal with when at least five hundred of the people watching all had oversensitive sniffers. But it was a real kiss—his hand cradling the back of her neck, holding her in position as he gave her his full attention.

That slow murmur of voices returned in a heart beat, the noise rising in volume as people gasped in shock or twittered out muffled laughter.

And under the whispers, a low, enticing rumble that made her toes curl.

Evan pulled back, grinning his fool head off, his gaze locked on hers. Caroline's cheeks steamed they were so hot. "You did that to yank his chain," she muttered as she attempted to pull herself back into a state of counterfeit calm.

"Yup," Evan admitted readily. "Just because there's a wedding about to take place doesn't mean you stop being my good, good friend."

"Ahem."

Goose bumps broke over her. The deep, growly voice rolling in her ears belonged to only one person.

She and Evan turned together to discover that the enormous shifter who'd strolled into Whitehorse and spun everything upside down had joined them, and now stood inches away. His big body close enough to heat her.

Caroline swallowed hard.

Tyler's expression was dark, none of his usual levelheaded diplomacy visible. "Good friends who don't *ever* kiss from here on. Just so we're clear."

Evan shrugged. "No problem. Got it."

Tyler stared for a long moment. Nodded. Then shifted his gaze to meet Caroline's. "You ready?"

He held out his arm, elbow raised high. She pulled herself together once more and rested her hand on his tuxedo-clad arm. Left Evan standing behind as she and Tyler walked up the short flight to the dais. Left her old life behind.

Oh Lordy, what had she done?

Chapter One

Whitehorse, Seven days earlier

“We’ll be landing soon.” Justin plopped himself into the oversized seat opposite Tyler and buckled himself in. “Should be no delays at the airport—I arranged our arrival so we land well ahead of the commercial flight the other delegates are traveling on.”

“Of course you did.” Tyler sipped the last of his wine and stared out the window, mentally ordering the next couple hours according to the least frustrating tasks he could remove from his list quickly. “Transportation organized?”

“Limo for the first days.”

A growl of annoyance escaped before he caught himself.

“I know, I know, but play along for a bit, okay?” Justin tugged the empty wine glass from his fingers and handed it to a male secretary walking in the aisle. “We have to stick with standard protocol until we get things lined up and all the security has been double-checked—”

“Justin. I wrote the security handbook. I know what’s in there.”

“Right.” Justin tapped his fingers on the armrest. “We’ve booked in at the Moonshine Inn. Your suite is—”

Tyler lifted a hand to interrupt the man. “I swear you’re

nervous or something, because you're rambling. You've already gone through the details of our accommodation as well as the schedule for the first two days of conclave. Verbally once plus you left me three copies to read."

"Sorry."

Pressure changed as the plane started its descent. Tyler examined his best friend, who happened to also be his personal advisor and bodyguard.

As if he, a bear shifter, needed a guard, but traditions weren't easy to break. So long as Tyler didn't have to put up with sycophants, he had no problem spending time with his friend as they dealt with the issues of clan security.

Still, there had to be something wrong. Justin was normally far more relaxed. "You got word of trouble brewing?"

Justin blinked then shook his head. "A bad feeling is all. There's been nothing but problems for the first two weeks of conclave between kidnapping and extortion, and plain old stupidity on the part of a few clans. I don't expect anything will get better for the final set of votes merely because we've shifted locations from Dawson City to Whitehorse."

"Of course there's still trouble coming." Tyler thought back through the notes he'd read on the previous territory-distribution talks. The events weren't held often, but the opportunity for an orderly exchange of resources and ideas was still the best way to stop the overaggressive bear shifters from methodically taking out most of their population and ninety percent of the other shifters in the north.

Bears on a rampage weren't a pretty sight.

"We'll deal with the troubles in a civilized manner. We aren't dogs to fight over a bone." Tyler spoke louder as the props on his private plane increased in volume. "Speaking of which, did you find more information regarding the wolf pack in

Whitehorse?"

Justin laughed. "Yes, from the strangest source, actually. You'll never guess who."

Tyler was tempted to make him lay a wager, but nabbing money from his best friend on a sure bet was far too unsportsmanlike. If he was going to gamble, he wanted the risk to mean something. "I'd never in a million years guess you spoke to my brother, Frank."

Justin's expression twisted in disgust. "You're not a lot of fun at times."

"I know everything..."

They both laughed as the plane touched down with a gentle kiss of the wheels to the tarmac. "Yeah, you have more resources than a gopher has holes. How did you figure out Frank was in town?"

"He texted me."

"Frank?" Justin's tone of voice was somewhere along the lines of hearing that Lady Gaga had flown a solo trip to the moon.

"Well, someone must have texted for him because I doubt he has a phone or a computer, but he's staying with the Takhini pack." Shocking information in and of itself, but true.

"You don't need my report, then?" Justin stood as the pilot smoothly taxied the plane toward the terminal.

"Oh, I need it. Frank was his usual loquacious self. 'At the Takhini pack house. See you for dinner. You're buying.' This makes me even more curious what kind of pack Whitehorse has that they welcome outcast bears into their midst."

"Curious situation to be sure. And it's two packs, not one."

This got stranger by the minute. "There are two wolf packs in the city? What kind of masochists are they? They must have total control over the media because I haven't seen any weekly reports of bloodshed in the streets."

Tyler joined his guard at the exit door. They waited briefly until the path was cleared, then Justin stepped out and looked around before giving the go-ahead. "Word is Takhini is in charge and Canyon has gone into hiding. We're staying at the hotel owned by the Takhini pack. Current Alpha is originally from the Hudson Bay pack."

Tyler whistled. "Impressive."

"Yeah, name of Evan Stone—took over about a year ago and seems to be controlling them okay. The other pack, all I could find was a name, Sam, and a lot of fuzzy rumours."

The mid-July sunshine caused heat waves to shimmer above the runway. The short walk to the waiting limo was long enough for Tyler to wish he wasn't headed for formal meetings, but finding somewhere comfortable along the river to ease back and relax. Maybe with someone soft and curvy to help pass the time.

The limo took off, the unfamiliar Alaskan highway disappearing rapidly as they headed into downtown. Tyler hadn't been to Whitehorse very often. His business trips tended to take him farther south into the US, or over to London or Europe. Staying in the smaller towns in northern Canada over the past couple of months had been a refreshing change from his long-range excursions to exotic or formal settings. "What did Frank tell you?"

"He likes them, that much was clear. He's been in town for a few days and he's still a guest in the pack house, so they're either very tolerant, or Frank has improved his manners since he used to live in Yellowknife." Justin peered out the windows, remaining alert as they traveled. "Also, he mentioned there was someone you simply had to meet."

"That sounds like a woman comment." Which was all kinds of impossible. "Don't tell me Frank's broken heart has healed."

"Don't think that's what he was implying." Justin grinned as they stopped at a set of lights. "Your brother said there was someone he wanted *you* to meet, emphasis on you."

"Good grief. He's trying to set me up?"

Justin shrugged. "Diplomacy will fill your days, but there are a couple of gala events planned—the organizing committee is striving to uphold the peaceful nature of the talks. You'll have a lot of time on your hands at night if you want Frank to introduce you to this someone special of his."

Tyler didn't bother to respond, instead glared at his friend. Justin grinned harder, then ignored him, whistling as the limo headed to their destination.

A downside of having money, power and a coveted position. Tyler didn't go long between offers of female company. Justin knew it well—the asshole rubbed it in all the time that Tyler's arms must get tired from fending the women off.

Tyler didn't fend them off. He simply took what they offered and let them leave. It might seem heartless, but physical pleasure was enough.

Although, once the territory issues were solved he'd consider putting more energy into finding someone permanent. A man with the kind of business and status he had needed to think of having a family to pass it on to someday, which would require a wife at some point. Right now, though, he had too many important tasks to be distracted by a pretty face.

His brother's broken heart and subsequent escape into the wilds of the Yukon was another good reason why Tyler avoided dating. Women wrapped a man up and tore them apart in ways that business and territorial claims never did. Those situations were logical and orderly, or at least when done correctly. Tyler had no intention of getting emotionally whipped through some kind of roller coaster only to find in the end he wasn't in control of anything—his family, his business or his heart.

In the meantime, he'd focus on the conference. Seven days and all this should be settled. Justin was right, though, there was an odd feel in the air, as if a storm was about to hit. Not unexpected, but Tyler would need all his wits about him for the coming time frame. If he could pull off the difficult task of winning the election and complete the territory shuffles without losing anyone—bear, wolf or otherwise—it would be a miracle.

Good thing he liked to play the long odds.

"You're looking for me to kick your ass into tomorrow, aren't you? Because...keep up the bad excuses and I'll totally help you with that."

Caroline glared as the wolf directly in front of her shuffled his feet and eased back a few inches. "We figured our work lists got mixed up."

"Mixed up?" She took a deep breath and counted to ten before slowly letting go. With every room in town booked solid over the next while, even pack members who weren't usually Moonshine Inn staff had been wrangled in to help. Wasn't their fault the two teenaged boys currently cringing at her displeasure weren't familiar with the tasks, but she thought the chore lists she'd prepared were pretty self-explanatory.

Only instead of cleaning the room as assigned, she'd caught Tweedledee and Tweedledum using the suite's gaming system to blow up the galaxy of Xerkon.

Getting mad wouldn't fix the problem, though. She lowered her voice and forced her body into a less threatening position. "I'll go do the final run-through on the rooms. You two go to the restaurant and work there. Got it?"

They'd still be helping, but she'd be less likely to kill them if she couldn't see them.

Total relief brightened the young wolves' faces. "That would be so much better. I mean, I'll pour beer or lift barrels of ale or—"

"Me too. I can rearrange tables and do manly things."

Manly things? Good grief, these boys were in for a lesson when she had more than two seconds to work them over. She caught each of them by one ear and towed them into the hallway. "Move. Both of you. We've got guests arriving any minute."

They took off at a sprint toward the pub, getting while the getting was good.

Caroline changed direction. Normally she'd delegate. She was the queen of delegation, but with the clock ticking there was no time to waste. She grabbed a cleaning cart and passkeyed her way into the executive suite.

Chatting about how housekeeping was something everyone should learn was obviously an agenda item for the next pack meeting. Not now when she wasn't sure the rooms that were supposed to be ready were even clean.

She dragged out her cell phone as she took a preliminary glance at the damages. Hopefully Evan wasn't busy or goofing off. Or busy goofing off.

"Hey, sweet thang."

Man, if she weren't so stressed the endearment would have given her a thrill, right before she planned how to get revenge. "If you are anywhere but in your office, I will make you bleed for using that nickname."

"I'm alone, finishing paperwork. You sound stressed.

What's up?"

"My blood pressure. I need you to give me a hand—and if you start clapping, I'll tie you to a stake and find ants to crawl all over you."

His even chuckle helped calm her. "What can I do?"

The suite wasn't as bad as she'd expected. She raced around tidying, the phone tucked against her shoulder as she worked. "I sent a couple of doughboys your direction. Put them to work scrubbing dirty dishes, or something gross and unglamorous."

He laughed. "They pissed you off, did they? Fine, I'm on my feet. Walking to greet them at the doors to the kitchen, and they will rue the day they messed with you."

"Thank you. Second favour... The head of the Harrison clan is due to arrive within the hour. Because I'm doing the job those brats didn't, you might have to greet our guests when they arrive."

Dead silence on the other end of the phone.

"*Pleeeeease*, Evan. I'll be there as soon as I can, but if I'm late, you have to do it."

"You want me to greet the Harrison delegation in my front lobby? You have any idea what kind of trouble this could cause? Two Alphas in the same space?"

"I'm sure you're much bigger than he is, Evan," she wheedled sweetly. "In character, if not in size. It's not as if he's coming here to take over your territory. Just welcome him in then take him to the suite. Talk about...the weather. Tell him the hours at the restaurant. There's already about fifty of his clan in the hotel, so boast about how much your pack loves you. He'll tell you about his fawning followers, only you know yours are better."

"You're managing me, aren't you?" Evan growled.

"Well..." She totally was.

"You're sexy when you're managing me."

She laughed. "I'll be real sexy in about thirty seconds when I stick the toilet brush in the bowl and get scrubbing. Can you handle it?"

"Piece of...*cake.*"

And with that, all her plans went to hell. Something had gone wrong. The final word he'd spoken was in his *irrelevant voice.* The one he used when something random and potentially dodgy was about to happen. It wasn't often the Alpha of the Takhini pack lost focus, but when he did, situations went to hell fast.

"Evan?"

He didn't answer.

Drat. So much for her last-minute bailout idea. Somehow she'd have to be the one greeting the delegation. She'd stuff Evan into his office with a glass or two of liquor to keep him out of mischief. Hmm, maybe pop the pack Beta in there as well, because when the two of them got together uncontained, bad things happened.

Wait. Oh, wait. Pack Beta—*yes*—there was her solution.

Caroline put down the cleanser and darted a glance at her watch. "Oh, silly me. I totally forgot. You never mind about the bears. I remembered Gem offered to help. You take care of the boys I sent, though, right?"

"Sure—dirty tasks." He was completely distracted. What the hell was going on? "I'm in the kitchen now. I'll make them work."

"Thanks."

As weird as Evan was acting, he didn't seem dangerous, so

Caroline hung up and punched in another number, the pack's female Beta answering on the second ring.

"Hello, Caroline. How are you?" Gem's impeccably polite southern drawl poured from the phone like soothing music.

Only there wasn't time to relax. "Emergency. You know where your mate is?"

Gem caught the urgency. "Yes. What do you need?"

"Send Shaun to help Evan deal with whatever is going on in the kitchen. Tell him it's important to keep Evan away from the front lobby. Then I need you to do your political-princess thing and charm the furry socks off the Harrison delegation when they arrive. I'm stuck doing the final spit and polish on their suite."

"Oh, you poor thing. Of course. I've got everything covered for you." Gem laughed softly. "I'd offer to clean, but I'm probably better off acting as hostess. I have years of training."

"Hey, you've learned tons since you arrived in the spring, but the pack needs your diplomacy more than they need you to have housekeeping skills."

"True."

One disaster neatly avoided. Caroline should have felt more pride, but she was too busy multitasking. "Thanks, girlfriend, I owe you one."

"You don't owe me anything. We're pack, we work together. Don't worry, I'll get the boys under control, and I'll give you a warning call once the group arrives."

Gem hung up and Caroline tucked away her phone.

She moved quickly through the tasks that still needed completing, cursing egotistical young men who thought they were above "women's work".

The entire time she kept the cleaning cart close at hand,

ready to vanish the instant Gem hit the warning signal. While Caroline was absolutely fascinated with the Bear Jamboree gathering, she didn't want the first time she met them to be while coated in eau de Pine-Sol.

Shifter politics had always been on her radar. As a human in a mixed shifter family, understanding why one wolf had more clout than another had been an important lesson. Surviving in the pack meant she'd learned young that power seemed inborn for some shifters.

As a human, she didn't have access to any built-in authority, but over the years she'd found something else that worked just as well. Humans called it chutzpah. Well, chutzpah in combination with the willingness to bleed or make someone else bleed.

Wolves liked their power games with a slice of pain.

She'd faked it until she'd made it. She'd even wrangled her way into a close relationship with Evan in a plot to help her less-dominant half sister. The good side of that ploy was she and Evan honestly liked each other, and the sex was on fire. The bad part?

There really wasn't one.

Their relationship was temporary. At some point Evan was bound to find his mate. In a way, she hoped it would happen soon, because he deserved to have the in-love-and-out-of-my-mind mate thing that had hit so many of her friends over the years. Shifter insta-mate wasn't ever happening for Caroline, obviously, but she wasn't stupid. She knew how much finding their soul connection meant to them, and as a good friend how could she not want that for Evan?

She finished the final wipe-down in the bathroom and manoeuvred the cart back into the living space of the suite.

Maybe she was twisted, but seeing people get in a flap over

her and Evan amused her far too much. What was wrong with having a good, hot sexual relationship that wasn't going anywhere permanent, but in the meantime delivered orgasms by the bucket load?

She didn't want to settle down. Not yet. While she'd achieved one goal—having her sister return to the north and find a place—there was so much more to do. Caroline flicked her duster over the floor-to-ceiling window treatment, lost in thought.

Travel, excitement, they called to her. Maybe once the bears had checked out, she'd think about booking an extended holiday somewhere warm. Three or four months exploring tropical islands, or getting lost in the markets of Europe, sounded intriguing.

She pulled the final pillows into position on one of the oversized couches gracing the suite. Satisfaction at having dealt with the most recent hotel emergency swept over her. The place was clean and the bears would be greeted by Gem, who knew way more about sweet-talking cranky diplomats into good moods than Caroline did.

On the way to the door to put away the cart, she glanced outside and noticed the hot tub lid was out of place.

"Damned windstorm."

She tucked the cart aside and dashed outside, attempting to tug the heavy cover back into place. Leaves floated on the surface and she muttered in frustration. Scooping out the debris was simple, until the wind picked up, swirling around the third-story balcony. The rubbish skittered away over the water's surface, disappearing under the quarter section still covered by the bulky lid.

Times like this she regretted she wasn't a shifter. Stupid, awkward, heavy contraption. She crawled onto the edge of the tub and put her feet against the cover, using her stronger leg muscles to thrust it out of the way.

The wind hit the French doors and they slammed against the doorjamb, the sound harsh and abrupt in the quiet around her. Caroline jerked in surprise.

"Crap."

She inelegantly slipped off the smooth tub lip and under the warm water, the back of her head rapping the edge hard enough for her to briefly see stars.

Then darkness.

Chapter Two

Tyler stepped through the hotel doors and paused, partly out of habit to allow Justin to get into position, partly because the place was far beyond what he'd expected from a northern inn. Exquisite decorations filled the expansive front lobby, one entire wall a virtual wilderness with plants, rocks and a floor-to-ceiling waterfall dancing down the barrier.

"Mr. Harrison?"

Justin moved closer, but Tyler waved him down. The beautiful woman approaching him with an outstretched hand wasn't a threat. "Gem Jacobs. How lovely to see you again, and in one piece."

She smiled, turning to welcome Justin as well. "I'm glad your delegation chose the Moonshine Inn as a base. Did you have a good trip?"

Tyler nodded. "Uneventful. Not nearly as much excitement as you got up to earlier in the summer. My personal apologies for the terrible way you were treated by some of my fellow bears. Have you recovered from the mishap?"

"Completely. Please, don't mention it any further. We all understand politics don't always go the way we'd like." She was the perfect hostess as she guided them through the grand foyer, pointing out carvings by local artisans, and Tyler hid his smile. He'd heard the southern belle was now Takhini pack, but seeing her in the setting was amusing. The last time he'd met her she'd been acting as hostess for her father in the far south of Georgia.

She turned from showcasing the lobby. "Do you gentlemen want to see your rooms or explore the town? We can arrange anything you'll need for the duration of your time with us."

"Thank you. If you could show us to our suite, that would be all," Tyler answered.

Justin interrupted. "If you'd let me know where we can park our limo, I'll inform the driver."

She handed him two envelopes. "The blue is room key and information for your driver, the other is yours for the suite."

Justin gave her a nod then turned to face Tyler. "You want to wait until I get back so I can escort you?"

The man was far too addicted to the guarding part of his job. "I think with Gem to protect me, I can make it to the suite without getting lost or shot."

"Half of your delegation has already checked in. They seemed pleased with our arrangements." Gem folded her arms prettily. "Let me assure you the Moonshine Inn is well protected. Between the security cameras and the pack presence, there's no one on the premises we're not aware of. Evan Stone takes safety seriously."

In spite of her promise, Justin waited until Tyler motioned him away. "Go on. Deal with the driver. Oh, and grab the information the organizers said they'd have waiting at conference headquarters. I promise to be a good boy and stay in the suite until you get back."

His guard nodded, leaving reluctantly.

Tyler offered his arm to Gem. "He's far too interested in making sure I'm coddled."

"It's his job. You can't blame him. This way, please." Gem

led him to the elevators and punched the button for the third floor. “Your initial security teams have already taken a look around the hotel and settled into their rooms.”

“Wonderful.”

She nodded. “Also, I’m supposed to pass on the message the Takhini pack is available for you. Anything you need.”

Interesting.

He’d give it more time, a few days at least, before seeking out the pack Alpha and getting a feel for where the man stood regarding the bear situation. Conclave wasn’t something Tyler wanted wolves poking their noses into, but with everything else his opponents had tried over the past weeks, he’d be stupid not to think they might also mess with the Whitehorse talks.

Someone might attempt to use the potentially volatile situation of two wolf packs in one place to set off some troubles in their favour. Having the ear of the ruling pack could help Tyler.

“Thank you for that. I’ll keep it in mind.”

She guided them to a single door at the end of the hallway, opening it before passing over the key. “I hope you have a comfortable stay with us, and successful meetings.”

“Pass on my greeting to your Alpha.”

She left him, and that sense of “wolf” faded as he watched her go. He slipped through the door, relaxing as he examined the space.

Other than a cleaning cart blocking one wall, the room was standard to what he was used to. He loosened his tie as he strolled in farther, peeking through the doors he passed to find a large bedroom with a decadent attached bath. There was a second matching door on the opposite side—he’d assume a matching bedroom waited there for Justin. Tyler stripped off his suit jacket and tossed it on the bed before wandering back into the main room.

The partially open French doors caught his eye. He dropped his tie, grabbed up an apple from the massive fruit bowl decorating the kitchen counter and ate it as he wandered to the balcony railing. An incredible view greeted him, with the mountains rising behind the city streets. The lack of skyscrapers added to the beauty, and he breathed deep to fill his lungs with fresh air.

A faint scent of human made him turn, but there was no one there. Only the door he'd left open behind him, and at the far side of the deck an open lounging area with a hot tub, the lid strangely askew.

A hand draped over the far edge, just visible from his new position.

Hell.

Tyler raced forward, reached into the water and scooped up the limp body of a blonde woman. Her head had been resting on a drink holder, the only thing that had kept her from becoming completely submerged.

"Wake up, little mermaid." Tyler cradled her against him. He nudged the door open and brought her inside, dripping wet, examining her face for a reaction. She was breathing, but shallowly. He lowered her onto the couch then pulled a handy throw blanket over her shivering torso. "Can you hear me?"

Her lips moved, eyelashes fluttering. Nothing but slight muttering to his question.

Damn it. He had to call someone, and now. He leaned over her to snatch the phone from the side table. Her arms flailed. In his unprotected position, one hand connected sharply with his nose, and he grunted in pain.

Ignoring the phone for a second, he tucked her in again,

holding down her arms to stop her from hurting herself or taking more pot shots at his face. "You don't need to hit me, I'm trying to help you."

"*Bear...*"

The word whispered past her lips, and Tyler paused. Leaned in closer and sniffed.

The scent of wolves clung to his waterlogged woman, but she wasn't wolf. Human through and through, yet the fact she'd just called him a bear?

Something was happening he wanted to get to the bottom of.

"Can you hear me?"

Her lips moved steadily, drawing his attention to them. For the first time he paused long enough to look the rest of her over. Her blonde hair stuck up in spots, the pale colouring all the way to the roots. Her skin was pale as well—whether from soaking in his tub or her natural colour, he wasn't sure. The deep red of her lips contrasted sharply against her skin, a delicate pout forming on their soft surface as she attempted to speak.

Speaking of bears, his was at full alert. The beast bumped to the surface, keen on him shifting for some reason. While he was the bear and the bear was him, there was one part of his brain that remained independent. His human side reasoning, rational. His animal side more...well, animal. Earthier and more connected to the wilder roots of shifterdom.

He understood why his bear was interested. Pretty face and pretty body, the swells of her breasts rose and fell as her breathing evened out and grew stronger. That was the reason he was staring at her chest, to make sure she was recovering from her ordeal. Not because he could see straight through the wet shirt and the bra underneath it. Not because the lush redness of her lips seemed to be reflected in the tips of those breasts...

Tyler shook his head to make his brains settle back in place.

Damn bear.

His mystery woman sucked in a deep breath, her eyes opening all the way. “Frack.”

He soothed her, attempting to keep her horizontal on the couch without actually forcing her back. “You should stay still.”

Her gaze darted over his face, and this adorable little crease appeared between her brows. “Who are you?”

Caution made him word his answer carefully. If this was someone planted by another bear clan, he wanted to know, so he used the oldest ploy in the book. His friend would understand. “I’m Justin. What’s your name?”

“Caroline.” Her eyes widened. “Why am I soaking wet?”

“I found you in my hot tub. I hoped you could tell me—”

“Oh, shoot.”

She would have surged upward, and this time he made contact, hands to her shoulders, to keep her from jerking to vertical. “Don’t. You nearly drowned. Until you remember what happened, you shouldn’t move.”

The fabric separating his palms and her skin warmed, and the scent of her skin grew stronger. She relaxed onto the overstuffed fabric as she tentatively touched the back of her head.

“I remember. I was finishing cleaning the suite and slipped on the tub.” She moved her fingers slowly but still cringed in pain. “There’s a goose egg to prove it.”

Tyler settled on his heels beside her. Cleaning staff. Okay, that was a possible solution to the question without turning this into some kind of political intrigue.

"Do you mind if I check?"

"Be my guest." She frowned. "You're Justin? You're the security man for Tyler Harrison."

Cleaning staff who knew details of the room's occupants? Tyler returned to being suspicious all over again.

He lifted her carefully until he could examine the back of her head. "I'm checking things out in the room. Everything seemed to be in order other than you doing unsupervised synchro."

"Can you get me out of here before he arrives?"

"You sure you're okay to move?" Tyler helped her upright, sitting next to her on the couch. He held one arm around her to stop her from shifting from side to side.

Caroline groaned lightly. "I'll be all right. I'm not nauseous or anything, which is good. I would hate to throw up and ruin the great cleaning job I did."

Tyler laughed. The conversation was far more blunt than he usually got to hear from people. "Well, yes. Let's avoid vomiting, shall we?"

It was rather comfortable sitting with her. Far more comfortable than he should be after rescuing a strange woman in a strange place. He wanted to be wary, wanted to remain alert to the potential troubles in the situation, but with her wet body cuddled beside him, his damn bear seemed to have taken control of his mind.

Her shirt had separated from the waistband of her pants, and a sliver of bare skin rested under his fingers. The sheer willpower it took to keep from stroking that soft section of skin shook him.

His human side pushed forward in defense with logic. "I

should call a doctor to check you out."

She frowned. "I'll go to the clinic. Let's not have ambulances at the hotel today. It wouldn't be a great way to start things off. Might set a damper on the meetings."

Curiousier and curiousier. "You've obviously worked at the Moonshine Inn for a while."

Give her a chance to admit she knew about shifters, and the game would change all over again. A tiny bud of a notion had burst forth in the last minute, probably planted by his bear, but damn if it wasn't a working idea.

She nodded slowly, wincing. "I've been on staff for nearly five years. Since before the Takhini pack bought out the previous owners."

And there was his answer. "You know about shifters, then."

She snorted.

His bear was far too charmed by her instant and honest response.

Caroline motioned upward. "Help me to my feet, and we'll see how I do. Yes, I know about shifters. Half-blood family, actually. My stepdad's wolf, so I've lived with pack most of my life."

A human who grew up with shifters. This might be the solution to one of his problems during the upcoming conference days.

Not to mention a lovely distraction, as long as she hadn't injured herself with that crazy fall.

He had her standing, his arms still around her in case she wobbled. Caroline clutched his shoulder momentarily as her knees gave way. He caught her around the waist and pulled her against him for support. She was tall enough to make him not feel quite as enormous as he usually felt around the ladies.

Other than that, he was desperately beating back the bear, who had just suggested they should peel her out of her wet clothes to make sure she wasn't hurt anywhere else.

"I think we should get that doctor in here."

"No." Caroline spoke firmly. "Damn, you shifters are all the same, bossy as all get out. I'm fine, and I really have to leave before your boss gets here."

His boss. Oh right, his little name game. They could drop that ploy. "Actually, I'm—"

The door opened, and Justin walked in. His best friend froze in midstep as he took in the entire scenario. From the open door, the trail of water across the carpet, the wet and disheveled woman, and Tyler himself.

Caroline swore and to his great surprise, hid herself against his side, arms curling around his torso.

Justin's eyes widened even farther.

Tyler had to say something before this got out of hand. Only with the reaction of the human, he didn't want to embarrass her further.

It wasn't his finest moment, but between his bear rumbling happily about having her in his arms, and everything else, Tyler made a snap decision.

Before his guard could speak and give him away, he opened his mouth and lied his ass off.

"Mr. Harrison, the room is fine, but one of the cleaning staff had a mishap. If you'll excuse us for a moment."

Caroline bit her tongue to stop from swearing like a fishwife. Way to make a great impression. Five more minutes and she'd have escaped without showing herself to be the total incompetent she felt at the moment.

Thank God for the sympathetic bear shifter she was unashamedly hiding behind. While he was damn impressive himself, a man who worked for a powerful man would understand some of what she dealt with on a daily basis, working with an Alpha. She felt a kinship, almost, with him.

Yet, *gack*, she must have hit her head harder than she thought. This wasn't her, she never hid. Certainly not when there was no good reason. I.e., soaking wet shouldn't be enough to make her lose her senses. Who knows, maybe being shifters they would think dipping fully clothed in pools was some weird human quirk.

She untangled her fingers from where they'd somehow become fisted around Justin's used-to-be-pristine white shirt.

White...shirt. *White*, like the uniform top she wore.

Caroline tilted her head to examine the full extent of the damages, but it was pretty much what she'd grasped in that one moment of blinding clarity. Her shirt had gone see-through. Great day to wear the sheerest bra she had in her closet.

She looked up to see her big bear studying her, the faint smile teasing his lips vanishing as she caught him.

Good grief. "Don't guys ever have anything better to do than stare at women's breasts?" she whispered in annoyance.

He chuckled. "Occupational hazard of being male. They're nice breasts."

Shifters. They were all the same. After years of dealing with the far more relaxed wolf-pack sexual attitudes, it was clear bears were no different. Still, she was human, and he should know better, so she secretly dug her fingertips into his side out of Mr. Harrison's view. "Stop it, and get me out of here without making a spectacle of myself."

Her benefactor dipped his chin. "Deal."

He tucked her behind his back, using his broad body as a block between her and the head of the Harrison delegation. Caroline peeked out, but Mr. Harrison seemed to have developed a great fascination in the carpet at his feet, strolling toward the bedroom without so much as a glance her direction.

She was across the room in seconds.

"I'll be a moment," the big guard announced. "Wait here."

"I can wait in the hall—"

"Right here," he snapped, still sotto voce, but despite the low volume it was clearly an order. "Or do you want to parade around the hotel in what you're wearing?"

Good point. She nodded. "Fine. Staying."

He grabbed her cleaning cart, rolling it over to the door. Then to her utter shock he stripped off his own shirt, broad chest revealed in a snap, plus the most incredible set of upper arms. Biceps like massive rocks, shoulders that could have been formed out of granite.

Caroline had seen her share of nudity, what with all the shifting going on from the earliest time she could remember, but this man wasn't a wolf, and he wasn't stripping to shift.

Her cheeks flushed. Whoa nelly, the man was built. She might have a bed partner, but she wasn't blind. The zing of attraction was natural enough, but other than enjoying it right here and now, that's all she planned on doing.

He thrust his shirt out, and bar being any ruder than she'd already been, she could hardly refuse. Especially when he was giving it to help deal with her frail human sensitivities.

His fingers slipped over hers. Caroline glanced up in time to catch him staring. Not like a guy merely fascinated with her boobs, but a *strip her down and ride her* expression on his face.

Oh hell, no. Not a complication she wanted to deal with in

this lifetime, thank you. She might think he was a looker, but she didn't cheat. Not on Evan, not on *anyone*.

Caroline turned her back as she tugged on the huge shirt, the tails falling to mid-thigh and more than adequately covering her important parts.

He opened the door and gestured her into the hall, dragging the cart with them.

She put the bulky thing as a block between them, self-defense kicking in. "Thank you, for everything."

"Not so fast." He tilted his head and eyed her. "I want a report that you've seen a doctor so I know you're fine."

She snapped off a salute. "Yes, sir."

"Smart-ass little thing." He laughed. "You're not what I expected."

Yeah. "I get that a lot. Please, extend my apologies to Mr. Harrison. I'll send someone in to dry off the couch and—"

"Don't worry about it. We'll sit on chairs until it air dries. Not as if we'll have to sit on the floor or anything."

"Thank you for being understanding." She grabbed the cart handle and prepared to leave. "I'll return your shirt as soon as possible."

There it was again—she hadn't imagined it. That red-hot flash as his gaze dropped over her, even though she knew damn well he couldn't see any thing. "Fine."

"You should go explain to your boss what happened. I promise you'll have nothing else to worry about for the duration of your stay." When he didn't move, she jiggled the handle, making the cart bump him. She smiled hesitantly, not wanting to encourage anything she'd have to defend against, but trying to walk the line between polite and *unavailable*. "If I didn't say it yet, thank you for saving me. I'm glad you came and fished me out of the tub."

He dipped his head and stepped aside.

She was halfway down the hall when he called, "Caroline…what?"

"Caroline Bradley."

She waited for him to say something else, but that was it. Silence. He watched her, though. Even as she widened the gap between them, she swore his gaze burned a hole in the back of her oversized cover-up. While she waited for the service elevator to arrive, deliberately fiddling with items in the cart, he was stripping her in his mind. The final glance over her shoulder as she slipped into the elevator proved he was still standing there, naked from the waist up, wearing a smile that spoke of amusement and sexual attraction.

She stabbed the button for the basement level before collapsing against the wall with a huge sigh.

Oh my Lord, what a mess.

Chapter Three

Evan clutched the kitchen countertop and held on for dear life.

Not possible. Not possible.

Freaking possible, he argued with his brain. It had to be possible, because the only other damn solution was he'd gone around the bend.

He leaned over and sniffed. Moved a foot to the right and repeated the action.

"Umm, Alpha?"

"Go away."

Nothing was going to distract him. This was far too important. He vaguely remembered shouting at the pack members in the kitchen to stay the hell back. Most of them had scurried like a bunch of mice as he'd stalked his way up and down the narrow aisles between the workstations.

The tantalizing aroma had hooked him as he'd left his office and led him in circles, desperate to maintain the trail.

There it was, just the faintest hint, but enough to drag him another two feet to the right where his head smacked into the chef's broad belly.

The man grunted in pain and stepped back. "Alpha, I need to use this section to make the orders. Do you suppose you could...do whatever you're doing on the other side of the kitchen? Please."

"Shhh." Evan dropped to his knees, following the fading scent. His wolf grew more frantic the fainter the aroma became. "*Damn* it all."

He lay full out on his belly on the floor, inching forward until his nose squished against the base of the counter. There. For one second he'd gotten a stronger whiff. Somewhere under this counter was what he was looking for.

He forced his arm under the narrow opening and fumbled until his fingers bumped a tiny, cylindrical object. A second later he was on his feet, staring at a plastic container of lip balm.

"Dude, if you've got chapped lips, there are easier ways to deal with it than disrupting the entire kitchen."

Evan snapped his head to the side to discover his Beta beside him. Shaun's relaxed grin and slouched body displayed a comfort level that was miles away from Evan's current state.

"It's not just a lip balm."

Shaun nodded sagely. "Sure. It's a *special* lip balm. I understand."

The scent had nearly vanished, but he still had one way to track it. There was no time to lose. Evan pressed the tube into Shaun's palm. "You will hold that for me with extreme caution. Do not use it, fondle it, hell, don't even look at it too hard, or I will rip out your throat."

Shaun curled his hand around the tiny object. "If that means something in secret Alpha code, I never got around to reading the manual. I'm lost."

Evan tore off his shirt and fumbled with his belt. "I'll explain later."

"You're shifting?" Shaun lowered his voice. "It's the middle of the day, this might not be a great idea."

"Cover me." Evan was naked, clothes abandoned on the floor. He changed forms even as his best friend and Beta continued to complain.

"Cover you. Great. Sure—just want to point out the last time I covered for you I ended up in the doghouse with my mate."

The change to wolf made the world brighter. Sharper. Evan loved the first moments after exchanging his human side for his animal one, and usually took time to revel in the differences. Today there was only one distinction between his forms he wanted to exploit with an urgency that made his heart pound.

He took a deep breath through his nose, his sharper lupine senses picking up on the scent. He howled his delight, then raced forward, ducking through legs as the trail meandered the length of the kitchen to the closed back door of the restaurant loading dock.

He smacked his shoulder into the metal in frustration.

"Slow down," Shaun snapped, hands on the door release. "You take off without me and animal services will have your tail in a sling."

Evan bared his teeth. The scent was vanishing, and he didn't care that it was his best friend blocking him. He was ready to draw blood.

"Fine, be that way. Just...don't bite anyone." His Beta pushed open the door, and Evan was gone, nose down, the wind and the other scents adding confusion to his target. If it weren't so very addictive, he might not have picked it up in the first place, but the aroma was now permanently branded on his brain.

He stretched out his stride as the path straightened to

follow the sidewalk. A few gasps of surprise escaped from the humans he brushed past. Tourists who weren't used to seeing wolves roam the streets of Whitehorse. The locals had grown more accustomed to the occasional sighting, although Evan's rule as Alpha had been to make pack keep a low profile.

What he was doing was in total violation of his own rules, but fuck that.

Rules were made to be broken.

When the sidewalk and his target turned a corner, hope rose in Evan's heart. They were only steps away from the pack house. Damn, his mark was under his nose?

Then the addictive scent cut off as if it had never existed, the pack house to his left, a single metal pole to his right, with the bus-stop route displayed on it.

Frustration knocked his hind legs from under him, and he sat on the sidewalk wondering how undignified it would be if his pack glanced out the windows and noticed him pouting like a two-year-old.

Loud footfalls slapped the ground behind him as Shaun finally caught up.

"Whoa, okay. There's a lady on the corner of Lambert and Fourth who got a shot of you, and I bet we're talking YouTube before the end of the hour. I hope the footage was worth it."

Evan snarled his displeasure, rising and heading for the pack house.

"Hey, don't get growly at me." Shaun followed him to the front door and opened it. "The only other option was knock her phone from her hand or steal it, and having to get bailed out of the slammer, *again*, wouldn't be a good thing for my record."

Seconds after entering the house Evan was back on two legs, dragging a hand through his hair in frustration. Pack members lazing in the common room picked up on his mood and vanished like an afternoon winter sun, leaving them utterly alone. “You’re right. It’s fine. Remind me to get Caroline to do a follow-up with our media contacts to make sure no one makes a huge deal of a lone wolf in the street.”

“What happened?” Shaun dipped his head to examine him closer, although Evan noticed his friend stayed out of swinging range. “You need me to help with anything?”

Now that it had finally happened, things made so much more sense. There was no use in beating around the bush. He stared at his Beta and straight out said it. “I caught a whiff of my mate.”

Shaun’s eyes widened. “Dude.”

“She was in the kitchen. Then she left.” Evan paced to the room he kept in the pack house, in search of spare clothing. “You got that lip balm?”

His Beta passed it back. Evan lifted the object to his nose and breathed in her scent, happy little hormones dancing along his spine and tying hundreds of yellow ribbons around his spinal column.

“Your mate.” Shaun whistled. “Well, congrats.”

“Yeah, thanks. Welcome to the coming shit storm.”

“Oh man, for sure.” Shaun sat on the edge of the bed as Evan dug in drawers and pulled out a pair of jeans and T-shirt. “She’s not from the Takhini pack, or you’d have found her before. What was she doing in the kitchen, and why did she leave? Does she know you’re her mate? Why did this have to happen while the town is full to the brim with bears and potential trouble?”

All those were minor compared to the one other issue scratching Evan’s nerves like nails on a blackboard. “You’re missing one item.”

Shaun choked off into silence, before clearing his throat. "So. How are you going to tell Caroline?"

Tyler closed the suite door behind him and leaned on the solid surface as he dealt with the intense need his bear had to chase down the delectable Caroline Bradley.

"If you're planning on abdicating from your position as CEO, I get dibs on your house and swimming pool."

Justin handed him a clean shirt, and Tyler pulled himself back to vertical to accept it. "Thanks for not giving away the little name thing there. Not often you see that kind of situation. A human who knows all about shifters—her family is half blood."

"And she always goes around soaking wet?"

Tyler shook his head. "She was floating dazed in the tub when I got here."

Justin stiffened as he moved for the door. "And you let her go off alone? She needs medical attention."

Tyler held up a hand. "I said the same thing, but I checked her vitals while she was recovering on our couch. She promised to see someone, but I think she'll be fine." He hesitated. "Now that's an odd response. I expected you would be more concerned with discovering a strange woman in our suite than advocating medical attention for them."

"You told me to trust your instincts. Obviously from the way you were eyeing the woman you don't think she's a danger to anything but your recently dead sex life."

"*Har-har.* Did you get the updated schedules for conclave?"

Justin paced to the bar counter and picked up a stack of papers. "The organizing committee is trying to keep it as simple and painless as possible. Two more votes, three at the most. The only trouble I see is if Clan Ainsworth manages to persuade Nakusp to support him. You could have a tight vote count if that happens."

Tyler nodded, still distracted by thoughts of Caroline. Why had he allowed her to leave the room without insisting she get checked? He could have at least accompanied her to find clean dry clothes.

His lack of consideration and mental clarity he would blame on his bear. Stupid beast had continued to grumble and send him far too vivid images of Caroline's breasts.

Focus on the task at hand. "Any suggestions on how to sweeten the pot in terms of Clan Nakusp? Ainsworth hates my guts—that won't change. But if we can swing Nakusp's vote our way we could kill two birds with one stone."

Justin leaned on the counter, tapping the schedule against his hand. "Well, there is one thing that could help. It wouldn't hurt."

"Sounds as if I'm not going to like your idea." He finished doing up his buttons and tucked in his shirt. "Wait, before you tell me, get housekeeping on the line and make sure Caroline is okay."

Justin made a face but followed orders, putting through the call. "You want to talk? I mean, you are the security guard who saved her."

Tyler was still scrambling for an answer when Justin spoke.

"Hello? Is Caroline Bradley available?" Justin's expression tightened. "I see. Thank you."

"What? Is she okay? What's wrong with her?"

Justin eyed him suspiciously. "She's gone home for the

day. You, on the other hand, have issues."

Tyler grabbed the paperwork and strolled to one of the oversized easy chairs, collapsing onto it with far more exhaustion than he should have at this point in the day. "I'm not allowed to be concerned about someone?"

He buried his head in the files, ignoring Justin. Because, dammit, his friend was right, something was wrong, and he had a good idea what it was.

Justin folded his long body into the chair opposite him. "I talked to your brother. We're picking him up for dinner at six."

"Fine." Tyler rustled more papers, pretending to be busy. He'd already memorized the damn things, but maybe Justin would pretend to go along with his pretending.

Nope. Justin was going to be the usual pain in the ass. "Back to the Nakusp issue, it could help to have a woman on your arm for the formal events. Not only would Mrs. Nakusp have someone to gossip with, *he's* always made it known your marital status is a detriment in his opinion."

"I'm not pulling a wife out of the woodwork in the next five days, Justin, not to try and impress Clan Nakusp."

His friend grimaced. "No, you won't find a wife, but even a date would make a difference. I was going to suggest you see who this special someone is that your brother is all keen to introduce you to. Having a local woman on your side wouldn't be a bad idea."

"You really think Frank found someone who can deal with the setting, let alone the politics? Frank used to be more impressed with the type who can guzzle a six-pack and then belch the alphabet."

Justin grinned. "Well, you never know."

"Wait, you said you *were* going to suggest that. What do

you have in mind now?"

Justin rose to his feet and paced to the windows, staring at the hot tub. "You could see if your mysterious Caroline Bradley is available."

The idea shouldn't have given Tyler such a thrill. "She's a human."

"Who knows shifters. She works at the hotel owned by the controlling wolf pack of Whitehorse. She's got to have some influence in the area, maybe even recognize some of the important players."

"You want me to take advantage of her for the connections she might have?" The suggestion wasn't outrageous; it was only good sense in light of the recent upheavals in the voting situations. Tyler wasn't sure why the idea made him so damn uncomfortable.

"Not really use her. Just see if she wants to help. I bet she cleans up nice. Buy her a couple of pretty dresses, give her a good time, and not only will it help our cause, but you'll have provided the thrill of a lifetime. She'd probably never get an invite to a gala like this otherwise."

Justin's words sat uneasily on Tyler. He checked his watch. "Then again, she could turn me down flat."

"Not likely." Justin waggled his brows. "I saw her reaction to your bare-chested bear-self. She tried to hide it, but she was interested."

"Still, your first idea is a good one. Contact Frank and see if he can rustle up his *someone* in time to join us for dinner tonight. Widen the pool a little."

Tyler excused himself before his friend's far-too-alert gaze told him more than he was willing to share.

He was looking forward to seeing his brother. Pleased to

meet this *whoever* Frank thought was so interesting. But his actions were all a cover-up for how much he really wanted to ask Caroline to join him for the galas.

The kind of reaction his bear had to the woman made him wonder all over again if something was fishy. If they'd slipped a love potion into his water on the plane. Or if an aphrodisiac of some kind was being piped into the air.

Now was not the time to have to soothe the beast. Not with votes to be won, not with shifter secrecy to be maintained. Now was the time he needed all his wits about him.

Instead it appeared he was being led by the balls, and his captor? A fair-haired human with a snarky attitude.

The idea she might still be wearing his shirt pleased him far too much.

Chapter Four

Caroline let herself into the apartment she shared with Evan, her fingers shaking with cold. Maybe she should have gone to the Medicentre to get checked, but other than a dull ache at the back of her head, she felt fine.

Embarrassed, but fine.

She draped the shirt she'd been loaned over the back of a chair en route to the shower. She'd drop it off at the dry cleaners as soon as she wasn't shivering. Steam rose as she cranked the water temperature as high as she could stand, her skin turning bright red under the assault.

Time to regroup. Get her brain back in gear. The next week was vital for the hotel, and the Takhini pack. She needed to be in tip-top form to remain a contributing pack member.

She stepped under the faucet to allow the water to run down her face. Of course, being pack was less important than it had been a month ago. Now that her sister Shelley had found her place in the north, Caroline's options had broadened.

And while she liked wolves, all shifters for that matter, there were times she wanted to kick their furry butts.

No, this gig at the Moonshine Inn wasn't permanent. Even the situation today with the delegation had shown that. At some point the hotel would have to learn to get along without her. Maybe it was time to consider the travel option and speed up the process. She didn't want to leave forever, but her soul screamed for adventure.

Her body temperature finally warmed to something near normal. Caroline shut off the water and grabbed her towel. No time to linger—she had to track down Evan and find out what had happened.

She stepped into the living area at the same moment Evan passed through the front door. Shaun hovered in the hallway behind him, guilt written all over both wolves.

"Guys."

"I'll...talk to you later." Shaun waved goodbye and attempted to disappear.

Her suspicions rose. "Going somewhere, Shaun? Come on in."

"Oh, well, actually." Shaun cleared his throat and jerked his thumb over his shoulder. "Gotta get back to my mate. Later."

He vanished.

Caroline examined Evan closer. He wasn't wearing the same clothes he'd had on when he left the apartment that morning. "Evan?"

He sniffed the air. She bit her lip to stop from laughing. Wolves—they did it every time, and every time it entertained her.

"Who's in our apartment?" Evan stared over her shoulder, looking for a hidden person.

"No one."

"There's a guy in here..." Evan's gaze narrowed and he stepped closer, sniffing her.

She shoved his head away, no longer amused. "Stop that. Jeez."

"Why do I smell bear?"

Whoa. He was good. Caroline reached for the shirt on the chair and held it up. "Long story short, one of the bears staying in the hotel loaned it to me. Your turn, what the hell happened to you while I was talking to you earlier?"

Evan stuttered to a stop. His entire *large-and-in-charge* attitude softened as he turned his mesmerizing eyes on her. There was a sparkle in the depths she'd never seen before. "She was here."

Okaaaay. It was going to be one of those conversations. "Evan, please. I'm not up for a wolf-of-mystery passcode-ring-needed explanation. She *who*?"

Maybe she should have clued in faster, but what with her own unusual morning and all, there was no reason for her to suspect. Not until he caught her fingers, squeezing carefully but with great enthusiasm.

"Caro, my mate was in the hotel this morning."

Her first thought became her instant response.

"Holy shit, really? Wheeeee!" Caroline tossed her arms around his neck and hugged until he gasped. "Oh my God, Evan, I'm so thrilled for you."

She let him go, an ear-to-ear grin firmly in position.

He blinked. "You are incredible."

"Actually, I'm confused." She stepped away. "Where is she? I mean, usually you guys find your mates—and I understand your loss of attention on the phone now—but I'd have thought you and she would be off on your wolfish honeymoon already."

His grin faded. "Yeah, well. She was in the hotel. I never really met her."

"But you sniffed her, right?" Caroline was pretty sure that was how it worked. "You at least know for sure she's out there."

"She's out there, yes."

Something was still wrong. "Is she...hiding on you? That doesn't sound typical either."

Evan dropped onto the couch. "Fuck it."

Trouble in paradise. This was not good. "Okay, back up and tell me if I've got this straight. You have a mate, or at least you smelt proof of her in the hotel this morning. Only you haven't met her, which is why you're here, and not off rocking both your worlds."

"Right." He leaned forward, elbows resting on his knees. "Help me find her?"

"Of course I will." What a nightmare this must be for him. "Come on, let's check the security cameras. I can access the feeds from here."

She darted to the computer desk and opened the hotel security system. Evan dragged a seat into position beside her, his hand resting lightly on the back of her chair.

"The only place I scented her was in the kitchen. Shaun and I took a second pass through the restaurant, but there've been too many bodies in the room in the past hour to catch anything."

Caroline punched in her password. "If you scented her in the kitchen, she had to get in and out, somehow. Unless she shifted into a mouse or something."

He choked. "Umm, no. Definitely not. She left through the shipping door."

"How long ago was this?" Caroline looped back through the feed that focused on the kitchen area. Evan's wolf reappeared, shifted back into his human and acted...interesting. "Whoa, were you ever pissy. Way to freak out the staff, big guy."

"I had reason."

She patted his knee. “You did. Come on, backing up shouldn’t take too long then. I’ll focus on the door and take it up to high speed.” A couple adjustments later the workspace was a blur of motion, uniformed cooks and assistants seeming to leap from position to position. “We’re looking for someone returning through the—”

“There.”

He stabbed his finger at the screen and she paused the motion. A body in a black hoodie was backing through the service exit, definitely not one of the staff, who were all dressed in white. “There’s no one else in the room, so no witnesses.” Caroline checked the time stamp. “Ten to ten. Someone should have been in there, no?”

“I would have thought so. Not sure why... What is she doing? And damn it, do we have another camera angle to check?”

Evan’s mate, if that’s who it was, had kept her back to the camera the entire time she paced past the workstations. She had a notebook out and wrote something down at one point. “I’m sorry, Evan, I can’t change angles because there’s only the single ceiling camera. We didn’t install them to monitor staff that closely, just...”

“Just for moments like this, when someone we don’t know tries to gain access to the hotel. Fuck it, Caroline. We’ve got a potentially volatile situation with a hotel full of bear diplomats, who aren’t known to be forgiving of indiscretions or mistakes. What does this mean in terms of them?”

Caroline spun her chair until she could catch his hands. “Hey. You’re rattled, and I get it, because you’re probably some kind of ticking wolf-time-bomb, but please, get it under control.”

The usually level-headed, hyper-bossy, always-in-control A-plus Alpha as good as bounced from his chair and into the kitchen, jerking open the fridge and hauling out a juice. She watched his throat move as he tipped the bottle back and drained it.

That's when the realization hit. They were finished.

She was happy for Evan, but now that he'd found—well, knew his mate existed—it was as good as a done deal in her mind.

Caroline didn't cheat, and she didn't fool around with other women's men. Her and Evan's love affair, as hot and intense and, *holy moly*, tons of fun as it had been, was over.

Something of what rolled through her must have shown on her face, because when their eyes met, his expression shifted. He put down the empty bottle and returned to her side, extending his hand.

She allowed him to pull her to her feet and accepted the hug he gave her, only she couldn't hold back a sigh of regret.

"I'm sorry for hurting you like this." Evan petted her hair gently. Even his touch had changed, from that of a lover heating her to the boiling point to a big brother offering comfort.

"Oh, Evan." She wiggled back far enough they were staring at each other so he had to witness her honest smile. "I don't regret one minute. Not of the time we had together, or that it's over because you've found your missing soul. How could I possibly be upset?"

Confusion lingered in his eyes. "But you sighed as if…"

"I sighed because I'm going to miss the sex, dammit." She wrinkled her nose. "You might have ruined me for everyone else in the future."

Evan grinned cockily. "I did warn you about that when we hooked up, you know."

She laughed. “Yeah, I think you did.”

He squeezed her again. “I don’t regret our time together either, although I am sorry it’s over. You’re a pretty cool human. Very devious.”

Caroline slipped back to the computer chair, considering the changes that would have to happen. “Only when I need to be.”

“Hey, I like devious. You’re more shifter than ninety percent of the pack, when it comes down to it.”

She went back to attempting to find a picture, a notable bit of information anywhere on the security tapes that would help him trace his mate. “I’ll get my things together. I can be clear of your place in the next day or two. I can use my sister’s apartment while she’s out of town.”

“No.” He leaned on the island counter. “You stay here. I’ll move into my room at the pack house until we can find you a new place to live.”

“Don’t be silly, Evan. This is your home. I’m not kicking you out of it.”

Evan narrowed his eyes. “Why are you arguing with me? Is it out of principle? Like you can’t possibly do what the Alpha says for once in your life?”

“Where would be the fun in that?” They smiled at each other, her sadness fading. “I mean it, Evan. You deserve this—to find your mate, and I’ll do everything I can to help you. And that sigh? Wasn’t *just* about the sex. You’ve become a super friend. I’ll miss being around you all the time.”

“Hey, you’re not getting out of my life that easy. We’re switching paths, that’s all.”

She nodded. “Friends instead of lovers?”

“Best friends.”

Her email pinged, but she ignored it. “One other question, though. How do you want to play this out with the pack? I assume while you’d love to hold a citywide search, you don’t want this broadcast. Or do you?”

Evan paced to the windows, messing up his hair with his fingers as he worked out his frustrations. “It’s not likely to stay a secret for long, but I don’t want to shout it from the rooftops. Any apparent weakness is an opportunity for others to take advantage of the pack through me. I won’t let Takhini suffer.”

“So…do you need me to stay here? Pretend we’re still together? I can sleep on a spare mattress in the bedroom. It’s nobody’s business what we’re not doing anymore.”

Evan turned, his gaze sharper, harder. “No, that’s not fair to you, or my mate. I don’t know if she’s unaware of me, but I won’t allow her to think I’m willing to be with anyone but her. Not even in retrospect.”

Caroline was at a loss. “Tell me how I can help.”

“Be yourself.” He gestured in the air, a wide encompassing circle. “Go with your gut instincts—they don’t seem to have failed you before. The hotel needs to keep running smoothly, and I…might need a few kicks in the butt. If I lose focus. Help me?”

“Deal.”

They paused. A moment of silence, almost as if they were saying farewell to what they had been.

Evan stepped to the window, hand clutched around something, his gaze focused into the distance.

Space. They might be committed to staying friends, and helping each other, but right now, they needed some space. She’d gather a few things and head over to Shelley’s apartment to settle in. Even though she was good with the change in their situation, not having Evan in her life was going to take some getting used to.

Maybe the invite to dinner she discovered in her inbox would be enough to distract her. Keep her mind off what she'd lost, and give her the chance to focus on all the good things it meant for her future.

Moving ahead with her plans—change might have come sooner than she expected, but she'd survive. A turn in the path, that's what Evan had called it.

If only she could peek to see what was around the next corner.

Chapter Five

Tyler stepped from the limo and into his brother's encompassing hug.

Frank didn't seem to care they were standing on the sidewalk outside the Takhini pack house, or that there was a horde of wolves watching with great interest as the two of them pounded each other on the back. Justin had a close eye on the crowd, so Tyler concentrated on enjoying being reunited for the first time in ages.

When the affectionate greeting was over, he paused to examine Frank closer. The years of hard living in the remote north had left a mark, but his brother seemed happy enough. Far better than when he'd left his broken heart behind and retreated from the family. "You've put on a few pounds."

"All in the last week, I swear." Frank jerked his thumb over his shoulder. "These wolves? They cook up a damn good table."

Tyler gestured toward their vehicle. "Climb in and we'll hit the restaurant. You can tell me all about your hosts while I do my part to fatten you up."

Frank settled opposite him, his honest face showing his curiosity. "You're all spiffy dressed. I told you it was a casual place."

"Can't be helped, I'm afraid," Tyler explained. "There are too many other delegates in town. I have to be on my best behavior at all times."

Frank made a rude noise. "Politics."

Tyler smiled. "Trust me, there are times I agree with you one hundred percent, only this one is important. It's not just people acting bigger than their britches, which is what I think you called politics when you were young. It's conclave, Frank. If I don't take it seriously, our people could get hurt."

His brother stopped playing with the automatic windows, returning his focus onto Tyler. "I hear you. Which is why I decided I should come after all."

Tyler had wondered about Frank's presence in town. "When I didn't see you in Dawson City, I figured you were too far into the bush to make it. Or tangled up with the strange illness that swept the north. I'm glad you're okay."

"Me too." Frank widened his smile, relaxing back in the seat. "I'm here to enjoy the good parts while you get to do the hard labour. Sounds like a wonderful distribution of work."

Tyler laughed. "We each have talents. Use them as necessary."

Frank nodded. "Speaking of talents, I've been thinking. This whole *brouhaha*—formal, you say?"

"Very."

"You need a bit of help." Frank leaned forward. "You need to know how to read these people, and who to impress, right?"

Diplomacy was what Tyler was good at, but he wasn't about to boast to his brother. Maybe Frank wanted to assist in the mediations. If he behaved it could work to their advantage. Frank wasn't the kind of bear anyone wanted to piss off unintentionally. Nearly seven feet of quick-tempered brute? Tyler and Justin were big, but Frank was in a class all his own.

"You want to join me?"

Frank brayed out a laugh. "Ha. Are you fucking kidding me? I'd have the peace talks down to wrestling and blood before the hour was out, and you know it. No, gentle massaging of egos and shit—not for me, big bro. Not anymore."

If Frank wasn't offering to help, Tyler was confused, but before he could get clarification, the ride was over. Justin pulled open the door and they crawled out, the Klondike Rib and Salmon Barbeque to their right. A long row of customers stood waiting to get in, the line wrapping around the corner and disappearing from sight.

"Come on, we have reservations." Frank cleared a path by simply pacing forward.

Tyler eyed the restaurant as he excused himself to the patrons they were butting in front of. Frank had said the place was casual, but this was lower on the relaxed scale than he'd imagined. Two disproportional buildings were smooshed against each other. The larger one vaguely looked like a tent, as if the original Whitehorse-gold-rush settlers had slapped up four walls and raised canvas over the top to make themselves a shop.

They paused inside the doors as the front desk staff cheered at the sight of Frank. Even the servers weaving between the tables with full hands grinned and called out greetings.

"Your brother doesn't give himself enough credit for knowing how to get along with people. He obviously has a way with them." Justin stood at his back, speaking over Tyler's shoulder as they waited for the spontaneous celebration to die down.

"He's only been here for one week. I can't imagine."

Frank motioned them forward. Tyler nodded politely to the girl holding their menus, then followed his brother toward the end of the room.

The tables ran in long rows, communal style. Red and green gingham tablecloths covered their surfaces, plastic ones, from what he could tell at a glance. The couple already seated at the far end of the table were digging into their food, plastic baskets with fake newsprint as their plates.

Frank settled into his seat with a sigh of happiness. "I love this place."

"They seem to love you." Tyler accepted the menu from the server. "How often have you been here in the past week?"

His brother grinned. "Some of the pack brought me in for lunch the first day I was in town, and I've been back every day since. I'm working my way through the menu."

No wonder the restaurant staff liked him. "Glad to hear you're having a good time. What do you recommend?"

"All of it." Frank nodded. "The ribs are fab, though."

Justin had directed Tyler into a seat that was as protected as possible, yet still presented a good view of the room. The lineup outside was explained as he realized every seat was taken but for the empty space to his left.

Popular place. Not only with locals, but tourists. While it wasn't always possible to spot a shifter from a distance, Tyler knew many of the bears who were in town for the next stage of conclave. He'd met them over the previous weeks in Dawson City, and at first glance, out of the hundred bodies occupying the main seating area, he'd guess fifty percent were bears.

There really was no getting away from it. They'd taken over the town.

Not all eyes staring his way were friendly, either. Supporters of his rivals glared. Those undecided which way to vote kept their expressions blank. The bear elected to the top would have enormous power for years, and even those without an agenda were rightly cautious about supporting some unknown.

A waiter shuffled down the narrow space between tables, filling water glasses and taking orders. Tyler was distracted by a rather venomous glare from a bear seated by the door.

“Justin. By the entrance at one o’clock. Remind me of the clan.”

His friend glanced over. “Radium. Bunch of hotheads. I don’t have proof, yet, but I have my suspicions they were involved in the kidnapping.”

That would make sense. Definitely a group to keep an eye on.

Tyler twisted to give his order to the waiter. “Now That’s a Rack.”

He was horrified to discover that instead of the young man who’d just stepped behind him, he ended up speaking to a familiar-looking blonde.

Caroline Bradley raised a brow. “You have a thing for my breasts, don’t you?”

He surged to his feet, his chair tipping into the person behind him. “I’m sorry, I thought you were the waiter.”

Her smirk widened. “Okay, then. I’ll make sure Anthony knows, but he’s already got a boyfriend.”

Tyler scrambled to dig himself out without looking more of a fool. “No, it’s not like that. There’s an item on the menu called *Now That’s a Rack*. It looks delicious.”

Her upper body, including her delicious rack, shook as she laughed. “I know, I’m just teasing. You have wonderful timing.” She leaned in front of him and gave Frank her hand. “Good to see you again.”

Tyler forced himself to remain in one spot and not *accidentally* lean into her. His attempt was made more difficult as Frank, ever the diplomat, tugged until Caroline was forced to move forward. Her torso rubbed his, every inch pressed to him for a second until she was yanked into Frank's arms for a hug.

Across the table, Justin was looking far too pleased.

"Shut up." Tyler mouthed the words, but that only made Justin grin harder.

Frank finally relaxed his grip on the woman and turned her with great fanfare. "Caroline, I want you to meet my big brother, Tyler."

Caroline cleared her throat and held out her hand—to Justin. "Nice to officially meet you. Sorry about the little incident earlier today, sir."

Justin paused halfway out of his seat. Tyler opened his mouth to explain.

Frank beat them both to it. He laughed and pointed. "Hell, that's not Tyler. That's Justin, his sidekick. The ugly one over here is my brother."

If she'd given him a *what the hell* look earlier for his unintentional sexual comment, her expression had grown miles more judgmental. All traces of amusement were gone. "Oh really. Gee, nice to meet you, *Tyler*. Frank has told me so much about you. He's been raving about how you're so honest and straightforward."

She held her hand steady until he had to accept it. If he'd not been a shifter, her grip would have hurt. As it was, the additional squeeze she gave to the handshake made his bear rumble in approval.

Feisty. *We like feisty*, his bear insisted.

When she let him go and greeted Justin, Tyler gave himself a firm scolding and shoved the beast further down. This was not the time or the place to have a discussion with his animal half about the kind of woman they were supposed to be consorting with at the moment.

Although the idea of consorting a lot more intimately? If he was honest, like Caroline had suggested he usually was, then *honestly*, getting more involved with the woman wouldn't be a problem for man, or beast.

She should have known this would be one of those days. From the disastrous start with housekeeping, to Evan's big revelation, to this wonderful twist on her relaxing evening, she couldn't get an even break.

Screw it. She was going to have fun tonight, and after discovering her bear with the grabby eyes was actually the head of the Harrison delegation, she wasn't nearly as worried about impressing him.

While she was grateful he'd saved her ass, he'd lied to her. That meant he owed her, as far as she was concerned.

"You find everything you needed in your room?" she asked the real Justin.

"Very comfortable, thank you. How are you feeling after your mishap?"

Tyler cussed lightly under his breath, giving himself shit for something.

Okay, that surprised her. She would have expected someone as high-ranked as he was to be able to keep his comments to himself. Maybe she'd only heard him because his chair had ended up closer to hers as they found their seats again.

"I'm feeling fine, thank you. I must have dazed myself for a moment or two. No harm done." She smiled at the waiter as he returned. "Full rack for the fellow beside me, please, and I'll have the usual."

"Sweet Caroline. Of course. And to drink?"

She faced the table. "Gentlemen? Did you order drinks yet?"

Tyler was glaring daggers at the server, a low rumble rising from his barrel-like chest.

Caroline's *give a damn* broke a little more. She'd accepted the invite to dinner as a distraction. She didn't want to deal with any more pissy shifters today, and that glower of his? Said something had cranked the bear's handle wrong in the last couple seconds.

She caught his face in her hands and leaned in, speaking softly. "You do *not* stare at the staff like they are scratching posts. Get it together."

He blinked, hard, refocusing on her face. He hooked his fingers around her wrists and lowered her arms until their hands were in his lap. His breathing slowed as he got himself under control then nodded. "Thank you."

Justin spoke up. "A bottle of red for the table, please. The merlot."

"Chilkoot beer for me."

"Double-sized. Of course, Frank." The waiter slipped away, not even aware he'd been one swipe from being knocked into tomorrow, if Caroline was any judge of shifter attitudes.

She jerked her arms back, trying to break Tyler's grip on her wrists. "You want to let me go, big guy?"

Tyler straightened in a flash. "Sorry."

Frank's gaze flipped back and forth between them like crazy. "You two know each other already?"

"Slightly." It was Justin who spoke again, smoothing things over. "Caroline was kind enough to help prepare our suite."

Frank grinned. “Damn, girl, you do take care of the details, don’t you?” He elbowed his brother hard enough Tyler coughed out a gasp. “See, she’s got the smarts to deal with anything. You should take my advice.”

Caroline leaned on the table. “What kind of trouble are you getting me into?”

The big bear lowered his voice, gaze darting around the room as if making sure no one was listening. “Told them you were good at dealing with shifters. You need to help Tyler here win this election so the rest of the rowdies will get out of Whitehorse sooner.”

Good grief. Was everyone intent on running her life? “Gee, thanks, Frank. Maybe I’ll talk to Tyler about what he needs, okay?”

The big bear shrugged happily. “Sure. Just, you impressed a lot of people. Your sister thinks you’re damn cool, and she’s like the queen of the north after making the vaccination that saved our butts. If she looks up to you, then you’re aces. You know what I mean?”

Conversation stopped as Anthony brought the wine to the table and poured three glasses. Caroline wasn’t discussing anything until she’d had something to drink.

Tyler caught her with the edge of the glass already to her lips, nearly desperate for a swallow of the soothing liquid. “A toast.”

She tipped the glass away, fighting her sigh of frustration.

He lifted his own glass and stared her in the eyes. “To new friends, and a successful visit to Whitehorse.”

Caroline clicked glasses with him and Justin. There wasn’t any choice in the matter without making a huge fuss.

The look in Tyler’s eyes, though? The one that suggested he

wasn't only interested in taking her out for dinner? He could hold off that anticipatory expression for another century or two. She might be a free agent after Evan's change of circumstance, but the last thing she needed was another head honcho to babysit. She loved Alpha males, but damn they were a lot of work.

She had to concentrate on the people who really needed her. Like Evan. And the pack.

Liquid swirled as she raised the wine goblet and imbibed long and deep. When she rested the glass on the table, a warm buzz had already begun at the back of her brain.

That was what she needed. To get good and tight. Something to help her forget she would be sleeping alone for the first time in months.

Tyler cleared his throat. "Perhaps we could start again. Caroline, I'm glad you could join us for dinner. If there's anything you need to make the evening more pleasant, let me know."

She took another sip of her wine as she considered his far more polite offer. Thank goodness the man had the sense to back off. "Keep my glass full and don't steal mushrooms off my plate, and I'll be fine."

He nodded. "What are you having, by the way?"

"Sweet Caroline."

His fingers tightened on his wine glass. "That's a menu item?"

She nodded, easing back in her chair slightly.

"Vegetarian pasta—they named it after me. I find I get a lot of meat dishes at the restaurant and pack house. You shifters tend to neglect your veggies." His expression of dismay was rather hilarious until she put two and two together. "You're kidding. That gruff-and-growly thing earlier was because you thought Anthony was sweet-talking me?"

"Well, I..." Tyler turned back to the table and straightened the utensils, lining them up with the grid system on the checkered tablecloth. "I didn't want him to treat you disrespectfully."

Good grief. Cute, but not necessary. Caroline held out her glass. "I need more wine."

Tyler topped it up, examining her closely as he poured. She drew in a deep breath just to watch his gaze stray from the top of the glass to her breasts.

"Whoa, Tyler." Justin leaned across the table and mopped up the spilt wine.

Caroline hid her smile as she took another swallow and checked out the rest of the room. Served him right for staring at her chest. Again. The man truly was obsessed.

Strangers filled the restaurant, Caroline noted. Not unusual for the tourist destination, but the ratio was off even from what she'd expect in mid-July. Human tourists were far outnumbered by the time their appetizers arrived, as the shifters kept coming. She chatted with Justin and Frank about Whitehorse, answering the typical questions that were always asked, but she also watched the door.

It was simple, really, to tell who was what. Visitors who hadn't been in the rib joint before paused to look around. They would sniff, the scent of barbeque and deep fried fish filling the air with wonderful aromas.

The humans would then turn to their companions and gush about the tasty smells. The shifters? Their gazes flicked to Tyler and Justin first, then farther into the room to examine the other shifters already seated. The newcomers even ignored the waitresses.

These were some tense shifters to ignore the pretty girls right under their noses.

Their meals arrived, huge platters of food lowered in front of Frank and Justin, the infamous rack of ribs in front of Tyler, and her pasta. They dug in heartily even while remaining alert.

Caroline nodded at Justin's question regarding the hotel, turning to see what Tyler wanted.

He'd pushed a rib to one side of his plate. "Would you like one?"

Maybe she'd had too much wine. Maybe she'd relaxed a tad too much after all the stress of the day. Perhaps she just wanted to cause him some pain for his earlier stupid moves. Whatever her reasons were, in the end she listened to the devil on her shoulder and not the angel. The angel promptly gave up and slung back the remainder of a teeny bottle of angel wine.

"Sure." Caroline stared at his face as she licked her lips.

Tyler hesitated, his fork hovering over the rib, his gaze fixed on her lips. She used her fingers to lift the savoury bone to her mouth and nibbled the meat from one side.

"Hmm, very good today." She licked her fingers clean one at a time, making sure to use lots of tongue.

His jaw fell open slightly, his breath escaping in light pants as she wiped the final bits of sauce from her lips. Okay, maybe the *no attention from him for a few centuries* was a little long to wait. He was attractive, she was interested. By the time the bears were done their business in town, she'd be ready for a night of adventure with him, as long as he wasn't into any furry stuff.

Tyler shifted uncomfortably in his chair, the wood creaking under his heavy mass. Caroline picked up her wine glass again, this time to hide her smile.

She still had it.

The volume of noise in the room had increased steadily over the course of their meal, laughter at times, but mostly voices. Male voices, and Caroline frowned as she examined the shifters.

Justin lifted his head. "Something wrong?"

"Your get-together. What is it, no females allowed?" She pointed into the room. "I don't see a single lady bear dining out."

Justin cleared his throat. "Well, yes, they are here in town—you should have seen them when they were checking in. But we tend to be protective of their more delicate..."

His words trickled to a halt about the time her brows hit her hairline. Good thing he'd stopped that nonsense before going any further.

Only she needed to know. "Tyler, you think the same way?"

His chuckle sounded sincere. "I believe in protecting those who need protecting, when they need it."

"Nice political answer. You didn't tell me anything."

He shrugged. "I'm a political kind of guy."

The twinkle in his eyes said more than *political*, confirming his continued interest in her.

Of course, that's the moment when the loud discussions at the front of the restaurant turned to shouting.

Chapter Six

Justin was up in an instant, physically blocking her and Tyler from the disturbance that grew louder by the minute.

Frank lumbered to his feet. "I can settle them down."

Tyler held him back, a hand on his arm. "Wait. It's not our battle yet."

Caroline leaned around the mass of bear between her and the fight. Tyler was right. People got in shoving matches all the time, and she didn't have to feel as if she needed to be the one to solve all the problems.

Only when she spotted who was involved, tables and chairs tumbled to the ground around them, things changed.

"Damn fools."

She ducked under Justin's arm, evading his grasp to scramble the length of the room and step in between the two biggest shifters facing off with raised fists. She glared at the wolf in front of her, one of the Takhini pack who had a bad habit of getting in trouble, wordlessly daring him to make one wrong move.

"If you have an argument, take it outside." Caroline held out a hand to the human waitress trapped against the wall, pulling the girl forward and sending her running for the safety of the kitchens. "This isn't the place for swinging fists."

The wolf in front of her backed down, he and his companions all making tracks for the exit door as if she might pull Evan out of her pocket and sic him on their butts. Or maybe they were scared enough of her without the threat of Evan, she couldn't be sure.

"Leave enough money to pay for half of what you broke," she called after them.

"Pussy-whipped." The word growled out behind her from the other half of the problem.

Oh, this would be fun. Caroline twisted slowly, reaching into her pocket as she moved. "You boys enjoying your visit to Whitehorse so far?"

The bear in front of her had a red welt on the cheek where something had hit him in the past few minutes. "Who are you, the RCMP?"

Close enough. She resisted the urge to pull imaginary guns from a holster. "Concerned citizen who wants to get back to my dinner, and all the noise is making it hard to concentrate. So why don't you guys call it a night as well?"

The bear laughed, then lowered his voice as he glanced around the room. "You and what army going to make us leave?"

She flicked out her left hand, and while he was distracted by the laser light she danced on the floor, she moved in and slammed her fingers around his balls. She squeezed hard enough for him to know she wasn't going anywhere.

He froze in position, not even breathing. A couple tidbits she'd learned from her years around shifters—dancing red lights were tough to ignore when they weren't expecting them. And balls made a dandy set of reins, no matter how big the beast.

Caroline leaned toward his ear. "I don't need an army. Because you're going to be polite, and not only leave, but you'll give the nice human waitress you scared a big tip to make up for being a jerk. And then, you won't come back here anymore."

Additional pressure from her fingers made him suck in a breath through his nose. "You're pretty cocky for a frail little thing," he croaked through his gritted teeth.

"You mean for a human?" She continued to whisper, the rumble of voices in the background covering her words. "That's the other item on my list. I see you making trouble again, I'll be in touch with your clan leader, and rest assured I know how to make shifters uncomfortable. Now, do you want to leave with your balls or without them?"

He let out a wicked snarl, but she forced herself to stay in one spot. Yeah, she wouldn't want to meet him in a back alley, but a huge part of dealing with shifters was never letting them know that. She adjusted her grip.

His growl broke off into a grunt of pain. "We're leaving."

His buddies shuffled out as he gestured toward the door, Caroline still holding him pinned in place.

"Remember the money you owe," Caroline tossed after them. She stared up at her captive. "Name?"

His nostrils flared as he glared at her. "Mick Lucerne."

"Mick. Tell your clan leader the Takhini pack is watching."

She released her hold on his groin but didn't step back, staying in his personal space, her chin held high, spine straight. The hush in the room ebbed and flowed as whispers broke out, or people gathered coats and fled.

Here and there, though, things went back to normal. Anthony gingerly stepped around them to pick up the fallen chairs, as he and another waiter set the tables to rights.

Mick adjusted his hips and broke off eye contact, lowering his gaze. "I'll pass on the message."

She didn't let down her guard until he was out of the room, pausing to press a wad of rolled bills into the wide-eyed waitress's palm.

Okay. Her heart rate was nowhere near normal. Caroline considered ordering a new bottle of wine for herself. Damn, she enjoyed excitement, but that had been unexpected.

Frank met her three steps from their table. "You were insane."

He didn't sound pissed off, he sounded impressed.

Caroline gestured him back to his chair. "Half the idiots involved in the rumble were Takhini. I knew I could get them to smarten up pretty quickly, which you couldn't. Thanks for wanting to help, though."

Justin held her chair. "I don't know if I should congratulate you or see if you're running a fever."

"Oh, just an average day in Whitehorse. Could I have another glass of wine, please?"

There was a bottle at her elbow before she finished speaking. The owner, gratitude on his face. "Caroline. I have to name something else for you, don't I?"

"Dan, you need to stop serving such good food. Look at what you caused—they were fighting at the tables for the leftovers."

Dan winked. "I'm sure. Well, whatever magic you pulled, I appreciate your help, as always. Dinner is on the house."

Caroline accepted the full glass from Justin and drank deeply, working hard to get back the relaxed and distracted sensation she'd had going. Now, where was she?

Right, flirting with Tyler.

Only when she turned to smile at him, he didn't return it. His expression seemed locked between admiration and horror.

She lowered her glass and examined him closer.

He had a death grip on the edge of the table.

"Something wrong?"

Tyler cleared his throat. "You do that often? Wade without blinking into a situation that could end in death?"

Her last straw broke. She didn't need a lecture. Not from him, not from anybody. "Why yes, I do. It's like this addiction I have. You're not truly living until you're one paw swing from a painful demise, you know what I mean?"

She reached for her glass only to find she was airborne, her belly firmly planted in Tyler's shoulder as he lifted her into the air.

"What are you doing?" She couldn't see a thing, her head dangling toward the floor, legs locked in his grasp.

Tyler stomped toward the door.

Caroline snorted in disbelief. What the hell was going on?

"Is there a problem?" The owner's voice.

Caroline planted her hands on Tyler's ass and twisted in an attempt to solve this situation as well, but the big bear who'd snatched her up had found his diplomacy. Sort of. He turned on the charm with her still suspended over his shoulder.

"Dan, thank you for everything. Caroline's a touch overwrought after the *showdown at okay corral* a moment ago. We're going to sit by the river for a while to calm down. Thank you for dinner. Please, allow my man to take care of any additional charges you have to repair things from the fight."

"Why, thank you." Tyler was moving again, but there was Dan, bent at the waist to dip his head to her level as she was carried past. "Caroline, always good to see you."

She wasn't about to call for help like some victimized heroine to announce she was being kidnapped. Not after she'd faced down a volatile fight. "Night, Dan. Wonderful as always."

The simple response—the only one she could make without turning this into a major situation—struck her as hilarious, and giggles set in hard. She folded her arms and rested her head on Tyler's strong back as he conveyed her across the road and into the park.

A set of fancy dress shoes and one beat-up pair of runners, both extra large, followed them.

Caroline got herself under control enough to speak. "Justin, does your boss do this all the time?"

"Not typically."

"Ty's gone out of his flipping mind," Frank suggested. "What the hell is wrong with you, bro?"

Tyler lowered her to a bench then shook his finger in her face. "You, stay."

Caroline had to be partly drunk. She curled her legs under her and made a face at him. "Woof."

His expression didn't break. He turned to Frank. "Thank you for joining us for dinner. It's been great touching base, and we'll get together again in the next couple days, deal?"

Frank nodded and stretched. "Nice evening. Think I'll take a walk before heading back to the pack house. See you later, Caroline. Justin—hang loose."

His brother ambled off happily as Tyler wrestled with the knot of tension inside him.

Caroline blinked at him from her spot on the bench, taking control of the wine bottle he'd grabbed from the table. She raised it in a silent cheer before putting the bottle to her lips.

He tore his gaze off her mouth and focused on his guard. "Go home."

Justin didn't move. "I don't think so."

Fuck it. What was the use of being the head of the biggest bear conglomerate when he couldn't get anyone to listen? "Justin. I don't need a babysitter."

"But you do need a chaperone." Justin motioned to Caroline. "Take your time, remember you're in public, and I'll be right over there just out of hearing, waiting until you get whatever the hell is wrong out of your system."

Tyler wanted to rip something to shreds, preferably his best friend's head, but the noncompromising stance Justin took forced Tyler to accept the truth.

As much as he wanted to vanish with Caroline, he couldn't. He'd been over the line hauling her ass out of the restaurant, and that was only forgivable because she'd laughed and made it all right.

He dipped his head briefly at Justin then joined Caroline on the bench, collapsing without much hope of holding up his limbs any longer.

She sat quietly, the two of them looking over the smooth flowing river. She held out the bottle, and he accepted it, swallowing down a number of gulps like some street person.

"What a day." Caroline stretched her legs in front of her and leaned back.

Tyler switched from watching the water to examining her legs, mesmerized. "It's been interesting, yes."

"So, what's the most recent thing on the 'this day can't possibly get any weirder' for you? Me, I got carried out of a restaurant by a cranky bear."

He went for honest. "It was carry you out, or shift in public."

"Shit." She leaned closer, peering into his face. "Really?

Well, I'm glad you went Tarzan on me then, but what the hell? I wasn't in any danger, you know."

Tyler wasn't as sure of that as she seemed to be. "You know why we're in town?"

She nodded. "Conclave. You guys vote for leadership then somehow the leader deals with territorial-distribution issues. You had the first part of the meetings in Dawson City earlier this summer, and you're supposed to finish them here."

Not bad. "You're well informed."

She wrinkled her nose. "I'm...kind of well connected in the Takhini pack. That was part of the reason I stepped in at the restaurant. I knew the wolves involved in the potential rumble would listen to me without an argument."

Tyler glanced at Justin, but his guard was being true to his word. He'd stepped far enough away he could keep an eye on what was going on around them, but he mustn't have heard her comment, or he would have given Tyler an "I told you so" look.

"Well connected means you understand how typical shifters react in power situations?"

"Considering I just had my fingers wrapped around a bear's gonads, uh, yeah. Violence is not the option of last choice, it's usually the first. Getting physical is like breathing to shifters, or at least to wolves."

Tyler watched her take another drink, wiping her mouth with the back of her hand as she offered him the bottle again.

"Bears are worse."

Her snort of disbelief only made his bear more agitated.

"I'm serious. You mention getting physical as a first option. Bears do that, step in and fight before trying to talk things through. But there's a violence built into us beyond protecting or wanting to win. Most bears don't give a damn if they get hurt during the power exchange, as long as their opponent ends up hurting harder."

She was thinking it through. "What does this have to do with you almost shifting?"

"My bear admires you."

Her eyes widened. "You guys don't do the mate thing, though, right? Like you're not telling me that—"

If only it were that simple. "No. Bears don't have fated mates, but my bear *likes* you. Not only physically, but your knowledge and your bravery. On an animal level he somehow senses you'd be good for me."

She slouched on the bench, staring out over the water. "Well, isn't that sweet. I'd be good for you. This day gets better and better."

Tyler considered his options, discarding them as rapidly as they popped to mind. Perhaps downplaying the physical attraction between the two of them was best, and he should appeal to her human side.

"Good for me as in *politically*. It's vital I end up on top by the end of the voting. Not because I crave the power, but because there are a few territories that need to be straightened out, and my main opponents are the ones who got them into trouble. If it were a matter of a cage fight, or leadership ripping out each other's throats, it would be different. These men aren't reasonable, though. We're talking communities of people—innocent women and children—who will be hurt if the wrong people come into power."

She rose to her feet, pacing in front of the bench. "I still don't see where I fit into this. Win the vote, then. Takhini pack will support you as much as we can, but that should mainly involve us doing a better job of keeping our hotheads out of fisticuffs with bears at large."

"Takhini's help guarding the peace is a start. There are also a few events in the next week where I'd be grateful if you'd act as my assistant."

"Oh boy." She crossed her arms and stared into space. "Well, that might be possible, but we have to talk to Evan, because he's usually got my schedule wrapped up."

"I'll speak to him first thing in the morning, then."

"Email is the quickest way to get hold of him."

She rubbed the back of her neck, and he remembered her fall. "You must be exhausted. Did you see a doctor?"

"Don't baby me. I'm fine, but I am ready for this day to be over." She smiled tentatively. "I must seem very unorthodox to you. Believe me, this day has been weird even by my standards."

He didn't care. His need to protect her and care for her was buzzing as his bear gloated over her *somewhat* agreement to act as his assistant.

Assistant sounded more professional than date, but at this point, whatever got him what he needed was fine by him. "Allow me to take you home."

"It's only a couple of... Oh, why the hell am I even trying? You'll probably pick me up and carry me if I protest." She turned and whistled at Justin who jerked in surprise as she gestured him closer. "We're done. You got wheels waiting somewhere?"

Justin glanced his direction, an unspoken question on his face. Tyler leapt to his feet and spoke before Justin could blurt out anything dire. "We're driving Caroline home. The rest of the details will be dealt with tomorrow."

Justin nodded and pulled out his phone.

Tyler offered his arm to her. "Walk with me?"

Her fingers curled around his biceps, and he slammed his lips together to stop a rumble of satisfaction from escaping. His desire to roll over her life and simply take control had to be fought. At least for now.

If she'd meet him in the middle, he could concentrate on his job and ease the beast within.

The ride to her apartment passed in silence as she stared out the window and Justin, fortunately, held his tongue. When they stopped, Tyler followed her out of the vehicle, motioning Justin back. His guard rolled his eyes but remained on the sidewalk.

She tapped in the security code at the front doors. "You don't need to walk me up."

"Humour me."

"I hope you realize if I weren't so exhausted, my answer would be *hell no*." She waited for him to push the doors open then led him to the elevator. "I'm capable of taking care of myself. Remember that, and we'll get along much better."

Tyler held his peace until they hit her floor and she had the deadbolt unlocked.

She turned in the doorway. "There we go. Safely home. Thanks for the lovely evening, and we'll be in—"

He twisted her to the side and pinned her to the wall. Frustration, hunger—it all came together in one moment of need that had to be answered.

"Maybe it's the fact you can take care of yourself that makes you so damn attractive."

He wrapped one hand around the back of her head, the other at her hip as he kept her completely under his control. He caught her with her mouth open as he kissed her. A rush of excitement roared through him at her taste, and his bear finally settled in satisfaction.

She hesitated, and he wondered if his balls were in danger, then she thrust her fingers into his hair and dove wholeheartedly into the kiss. Tongues tangling, bodies pressed tightly together. She wrapped a leg around his thigh, opening her body to him. He used both hands to lift her, lining up their mouths better while easing his erection between her thighs.

Caroline groaned as his lips left hers, kissing his way along her jaw to her neck. The sound fluttered as he took hold of her earlobe and sucked lightly.

“How hard did I hit my damn head this morning?” Her muttered complaint was negated by the fisted grasp she maintained on his hair, holding him to her throat. She was nearly purring with satisfaction as he tasted her skin.

He licked, once, and her full-body shiver made the hair on his arms stand on end with the desire to take more.

To hell with restraint, he wanted to take it all.

Control fled as he latched his mouth onto her neck and sucked. He played her with his tongue, tormenting them both as he rocked against her, taking the final liberty he’d allow himself this night.

She swore and jerked his hair, tugging hard enough to break the seal between them, but not soon enough to stop him from leaving a mark on her pale skin.

His bear gloated, then retreated like a coward leaving him to face her alone.

They stared at each other, still breathing heavily, still smashed together in the open doorway of her apartment.

She tried to settle her gasps. “I should be pissed.”

“Don’t kid yourself. We both needed this.”

“That’s what makes me upset.” She loosened her death

grip, lowering her leg toward the ground. “I know better than to act without thinking.”

He slipped her down the front of his body, the tight run against his cock driving him wild while strangely filling him with peace. Somewhere, not too far down the road, they would answer the physical craving between them. Even knowing that made it easier to wait.

“Instincts are rarely wrong.” He stepped back and dipped his head politely. “I look forward to exploring that concept with you.”

He waited until she’d closed the door and the deadbolt had turned before making his way back to the limo.

Justin held the door for him. “You smell like the human. I take it she agreed to be your date for the galas?”

Tyler settled into the seat and wondered at it. “I have no idea what she’ll do next, and somehow that amuses me far more than it should.”

Not even Justin’s expression of dismay could bring him down from his high. The next round of voting would begin the following afternoon. He should be obsessing over numbers and finding new ways to gain allies.

Yet all his gut instincts were wrapped up in one fiery-tempered blonde with a penchant for speaking her mind. Who kissed like she could suck his soul from his body.

He was one out-of-control bear, and he liked it.

Chapter Seven

Evan paced his office three times, pausing at the window to examine the parking lot for her car before repeating the motion. Every time the computer announced there was another email, he slipped over to read what was fast becoming a joke of cosmic proportions.

A yawn escaped him, and he scratched his jaw, wondering if he needed a second shower to knock the cobwebs from his brain today.

Sleep had eluded him for most of the night. While he'd been honest with Caroline about his need to start a new direction between them, he'd missed her, damn it. Missed having her complain about the pack. Missed seeing her walk naked from the tub into his bed. Missed how she hogged the covers and then cursed when he tugged them free.

If his mate had already been on the scene, he would have been distracted, but all Caroline's absence did was showcase even more what was missing in his life.

He wanted his mate, for fuck's sake. Wanted her to be the one wandering his apartment naked, jumping into bed with him, leaving him breathless and satisfied. What he and Caroline shared had been incredible, but only a shadow of what his life would be.

Lost in limbo between what he'd had and what he had to

find was a fucking unhappy place.

He peeked out the window again. Where the hell was she? Caroline was never late for work. Maybe he should phone her. He glanced at his watch and growled in frustration. Only seven thirty. He couldn't expect her for at least thirty minutes.

Another email pinged, and he swore. He had to do something to pass the time.

Cueing up the security tapes simply aggravated him further. Not only did it take him four tries—he fucking *hated* computers—but when he did luck out and open the right program it remained a dead end. Lots of little details like his mate wore her nails neatly trimmed, and she had a freckle on the back of one hand. And she was short. That much they could get from the tapes, but nothing else.

The office door swung open at eight and he snapped to his feet. Caroline walked in and this familiar aroma wafted in with her. Familiar, but unexpected.

She clicked her tongue sadly. "Still looking for clues? I wonder if we contacted a few of our neighbors and asked to see—"

Evan moved in closer. "What the hell have you been up to?"

She paused in the middle of putting her purse away. "Hello?"

There was that scent again. "Bears."

She did *exasperated* well. "Oh, *God*, you would not believe the trouble those creatures are."

"I bet I would."

She dropped into her computer chair, misery written all over her, and his gut did a triple backflip.

"Caro?"

She paused, gaze fixed on the empty screen. Then she

lowered her hands into her lap and twisted to face him. Confusion painted her features. “Never mind me, I had a rough evening.”

“Me too.” Plus, he missed kissing her good morning. “Fuck it all, come here.”

He held his arms open and willed the part of himself to the surface that was pack, and nothing else. The care-for-everyone-and-make-them-happy part.

She curled against him, and he held her tight, her warmth settling on his chest like a cuddly kitten, without the sneeze-inducing allergies. Having her there only increased his confusion, though, as he fought the urge to blurt out the questions flooding his brain.

Instead, he soaked in the companionship she offered, the deep comfort of holding someone who cared for him, who was part of his family. Turning it into a pack issue saved his butt and put things into perspective. He could ache for her without the feelings turning sexual.

Which made it easier to cradle her until she finally sighed, far more relaxed than when she’d basically thrown herself into his arms.

“Better?” he asked.

“Yes.” She leaned back and smiled. “Oh, what a tangled mess I’ve gotten myself into.”

“Really.” Evan considered the dozen emails sitting on the computer and wondered if she already knew, or if they were in addition to her troubles. One thing he had to ask. “Does the tangle involve bears? I mean, at least one male bear?”

She laughed, backing out of his arms. “I had a shower last night, and this morning. I used shampoo, conditioner and body wash, and you can still smell him?”

"That's not an answer. An answer would involve name and clan affiliation. And a detailed list of why you smell like him after the scrub down. Or don't I want to know?" He leered.

Damn if she didn't flush. "Nothing happened."

"Oh, *really*?" He brushed a fingertip over what he would have sworn was a hickey on her neck.

"Nothing much, at least." Caroline collapsed back into her computer chair and stared at the ceiling. "I swear you guys are so damn complicated. I'm doing a Google search for a part of the world where there are no shifters and holidaying there, first chance I get."

"New York City is shifter free."

She snapped halfway upright. "You're shitting me."

He grinned. "Yeah, I am. Sorry, Caro, you're stuck as one of the most shifter-educated humans in the world. You get to enjoy our glory no matter where you go."

"Bastard."

He pulled a chair up beside her. "Want to talk about it?"

"Not really."

"I think we should."

She stared him down. "Did you get an email this morning naming you master of the universe concerning my life?"

"You were expecting emails?" Because if she was expecting them, that changed everything.

Only she frowned. "Emails—no, one email. From..." She spun toward the computer and shifted the mouse to wake the screen. "Holy shit, what are all those?"

"Emails to the hotel-slash-Takhini pack with the subject line *Regarding Caroline Bradley* and *Urgent request for C. Bradley* and my personal fav..." He leaned over and clicked open one of the messages.

Caroline leapt back as a GIF flashed across the screen showing a nearly naked male, hips pulsing in what he must consider a sexy move with the words *make my day, baby* pasted across the bottom of the picture.

"That one is from Clan Miette. Classy."

"Oh my God, what is going on, Evan?"

"You seem to have done something last night that impressed or freaked out, I'm not sure which, all of the visiting bear clans. You've now been asked to join..." Evan slid his finger down the computer face and counted, "...wow, it's up to fourteen different clans as an 'interested party to the proceedings'. You want to tell me what this *tangled mess* you mentioned involves? Because it looks as if you've hauled the Takhini pack full force into the bear conclave, whether that was your intention or not."

"I didn't do anything..." he gave her a look, "...out of the ordinary. Stop that. You know I don't make trouble for trouble's sake. That's Shaun's job."

"True." He moved toward the coffee machine.

"I interrupted a rumble during dinner. Lance and Toby are on the shitlist, by the way."

"That's not unusual news either. I take it the fight involved bears?"

"Yes. I was out with Frank at the time."

His hands jerked, and Evan slopped coffee over the edge of the cup. "Whoa. Really? You and Frank?"

He didn't want to picture it. Not the big, rustic, half-wild visitor.

She snatched the cup from him and gave him a glare. "No, you dirty-minded shifter. I was not fooling around with Frank. Good grief."

"Well, that makes it so much better. Which bear were you fooling around with?" Not that he was jealous or anything.

Much.

She sighed. "Frank's brother kissed me. He's rather exasperating, in this sexy, overbearing, luggish way."

"You do like them luggish."

"Ha!" She lost her pout. "You should know. Neanderthal."

He nodded slowly. "Okay, this makes more sense. You did something hugely unexpected and out of character for a human, followed by showing a marked interest in one of the powerhouses involved in conclave. Now all the clans are taking a shot at you in the hopes of neutralizing whatever advantage you bring forward, if nothing else."

She stared at him. "You're joking. It was a public dinner with Tyler, his bodyguard and his brother, and one bloody kiss—that no one saw, I might add."

"I'm not so sure. Check the fifth email."

She scrambled for the mouse, swearing as that particular email turned out to have an attachment link to a newsletter. *Be Bear Aware*. "This is some kind of joke."

"Well, they don't have great skills as paparazzi, but I think that grainy JPEG is you and him sharing a memorable first date on the park bench. Once again—classy. You should have told me I needed to wine and dine you more."

"Asshole." She pointed at the screen. "We weren't doing anything but sitting. The kiss happened…elsewhere."

"Doesn't matter where, it happened and word got out. So the question becomes, what are you going to do about it?"

So much for her nice, simple life. Every hour that passed seemed to bring more twists to the program instead of less. "I need to brainstorm with you. I need your perspective, okay?"

Evan lowered himself into his favourite leather chair, draping a leg over the arm. "Storm away."

"I could say no to them all. Remain neutral." She pressed back into her computer chair, rocking it slowly. "That's one solution."

"Remaining out of the picture is one choice." He eyed her. "Is that really an option, though?"

"What do you mean?"

He took a long obvious sniff.

She wished baring her teeth and growling would make an impact on his stupid ass. Instead she threw a pen at him. "Stop that. Yes, even though one of the clan leaders kissed me, we're not handfasted or something. I could delete all the messages or politely tell them I'm otherwise occupied."

"Okay, so what's the advantage of you staying out of it?"

She thought longingly of a sun-scorched beach. "I can keep up with my job here at the hotel and help you find your mate."

"Hmm. Both worthy tasks. What's the advantage of you getting involved with the bruins?"

She was trapped. "Damn it, Evan. Being a part of the conclave is like a front-row seat to keeping the pack informed and safe. And last night..."

The information Tyler had shared regarding why conclave was so important had made sense. There were shifters out there she didn't want in control of anything bigger than a toaster.

Evan's foot bounced as he scratched his chin. "I see lots of reasons why it's a good thing, Caro, you accepting an invite. This is bigger than me and my current issue, or the hotel for that matter. If you're willing to sacrifice some personal time and suffer through political bullshit for a week, I think it's worthwhile for the pack. But I'm a little biased."

"Well, yeah you are, but you're also right. This is big, and I'd be stupid to ignore the opportunity."

He cleared his throat. "Then you simply need to decide which one of your bear beaus you want to go to the ball with."

"Shut up." She tapped the arm of her chair with her fingertips as she considered. "How much do you know about Tyler?"

"Other than you swapped spit?"

Gah. "You are so annoying at times."

He grinned. "You love me, you know you do."

In her way, she did. "Tyler shared information last night that made me think he's one of the good guys. Does what you know line up with my instant appraisal?"

Evan leaned forward, his expression sharpening. "I checked out all the clans before conclave moved. He's clean from what I could find. Hard working and runs a fair company. Head of his family. No shifter issues in his territory, unlike the reports from a few others. This might be your decision, but you are not getting involved with Clan Ainsworth or Lucerne. I won't allow it."

Well. "You won't allow it. Really."

He rose to tower over her. "You might not be in my bed anymore, but you're still mine. I forbid you to get involved with anyone I suspect cares less for your survival than what they can squeeze from you in short-term benefits."

As a human, his shifter power didn't hit her the same way it would affect a fellow wolf. Didn't mean she couldn't feel the effects, especially when like now, he had his dominance cranked on full blast.

To a human who'd never experienced it before, even a

gentle touch could make them uncomfortable. Perhaps have them running from the room as if they'd felt a ghost. Caroline stiffened her spine. She raised an arm to admire the way her hair stood straight on end. "Whoa, you're like a twelve on the Richter scale with that order."

"I don't want you dead."

Whoa again. She laid her hand on his and tried to soothe him. "Hey, this is me. You don't need to get all growly so I'll listen to reason. Don't make the situation bigger and scarier than it has to be for shock value."

He shook his head. "You're not getting it. If anything, I'm playing down the dangers. Yes, I'd love to have you as a fly on the wall to keep things safe for Takhini, but these are bears, Caroline. For all my and Shaun's joking about the 'wimpy bears voting instead of ripping out throats like us macho wolves', there's a reason they moved to this method. It saves a fuck-ton of lives. This won't be a walk in the park. You will be vulnerable, and if something happened to you, I'd never forgive myself."

Caroline nodded slowly. She touched his face. "I'll be careful, and I'll take this seriously. And if I feel as if it's getting too much for me at anytime, I'll step aside, okay?"

"Promise me."

Evan turned down the Alpha vibes and her body stopped pulsating.

She raised her hand in the air, palm forward. "I solemnly swear I will protect my ass at all times."

He narrowed his gaze. "Well...maybe that will do."

She flipped her hand around and turned the vow into one, lone finger.

"Don't push me, Evan. I've had a seriously weird twenty-four hours." He raised a brow, all Spock-like and she snorted. "Okay, fine, you're in the same boat, and you don't even have a paddle."

He laid his arm around her shoulders and tugged her in, resting his chin on her head. "We'll get through this, you and I. We're strong, we're smart."

"And we don't take shit from anyone." Caroline squeezed him tight. The path had turned the corner, and she was almost at the point she'd be able to spot the coming obstacles.

Because if she'd learned anything, obstacles went with the territory.

Evan pushed her toward the computer. "You're going to accept Tyler's offer, I presume."

She glanced down the list of names, shocked to see them all. "If we eliminate the ones you know are rotters, should I do more research before accepting anyone?"

He paused. "What's your gut telling you?"

Tyler's deep rumbled words about instincts flashed through her brain, bringing the smooth slide of sexual anticipation along for the ride. "You don't want to know my gut right now."

"I love it," Evan chortled. "You are such a weird human."

"Enough." Caroline dragged her hands through her hair—one of the fidgets of frustration she'd learned from Evan. "Who am I kidding, though? What Tyler said to me last night regarding power seemed completely honourable. The fact he's attractive isn't a hardship." She glanced at Evan. "I'm not trying to replace you. I hope you know that."

He seemed lost for a moment before his face brightened with comprehension. "Oh, Caro, you don't have to explain away animal attraction or justify getting involved with another guy. There's no statute of limitations that wolves adhere to."

"I don't need to go through a period of mourning before hopping into another man's bed?"

He laughed. "I'm not dead, and neither are you. Stop worrying about if you and Mr. Teddybear are going to fuck around. Worry about how to survive whatever weird things bears do."

His phone went off, and Evan answered it, swearing starting shortly after he lifted it to his ear.

"One second." He leaned down and kissed her cheek. "I gotta run. Someone mucked up the kitchen orders and the chef is getting spirited."

"Spirited?"

"Literally. He's drinking already, and if we want to survive the lunch rush, I need to go coddle him."

She nodded. "I'll find out what's involved in the bear deal and get as much done of my job in advance as I can."

He waved from the door. "Give it a break. You're indispensible, but we'll manage."

Caroline waited until he was gone, rising and double-checking the office door was locked before returning to the computer and pausing.

Yes, Tyler's invite was there, with an eight p.m. appointment time. Hmm. An evening meeting?

She pushed aside her curiosity to deal with other issues first. She flipped through the hotel to-do list, delegating items for the coming week to others.

There was one thing she couldn't delegate. She opened Skype and checked for the green light to see if her contact was on.

Who was she kidding, though—Amy was always online.

Got a minute?

A pause, then Amy's response. *Yeah*

Can we talk?

The video part of the program rang, and Caroline stabbed at the volume button. She answered, then held a finger to her lips as she scrambled to plug in her headset.

"I need to touch base with you, and I can talk faster than I can type."

The woman on the screen nodded. Her short hair spiked upward, dark against the plain white background behind her. "I have to take a call in a minute. What's up?"

Caroline struggled for inspiration. How was she supposed to walk the line here between helping Evan and revealing too much? "Amy, when we first got in contact, I promised I'd keep your identity a secret. I'm not breaking that vow, but I need you to consider adding one more person to your trust list."

Amy's mouth tightened. "You want to tell someone else in the Takhini pack about me?"

Caroline nodded slowly. "I'll be busy for a week with some new developments and might not be around a lot. I figured if you needed to talk to anyone, in an emergency, you should have someone else you're okay with."

The wolf fidgeted with her hair. "I don't know..."

"You want to help amalgamate the packs, right? That's what we've been talking about for the past month."

"Yes. There really is room for only one pack in Whitehorse."

Caroline nodded. "That's what Evan says as well, so why not talk directly to him if you need anything? Or if there's anything you want to give him a heads-up about."

The woman's eyes widened. "You plan to tell the Takhini Alpha you've been talking to a mole in the Canyon pack? He's the person you want me to contact? Are you *nuts*?"

Another email pinged into her box from yet another bear clan, and Caroline's frustration level rose to near breaking. "Not completely nuts, not yet. Who else would be better, Amy? Evan's got the best interests of all local wolves at heart. I'm not passing you over to the Beta, because while Shaun is a great wolf he's not...as diplomatic. He'd probably order you to give up names and places and stuff. I understand you've got to be careful."

"And Evan's not going to simply order me to spill all the Canyon secrets?" Amy shook her head. "I don't mind talking to you, but you're a human."

"Then don't talk. Text only, if you're afraid of shifter hierarchy kicking in. I'd hate to see the motion we've made toward unification come apart because I'm tied up."

A phone rang in the background, and Amy jerked upright. "I have to go. But...fine. Give me his email, and tell Evan he can contact me."

"Thanks. And don't worry—Evan is a great guy. You can trust him."

Amy wrinkled her nose. "We'll see."

The Skype screen went black as Amy hung up. Caroline breathed a sigh of relief, even though she had one more issue to deal with before turning herself over to Tyler for the duration of conclave. She wondered what Evan would think of her little secret-sharing undercover wolf from the Canyon pack.

Amy was so sweet. Caroline hoped Evan would be able to help ease the girl's fears while he kept the integration of the packs headed the right direction.

The list of emails from the bear clans distracted her from focusing too hard on that mystery. Now she had to find out exactly what an assistant to a bear did.

Anticipation danced inside. She was somewhere between

being disgruntled that she was *good for Tyler politically* and fascinated with the chance to be involved with something brand new. Whatever happened in the next while was sure to be a lot different than emergency room cleaning for the hotel.

She clicked open Tyler's email to formulate an acceptance.

Part Two

Ye who know the Lone Trail fain would follow it,
Though it lead to glory or the darkness of the pit.
Ye who take the Lone Trail, bid your love good-by;
The Lone Trail, the Lone Trail follow till you die.

Bid good-by to sweetheart, bid good-by to friend;
The Lone Trail, the Lone Trail follow to the end.
Tarry not, and fear not, chosen of the true;
Lover of the Lone Trail, the Lone Trail waits for you.

"The Lone Trail"—Robert Service

Chapter Eight

The hushed voices around them were a good thing. Tyler sat in his appointed section, high along one side of the room, Justin at his right. All around the perimeter were special seats for the nominees to use as they observed the proceedings. The rest of the space was filled with a mass of bears sauntering in to disappear behind the screen and mark their choices in this round of the elections.

"Everyone's behaving so far," Justin noted, moving his gaze around the room, keeping alert for any surprises.

"There's no need to make a fuss at this point. We're still using approval voting. Out of the eight clans left, there are clearly four who have the power to not be eliminated."

"Agreed. After this vote is complete, the real juggling begins." Justin turned to face him fully, his voice lowered. "You done being distracted? Ready to get your mind on the task of winning this thing?"

"Shut up. I'm not distracted."

Justin snorted, then went back to sweeping the room for trouble. "Sure, that's why you were singing in the shower this morning. I kept waiting for you to break out into Julie Andrews or something."

No one was supposed to have heard that. "Mention it again and I'll shove a spoonful of sugar down your throat until you choke."

His friend chuckled, but Tyler didn't bother to correct his manners. He was too busy being distracted by the phone vibrating in his pocket. He whipped it out and snapped to messages.

Oh, yes. Finally, Caroline's response.

"Does that *'fuck, yeah'* you just muttered mean you got an answer from the elusive human?" Justin asked.

"She's on board." His bear did the equivalent of a fist pump. Tyler glanced around the room. "How much longer do you estimate?"

Justin scratched his side. "An hour until they close the poll. Another thirty until they lock down the official counters in the safe room, and we can leave. Why?"

"She wants to know our plans for the evening."

Justin whipped out a plain black book. "You are so lucky you hired me. Here. Everything you need to keep you far too occupied until we're set free."

"I didn't hire you, my father hired your father. I inherited you, like the family estate, so don't blame me. And a black book? How is that—?"

Holy fuck.

Tyler had slipped open the notebook, not expecting the lacy underwear and skimpy bras that assaulted his eyes. He slammed the cover tight and glanced around the room to see if anyone seated near them had noticed.

Good so far. Clan Fairmont on their right were busy chatting, and Clan Riondel on the left were busy moping, utter dejection in their body language and faces. They were certain to be eliminated this round.

Tyler had other issues to deal with. He leaned closer to his friend. "What the hell did you hand me? A Victoria's Secret catalog or something?"

Justin grinned. "Well, you have a couple of hours to waste. I figured you might want to get started on that 'sharing the plan for the evening' thing with your woman."

"You're going to get me killed." Still, Tyler cautiously opened the pages, this time realizing there was a fake cover over the official sale catalog. "Oh, mercy..."

Justin tapped the pages, seemingly uncaring his fingers were covering a mostly naked woman. "Local shop. You can order things, or text in your favourites, and send Caroline to get fitted. Unless you think you know her size well enough to order for her?"

Right. He wished he had more than a rough estimate of her size. Wished he had a much more intimate knowledge of exactly how those breasts of hers looked without any layers between them, even soaking-wet ones.

Holding out his hands at approximately the shape of her ass wouldn't help her fit into a formal outfit, though. "I should probably warn her it's a social event tonight."

He turned the page, and his tongue got stuck to the roof of his mouth. The lingerie bursting from this page included a corset. One piece, barely there, hot pink. All thoughts of warning Caroline about *anything* fled as he held his phone to Justin. "Take notes for me."

"Nothing doing. You be distracted, I have to stay alert to keep your ass intact."

Fine. Tyler felt a touch of guilt at not giving the proceedings his full attention, but this was important as well.

Strange how his conscience was far too easy to appease.

He settled in, his big thumbs hovering over the tiny

keyboard as he prepped a greeting message to the shop. Then he flipped through page after page, slightly incredulous at the variety of garments available for a remote location. "We don't have a shop like this in Yellowknife, do we?"

"No."

"Look into sponsoring some eager entrepreneur. This could end up as lucrative as the family business." He spotted the prices discreetly written in full numbers at the base of each garment's description. "Correction, they could end up richer than me."

He fell silent for a few minutes, adding page numbers to the email before sending it off, along with a message to his limo driver.

He'd just tapped out Caroline's phone number when a rumble began in the line. A bit of push and shove. Justin stood immediately, stepping forward.

"Hello?" Caroline's sweet voice sent a shiver down Tyler's spine.

Someone swung a fist, and Tyler swore. "Sorry to call and run, but there's a fight starting. I can't explain. Limo will pick you up at the hotel at five."

A loud clatter rang out as one of those lined up tackled the two bears in front of him, and the entire group crashed into a set of decorative tables at the edge of the room.

"Shifters. Stay safe—I'll meet you later." The call ended, and Tyler was so stunned he almost forgot to duck, snapping his head to the side at the last moment as a vase flew past him.

She'd hung up without asking any further questions regarding the time change. Obviously, she did know shifters.

He tucked away his phone and waded forward to help bring order back. "Ten minutes left, you think?"

"Yeah, about the right timing." Justin slammed a fist into a shifter's face, and the man teetered on his feet before folding to the floor.

"I'll take care of these, you make sure the rest of the line gets to the voting booth before it closes." Tyler didn't wait for his friend to acknowledge him. Justin would obey. At times like this, the situation wasn't about protocol and prestige, it was doing the job you were trained to do.

Tyler might look pretty in a suit, but he had a whole lot more to him than a head full of numbers.

He caught one fighter under the ribs with a jab, hard enough to bend the man over and make it simple to grab him by the hair and toss him to one side. An elbow to a chest, a strategically placed foot followed by a sharp uppercut. In only seconds, the troublemakers who'd snuck in to disrupt the final votes were either groaning on the floor or backing away from Tyler, far more wary than they'd arrived.

A shifter stepped down from the opposite side of the room, his expensive business suit perfectly in position as he avoided participating in any of the fighting. Threads of grey in his hair, a sneer on his face, Todd Ainsworth looked as if he'd smelt something foul. "Tyler. Once again your low-bred roots come to the foreground at the most inopportune moments."

"Ainsworth. You pay these men to come get their asses kicked?"

The bastard shrugged. "Riffraff. Never sure what they'll get up to next." He kicked one of the fallen aside. The man groaned and crawled out of reach of the perfectly polished black leather shoes.

Ainsworth stopped directly in front of Tyler, his smaller body made up for with his arrogance.

Tyler held his fists with great difficulty. "Did you get a

chance to cast your ballot yet, Ainsworth? The boxes will be closing soon, and I'd hate for you to lose out so soon."

"I, and my wife, cast our votes this afternoon." Ainsworth made a big deal out of motioning across the room to someone. Tyler refused to take his eyes off the shifter—he couldn't trust him to not pull a knife or something equally stupid.

And yes, there he went with the wife thing again. Playing up every advantage possible. Tyler looked forward to rubbing Ainsworth's nose in his change of situation. "The ladies do enjoy these little get-togethers, don't they?"

Ainsworth snorted. "Bachelor bears—what would you know of the joys of caring for the tender sex?"

Someone stood behind Tyler, probably someone Ainsworth was attempting to impress with his syrupy gag-worthy bullshit. While the taunting was ignorable, the chance to make an impression wasn't to be lost. Tyler couldn't afford to let any opportunity pass him by. "My personal relationship isn't something I flaunt in public. Unlike some."

The person behind him cleared his throat, and Tyler twisted, feigning surprise at the appearance of the head of Clan Nakusp.

The elderly shifter nodded politely. "Sounds as if you've got a woman hidden somewhere, sir. Why did I not know this?"

Because you failed to listen to the gossip this morning? Tyler kept his mouth shut and held out a hand. "Nakusp. Good to see you again. And yes, there are times I feel it's prudent to keep my lady out of the spotlight, so to speak."

Ainsworth narrowed his eyes. "You'll be bringing a woman to the event tonight, then, will you?"

Both feet forward, all barrels loaded. "Of course." He turned to Nakusp, ignoring Ainsworth as if he were nothing more than a cub squalling on the floor. "Caroline will be delighted to meet you. And your wife."

From pounding knuckles into rowdy bears to polite diplomacy in under two minutes. Bear politics were weird to the extreme. Even Tyler thought so as Justin rejoined him, and the two of them made their way back over the bodies struggling to find their feet.

"No one called the RCMP on us?"

"Head of the local division is sitting over there." Justin pointed at one of the men holding an icepack to his head, a couple of his clan pulling him back to vertical.

Ahh, politics. The sweet scent of chaos couldn't be finer.

Tyler tucked the black book under Justin's arm. His friend looked at him questioningly, and Tyler smiled. "I won't need it any longer. I'm meeting Caroline at the shop in an hour."

The real thing would be so much better than any slicked-up, shiny magazine images.

He could hardly wait.

Caroline stared at the closet in front of her. There was a suitcase on the floor she should be filling as she debated her options, but she couldn't seem to make herself move.

"You waiting for something to jump out and attack you?" Evan strolled in and tossed himself on the bed, all long lean limbs and relaxed shifter as he folded his hands behind his head. "Whatever you wear will be fine."

"I wish I had more of a clue what's happening tonight." She pulled out a business suit, pausing as a furrow appeared between Evan's brows. "What?"

"Not that. That's a nice outfit for bailing the boys out when they get arrested. It's not a 'take notice, I am a woman with balls' outfit."

Caroline tossed it on the bed. "And I'm a woman with balls, am I? You make me sound so appealing."

Evan stared her down. "Don't go fishing for compliments. You know damn well you're an attractive woman physically. Your power in the shifter world, though, is your fuck-it-all attitude. Don't downplay it, or I'll tell your new beau you need a spanking."

That suggestion shouldn't have caused a shiver to race along her spine. "Nasty boy."

Evan winked. "You have your phone with you, right?"

"Of course."

He sat up, paying far more attention than his seemingly off-the-cuff self would suggest. "I've assigned a wolf to follow you. He'll stay out of sight—"

"No way." Caroline ignored the dress clutched in her hands as her fists ended on her hips. "You are not babysitting me."

"This isn't up for discussion, Caro. You're still pack as far as I'm concerned, and someone will be on hand if you need help. Argue if you'd like, it's your breath you're wasting."

She glared, but she understood too well what he was saying. A huge sigh escaped. "Okay, I won't argue, but what are you going to tell my watcher about us? Because you know damn well if your spy spots another man acting...solicitous toward me, there will be hell to pay."

Evan nodded slowly. "Tonight, it's Shaun, so there's no explanation needed."

Lordy. "This is one for the diary. I've got the pack Beta acting as a mother hen."

"Be nice, or I'll make him stick to your side like a burr. Which could make Tyler acting...*solicitous* toward you awkward."

Asshole. Caroline stuck her tongue out at him. Then she ignored him and got dressed.

The limo was waiting as promised, and Evan handed her into the back with far more grace than she expected. "Hey—whatever is up tonight, remember what I said. Trust your gut. You've got a way with people. Don't ignore your first reaction. And don't hesitate to call if you feel uncomfortable."

She settled into the plush leather and waved as Evan closed the door. It wasn't her usual tumbled-down jeep, that's for sure. She relaxed, enjoying the contrast.

She could get to like this kind of lifestyle far too easily.

"Where are we headed?"

The driver tilted his head a touch. "To the central mall. Mr. Harrison will meet you there."

Strange.

Distances being as small as they were in Whitehorse, it was only moments later they pulled to a stop in front of the building. The area wasn't one Caroline usually frequented, and she glanced around with curiosity. The door opened, and an immaculately dressed female attendant waited for her to crawl out. "Ms. Bradley?"

"Yes?"

"Mr. Harrison has been delayed. If you'll come with me, we'll get started."

Caroline followed the girl, wondering exactly what she'd gotten herself into. And when they slipped into an elevator, she waited on pins and needles. Having the doors slide open on a room full of mirrors didn't answer many questions, either.

A lean gentleman with a trimmed goatee stepped forward, hands open in greeting. "*Ahh*, Ms. Bradley. So good to meet you. I have heard much about you."

She was captured before she could respond, his elegant whiskers teasing her as he kissed both cheeks. "Umm, hello."

He straightened, every inch of him screaming high fashion. "I am, of course, Monsieur Stephan. I will be assisting you this evening, and any time you return to us in the future."

Had she stepped into some kind of transportation device and landed in Paris? "Well, that's lovely. But, what are we doing, again?"

He held out a soft terry robe. "Strip, please."

Her forehead cramped, her brows shot upward so fast. "Excuse me?"

Monsieur Stephan wiggled his hand at her. "To your underthings, so I can measure you properly. Come..." he clapped his hands together sharply, "...we have a deadline to meet."

Caroline held up a finger to motion him to wait as she dug in her pocket and pulled out her phone.

Tyler's number went to his voice mail, which might not have been a bad thing because who knows what she would have shouted at him at that moment. She switched instead to more feminine help.

"Gem?"

"Yes, darling. Have you gotten in trouble already? Shall I alert Shaun?"

"Oh, ye of little faith. No, I don't need Shaun. I need your diplomacy." Caroline turned her back on the stripper man and lowered her voice. "I was supposed to meet Tyler, yada, yada...you know this. But instead of the furry brute, I've got some guy with a French accent telling me to strip to my skivvies so he can measure me. Is there any part of this that makes sense to you?"

Gem laughed. "How you get involved in these situations, I'll never understand. You are seriously talented. But yes, I can reassure you on at least one point. You must be in Boutique Boulanger. That was Monsieur Stephan who freaked you out, right?"

Caroline eyed the man who had his arms folded, his foot tapping. "You know him."

"He's safe. One of the finest distributors of lingerie and evening gowns in the world, but he's a mink, and fond of the Yukon, so we managed to score him."

The temptation to make some comment about Gem being a pampered princess was tempting, but Caroline made a point of not pissing off the people who were helping her. At least not while they were in the process.

Still she wondered. "How is it that you know this, and I don't? You've only lived in town for two months."

"Caroline, you tend toward the boy's department of MEC and the thrift shop for your clothes. Do I really need to explain why we don't go shopping together?"

Not really. The one time they had tried, Caroline had wanted to stab her eyes out with forks before they were done. Gem took on shopping like a professional sport.

"So...I strip?"

"Why not?"

Caroline caught herself growling and made a mental note to stop hanging out with so many shifters. Their bad habits were growing on her. "Because Tyler asked me to join him for some conclave events, right? If he thinks getting the human to wander around in her underwear will be part of the program, I don't care what Evan said about bears being aggressive. They ain't never seen me livid."

Gem made soothing sounds over the phone. "I wouldn't rip his arms off just yet. I assume there's a formal event happening, and if he's any kind of a host, Tyler wouldn't expect you to splurge for the correct attire. Does that make sense?"

"I suppose."

"And if he's buying you a dress at Boutique Boulanger, you are not wearing your Walmart sports bra under it. Trust me on this."

Blah. Logic. It did make sense. "Okay, he can keep his arms. Thanks, girl."

"No problem. And now that I know you've met Monsieur Stephan, I'll invite you along the next time I go. We'll have a blast."

"Oh, wow. That would be peachy." Caroline bit back the final words, but it was too late. Gem laughed, then hung up.

Caroline turned to face her soon-to-be-far-too-intimately-acquainted-with-her-anatomy tape-measure-wielding foe. "Hi."

His long-suffering expression turned more hopeful. "And now, you strip?"

Caroline shuffled forward. "Yes, I suppose. Where should I put my clothes and purse?"

Monsieur Stephan sniffed. Caroline wasn't entirely sure, but he seemed to have muttered *in the trash* before pointing to a basket.

There were a hell of a lot of mirrors in the room. Caroline didn't have much time to feel self-conscious, though. She was tugged here and there, twisted in circles on her raised platform as not only Stephan but his assistant measured and pinched, announcing numbers that were noted down by the woman who'd first greeted her.

A few moments later she was wrapped in the extraordinary soft robe, a warm cup of tea in her hands. "Well, that wasn't so bad."

Stephan smiled at her, indulgent now that he'd gotten his way. "I'm so glad to hear it. Please remove the rest of your garments. I'll have what you need to try on brought—"

"Is there a change room?" Caroline broke in. "Because, I'm kind of used to dressing myself."

The mink's lip quivered.

"It's not that you're doing anything wrong, it's all me. You know us humans. Strange habits, things like that."

"But how can I be sure the items fit?"

Caroline had a brilliant solution to that issue as well, she was sure she did, only the door opened behind them, and Tyler burst in. Any thought of talking sense into Stephan vanished as she took in Tyler's appearance. "Holy cow, what happened to you?"

She hurried across the room, brushing his hair off his forehead and away from a bleeding gash.

He caught her wrist. "I'll be fine. Some of the less considerate bears voted after the polls closed, only they used baseballs bats and hockey sticks."

Caroline snapped out orders. "Stephan, get someone to fetch a wet cloth. And another cup of tea, with extra sugar."

"Caroline, don't fuss. I'm fine." Tyler's gaze trickled over her, appreciation in his eyes, and her current wardrobe choice snapped back to mind.

She tightened her belt. "You can't bleed all over the boutique. It's inconsiderate."

Tyler smiled, the right side of his mouth hitching upward faster than the left. "Are you having fun?"

Snapping her fist into his gut would be inconsiderate as well, so she kept her hands to herself. "I would have appreciated a heads-up what you were doing. I had no idea why I was here."

His nose wrinkled in this totally adorable manner, and Caroline glanced away in self-preservation. He was sexy enough without adding adorable to the list of his charms.

She changed the topic. "Is Justin okay?"

Tyler nodded. "He's headed to the Takhini pack house to get patched up. Your guard is taking a momentary leave of absence to escort him."

Whoa. "You knew I had a guard?"

"You are a part of the Takhini pack, are you not? I assumed you'd be guarded. Any Alpha worthy of his position would care for his own."

For someone who prided herself on staying in control at all times of her life and situation, something had gone radically wrong over the past couple days.

She practiced her deep breathing as the staff swarmed over Tyler, wiping his face and knuckles clean. He seemed totally unperturbed by the fawning attention. The short pause was enough to allow her to realign her thinking, and as the area cleared around them she spoke firmly.

"If you tell me more about the meeting at eight, then you can leave, and Monsieur Stephan here will get me froo-froo'd in no time."

Instead, the annoying bear lowered himself into one of the luxury leather chairs strategically placed at the side of the room. "I'll stay. In case you need me for anything."

He had that air about him, the one of *I'm in charge*, and it put Caroline's back up far more than it should have.

"You plan to stay while I try on underwear and dresses."

His eyes snapped with amusement, a sparkle in the depths of the black. "You have a problem with that?"

Yes, but damn if she'd let him take the advantage in this round. Somehow in the past couple of minutes, things had changed. This assignment of hers wasn't some favour she was doing for him. Or a job that would protect the Takhini pack.

This was a war on a personal level, and Caroline meant to win. Just like she never allowed shifters to know when she was afraid, he couldn't find out how much having him here freaked her out.

So she did the only thing possible. She lied her ass off.

"No problem. Not for me."

Then she loosened the robe and let it fall to the floor.

Chapter Nine

It was a good thing he was sitting down or Tyler would have fallen over.

Never in a million years would he have predicted her to be so bold, and yet—perhaps he should have. She'd done nothing but the unexpected since the first moment they'd met.

His bear poked him, eager for a glimpse of something more than her ankles. His gaze had dropped with the robe, so he started at her toes and worked his way up, slowly. Savouring.

She stood like a warrior, not a model, both feet planted firmly. Her strong legs had visible calf and thigh muscles, noted in passing as his gaze landed on the plainest pair of cotton panties ever. Cream coloured, they were thin enough the pale curls over her mound could be seen through the material.

He subtly adjusted position to allow room for his growing erection.

The visual tour increased in pace as his gaze rose past a trim waist he couldn't wait to wrap his hands around. He barely allowed himself a glance at her chest, because getting lost while staring at her tits might be the equivalent of falling into horizon blindness.

So he ended up at her mouth a lot sooner than he'd expected where her expression could be labeled nothing less than a smirk. Her eyes said it as well. She was laughing at him.

Yeah, he pretty much deserved that. But then again, this was only the beginning of the evening.

"Did you get my list?" he asked Stephan, not looking away from her mocking gaze.

"Of course, sir."

"Let's try the blue set first, then, with the full-length gown. That will give you time for adjustments if needed."

Her mouth tightened slightly as Stephan stepped in front of her and slipped off one bra strap. Then, damn it, there were too many bodies between Tyler and her for more than momentary glimpses. Flashes of naked skin that did more to tantalize than satisfy.

When the proprietor of the shop finally stepped away, Tyler found himself on the edge of his chair, a mere second away from bolting to his feet.

The view was beyond spectacular.

Caroline had been eased into a one-piece outfit with a corset-like top that emphasized the flare of her hips. The cups that held her breasts—he'd never been envious of a piece of fabric before. Only he was, the gentle swells of flesh rising above the shimmering silk moving slowly as she breathed.

Her blonde hair fell around her shoulders like she'd just crawled out of his bed, all soft and warm and satisfied, and damn it—

His bear was really working the imagery.

Tyler cleared his throat. Fought to use his vocal cords. "Lovely."

It shouldn't have come out so growly and lust-filled, not if he'd been in control, but that was the issue. He *wasn't* in control. Not since he'd met Caroline.

He moved his gaze to the proprietor, catching his eye before flicking a glance toward the door. This probably wasn't the first time Stephan had been silently ordered out of his own shop. The owner dipped his chin before gesturing to his assistants.

"We will be back in a moment," Stephan declared.

Once the room was down to just Caroline and Tyler, the classical music playing in the background was softer than his panting, damn it.

Caroline shifted her stance. When she spoke, her words came out low and lusty, teasing his eardrums like they were erogenous zones. "I take it there's a reason I need to have a fancy dress?"

He didn't stop appreciating the view. "Next week Tuesday. There's an event for the heads of the clans every few evenings beginning tonight, concluding in a formal dance."

She glanced at the door the shop workers had vanished behind, then stepped off the platform and paced toward him. Slowly. Hips swaying as she moved, breasts wiggling just right, her naked flesh pale peach-coloured in the soft lighting. "So this *assistant* position you need me for. You want me to take notes?"

She was nearly close enough to touch. "No notes. There's a secretary who does that. I need you to help me impress those clans who think I'm too impulsive because I'm single."

Caroline planted her hands on her hips before easing her palms upward. He watched, mesmerized, as she caressed her rib cage, along the sides of her breasts, not stopping until she'd threaded her fingers through her hair.

He was going to die of a lack of oxygen. He seemed to have forgotten how to breathe.

When she pressed her fingers to his chest, he swore his heart stopped as well. Yes, he was going to die here and now, one body system shutting down after the other.

His cock would be the last thing to succumb.

Tyler shoved himself back as she wordlessly demanded until he was fully seated on the couch. Then, hallelujah, she climbed on top, her shins resting on the leather on either side of his legs.

"So, this is a date?" she asked.

Tyler attempted to focus on her face. "What's that?"

"A date. You asking me to join you for the conclave isn't a political arrangement, it's a date."

He'd swallowed his tongue. A second earlier he'd glanced down far enough to notice the material of her outfit, when she was in that knees-spread-wide position, barely covered her pussy. "Not a date. Political. Necessity."

The words surprised him as they slipped past his lips.

"Really?"

Caroline eased herself closer. Closer. Until her torso rested right against his.

Their faces were only inches apart, the rest of them touching. The warmth of her sex centered squarely over the erection that bulged the front of his trousers. He was unable to resist sliding his hands onto her hips.

She licked her lips. "Political necessity. Good to know."

He wasn't sure what he wanted to touch next. Taste next. Her lips were so close. The scent of her attraction rose like a siren call. She undulated her hips, only a fraction of an inch, but it was enough to drag a groan from him as she rubbed his cock.

Caroline brushed her fingers lightly over his forehead, careful to avoid the cut. "Dangerous business, getting involved with bears."

"I warned you." He held her hips tighter and ground her

over his aching length. So good, yet a million miles from what it was going to be like to sink into her warmth.

She thrust her fingers into his hair, her cheek against his. Her breasts crushed to his chest, intimately close but for the scrap of material she wore and his clothing.

He'd never wished for the magical ability to strip so hard before in his life. Not even the time he'd woken as a teen choking on his own T-shirt after accidentally having shifted in the night.

He moved her again. And again. This throaty little noise escaped her, and lust flared like a white-hot poker. One second more, and he'd forget all decorum and have her naked and bent over the back of the chair. He'd take her and make her scream.

She nibbled on his earlobe, and he fretted perhaps he wouldn't even make it to the *strip them down* part. He was about to come right there, right then.

Her regretful sigh surprised him.

"Too bad we're only getting involved for political reasons." Another sigh, air brushing his cheek as she sat back, opening a space between them.

His bear screamed *noooooooooo.* His human mind boggled and attempted to make sense of her comment.

She cupped his cheek. "I understand though. Politics are very important, and you can trust me to do everything I can to help you."

When she would have wiggled off his lap, he held her immobile. "Where are you going?"

She rolled her eyes. "To try on the gowns and stuff that I need to be a pretty political assistant to you. D-uh."

Somewhere this had taken a wrong turn. "Wait..."

He couldn't hold her in position without hurting her, so he

released his grip, her warmth fading as she stepped back, hands folded demurely in front of her.

"See, if we were actually dating? Then we might have a few other things to discuss, but since this is all political, well. I'll just have to keep my disappointment to myself."

Oh fuck. "It's not that I don't—"

"What? Find me attractive? Of course it's not. We did kiss yesterday, and it was kind of fun, but I find mixing work and play isn't a great idea. No problem. Glad to have that all straightened up. I'll be the very best political assistant you could wish for."

She stepped onto the platform. Tyler dragged a hand through his hair feeling a little as if a train had just hit him. Especially when she squatted, knees wide, finger raised to her lips. Every part of her open to him, her breasts nearly spilling from the corset top.

"And Tyler?"

"Yes?" He somehow dragged his gaze back up to hers.

"Don't think you can take any liberties while I'm assisting you. No kisses out of the blue, no secret groping. I'm the one in charge of this, and unless I decide I want you, hands off the goods."

She rose to her feet, one hand presenting herself like the treasure she was. The sexy display ended when she planted her fists on her hips again. The bold move at the finish was racier than she probably realized.

Well, hell. That hadn't gone nearly the way he'd expected.

The limo brought them up the winding mountain road toward their destination for the evening. The windows of the distant manor glowed amber and gold in flashes through the trees.

On the bench seat to her right, Tyler had remained silent for the past twenty minutes of the ride. After helping her into the limo, Justin had taken the seat across from them, and alternately grinned or fought to keep his amusement from showing.

Caroline ignored them both and folded her fingers together to stop from fidgeting. The dress she wore had a slit up one side that kept falling open if she didn't keep her knees pinned to the leather seat. The dress itself was gorgeous. Soft silvery silk that clung to her curves, the deep V of the neckline magically staying in position over the bra Monsieur Stephan had fit her in, and she had to admit, the man knew how to make the girls look the best they ever had.

From the elaborate hairdo one of the shop assistants had created for her unruly blonde hair to the tips of her freshly manicured toes, Caroline was a fancy woman. A soft shawl lay over her shoulders to keep the chill in the air at bay. The three-inch heels on her feet were frighteningly comfortable—she would have sworn they were old and broken in, and not brand new from the box.

Yes, in an hour and a half flat she'd been packaged prettily for the evening. Still had no bloody idea what was coming next, though.

After her little ultimatum in the lingerie shop, Tyler had nodded curtly then vanished with a final comment he'd be back for her at six thirty. Even the fact he'd walked out with an obvious erection hadn't been enough to satisfy the frustration raging through her.

Shifters didn't think of intimacy the same way most humans did. She understood that. She really did.

Easier attitudes toward sex she could handle. But totally ignoring attraction and making it all about a job? Fuck that noise. Even when she'd gotten involved with Evan, the relationship hadn't been completely about what they could do for each other outside the bedroom. There'd been an honest attraction between them.

Caroline resisted the urge to swing a fist and thump Tyler on the chest. She'd thought there was an honest attraction between her and the bear as well, but it seemed Mister High and Mighty couldn't even confess to that.

No. She wasn't about to become some kind of *political advantage* and hand over sexual treats on the side. Not if Tyler didn't man up and admit he wanted both her and her help.

Why couldn't someone want her for *her*?

She kept her woe-is-me sighing to a minimum, but the truth remained. After spending so long around shifters, after knowing how she had to act to impress them, she was tired of being taken for granted.

Evan suggested she trust her gut instincts. Right now her instincts told her there was a big *big* game about to go down, and she wasn't sure she was up for more playing.

The realization should have scared her out of her mind.

They were still about ten minutes from their destination when Justin broke the silence. "Tyler updated you on all the clans you'll see tonight?"

Caroline twisted to stare at Tyler. "Gee, no. Was he supposed to?"

Tyler's gaze narrowed in warning. The rampant who-gives-a-shit rising inside made her glare back.

Justin cleared his throat. "Well, yes. But—"

"Tell her," Tyler cut in.

Justin held up his hands, eight fingers raised. “The vote today was between eight clans. Four go on to the next round, and it’s almost a given which they will be when the count is completed tonight.”

He dropped one hand and flicked fingertips as he named names. “Harrison, Ainsworth, Nakusp and Halcyon. Each time we vote, the clans who are eliminated become a bigger factor. It makes a difference who they rally behind. Tyler has his supporters, but unfortunately so does Ainsworth.”

“Makes sense. Who will be here tonight?”

“All eight clans from today’s vote.”

Caroline tossed her mad away and focused on Tyler. “You hope to convince some of Ainsworth’s followers to switch sides?”

Tyler shook his head. “Unlikely. Even if they wanted to, he’s got a tight-fisted grip on most of their lives. No one will attempt to rock his boat from the inside.”

She wasn’t getting this. “We are talking Canadian shifters, right? You make it sound as if he’s got his clan in slavery.”

“You think people have to live in foreign countries to be cruel tyrants?” Tyler snapped, and Caroline blanched.

“Gently, Tyler,” Justin admonished. “She’s used to dealing with wolves.”

Wolves who, it appeared, were some of the best controlled in the land. Evan had been doing a wonderful job—she had to remember to let him know that.

Caroline’s doubts rose, yet there was no time to turn the boat around and retreat as the car passed through enormous rock-hewn gates. “Top three people we want to impress?”

Tyler spoke softer than a moment ago. “Definitely Nakusp. He’ll be part of the final four, but chances are high we’ll end up going for a final two, and we’ll need Nakusp on our side. Talk to his wife, get close to her, and see what topics she's heard him mention as key interests."

"Liard is a loose cannon—they tend to switch votes in every round and play games until even they don't know what they'll do next." Justin touched the fading bruise on his temple. "They can get rough while playing, so be extra careful around them."

Tyler nodded. "Also, Halcyon already mentioned he'd support me. I'd like confirmation the offer is still in place."

The limo pulled to a stop as Caroline tucked the names into her brain. Justin slipped out the door, but when she would have followed Tyler held her back.

"I hope we avoid any wild antics tonight, but in case things go wrong, retreat to a safe corner and I'll be there as fast as I can to help you. Understand?"

Goodie. They would keep this totally on the professional level. Her disappointment was complete. "Yes, sir."

Tyler caught her fingers in his, stroking her knuckles with his free hand. "Caroline, I'm sorry for upsetting you."

Whoa. A guy who apologized? Hope rose slightly that the evening wouldn't end up a total fail in the personal department. "Really?"

He nodded. "I should have explained ahead of time what was going on. You need to know who to talk to. Who to gather information from."

Oh.

Well, yes, that was another place where he'd gone wrong, but the shadow of sadness inside her grew as she stomped her attraction into a tiny little box and duct-taped the lid shut. "I might have good instincts, but information helps."

She wiggled, heading for the door. He refused to release her fingers.

"Wait." Tyler paused until she faced him again.

Damn, why did his eyes have to have that mesmerizing quality to them? "What?"

There was no smile on his face, just full-out commanding concentration. "I expect you will behave properly in public."

Oh no. He did not go there. "Excuse me?"

"As far as any of the clans know, you are here as my date. As such, I expect you to remain by my side when appropriate. If I take you by the hand or embrace you, there will be no negative responses on your part."

His words rattled in her brain as she attempted to line this up with his earlier comments. The ones he'd pantingly got out about Political Necessity etc. etc. "Are you serious? You do realize I got invitations from damn near every one of the other clans to join them. Are you telling me they expected me to be their dates?"

"I have no idea what their intentions were. These are mine. You will be introduced as my date."

Caroline caught herself growling. "You didn't think this was important to tell me back when you were ogling me at the lingerie shop? When you specifically told me this was business?"

"I was...distracted."

"You were an asshole," she snapped.

He frowned. "That's exactly what cannot happen. Do not speak disrespectfully to me while in clan presence."

"How about I get it out of my system, then?" Temper flaring, she yanked her hand free then poked him in the chest, once for each word. "Make. Up. Your. Bloody. Mind. We're not dating, but you expect me to, what? Fawn over you like I'm some kind of arm candy for you to show off? You say you want my help and then you basically insult me with your warnings? You're a jerk, Tyler Harrison."

He folded his arms and stared her down.

"Justin is waiting outside." She pointed out. "We should go."

"You're deliberately misunderstanding me..." he pulled a box off the back window ledge, "...and we don't have time for more discussion. Put these on."

She jerked open the slim case to discover a set of dazzling diamond jewelry. "What in the world?"

"Family workmanship. You will, of course, wear a sample of our craft any time we are in public." She was still staring at the earrings and ring even as Tyler pulled the necklace free. "Turn your back so I can put this on you."

Whoa. "Diamonds?"

"I'm the head of Dzinsen Diamonds. I assumed you knew."

"You assume a lot of things." Migrating moose on a pogo stick. She couldn't even begin to estimate the value of what he'd so casually tossed her direction.

The cool weight of the stones landed on her chest, and again Caroline was caught off guard. She ignored the warnings, and the words of frustration she wanted to speak, instead removing her plain pearl earrings and replacing them with the dangling falls of diamonds, long enough they brushed her neck when she twisted her head.

Tyler had her hand, and before she could protest, he slipped on the immense ring that was part of the set. The motion made her uncomfortable for so many reasons.

Tyler's face was unreadable. When he brushed her cheek she twitched before deliberately relaxing with a long exhale. He nodded in approval, his finger continuing down the side of her neck then along the cluster of shimmering diamonds. The end of the cascade nestled between her breasts, and she skipped a breath as his touch lingered there.

Why did she have to be so attracted to the damn beast when it was obvious he wasn't a good match for her future?

He lifted his gaze to meet hers, and for a moment, just a moment, there was something there other than professionalism. Then a shadow rolled in, like he'd lowered a curtain, and the cool, collected man without a trace of humour was back.

Caroline pushed her questions aside and exited the limo. The only thing she was sure about was this evening was more complicated than she'd expected, and they were only starting.

Chapter Ten

He'd dealt with Caroline all wrong, but there was no changing the past few hours. No time to thrash himself for being an ass instead of allowing the fascination between them to run its course naturally.

Knowing why he'd been an idiot was one matter. Fixing his mistake was another, and in the middle of escorting her into the presence of his enemies wasn't the time for self-flagellation.

The cool of the evening settled around them with the warning that even now winter was on its way. Caroline held his arm, but all her focus was on her feet as he guided her up stairs formed from vast chunks of granite.

Tyler tucked his elbow in, trapping her fingers between his arm and his warm torso. Her fingers rubbed the fine fabric of his suit, and he bit back his hum of approval. She was enjoying the intimacy of their position. There was no denying her body's response. Even though she'd fussed and told him no, she was still interested.

He wouldn't act on it immediately, but knowing the attraction was still there made him hopeful he hadn't mucked up beyond all repair. Once they were in a better position to do something about their mutual fascination.

White-suited attendants opened doors and took her wrap. Justin crowded close as they were led out of the grand foyer toward open doors at least ten feet tall.

If an attendant had banged a mallet on the floor and announced their names *a la* royalty, he wouldn't have been surprised. Their hosts for the evening had pulled out all the stops to make an impression.

The magnificent hall they entered was filled with delicate music, a four-piece ensemble tucked into the corner providing a live performance. The sparkle and shine of jewels twinkled everywhere. He bet Caroline had never seen a setting like this outside of a movie.

He was right. She whistled softly before muttering, "We're not in Kansas anymore, Toto."

"What's that?" Tyler leaned toward her, eager for a closer touch.

Caroline placed her lips an inch from his ear. "This is more elaborate than I expected."

Tyler rested his fingers on her hand and squeezed reassuringly. "You can handle it. I know you can."

She was tense, though. He regretted more than ever his screw-up during the planning portion of the evening. His bear snorted, pointing out that so far she hadn't seemed to fail when it came to going completely on impulse.

"Tyler. There you are."

Tyler turned them both to face the young man stepping closer, an impeccably dressed redhead on his arm. He spoke softly before the couple could reach them. "Jim and Lillie Halcyon. Our hosts."

"Got it." Caroline nodded, her face lighting up with an incredible smile.

Hosts, and his promised supporter. From Jim's enthusiastic approach, it appeared the positive sentiment was still there. The men shook hands before Tyler introduced her. “Jim, Lillie. I don’t know if you’ve met Caroline Bradley before. She’s also local to Whitehorse.”

Jim lifted Caroline’s hand and kissed her fingers, his gaze pinned to her face. “I haven’t had the pleasure.”

Caroline remained polite, but her gaze darted between Jim’s wife and Tyler to see their reaction to what must have felt like an over-the-top greeting.

Lillie didn’t seem the least bit concerned, and Tyler made sure his own response remained neutral. Old-world charm was another built-in response bears used to stay in control.

In fact, their hostess clapped her hands in delight. “It’s lovely to finally meet you. I have heard your name. You spend time with the local wolves, correct?”

Caroline’s smile now contained a hint of amusement. “The Takhini pack and I go way back.”

Lillie threaded her arm around Caroline. “Let’s go find somewhere to chat, so the guys can do the political wrangling they are longing to get into.”

“They only just got here,” Jim admonished. “We can’t monopolize them this quickly.”

Lillie sighed dramatically as she released Caroline, and Caroline laughed.

Even as he corrected her, Jim made his words softer by pulling Lillie close and kissing her cheek. The honest affection between them confirmed what Tyler had heard. It also made him slip against Caroline, sliding a hand around her waist.

She tensed for a second before adjusting her stance to press closer. One palm skimmed his chest in plain view of their hosts as she adjusted his tie with familiarity. Warmth spread from where her breast nudged his open dinner jacket.

He wasn't sure he liked how good she was at picking up clues, or if her astute moves would kill him by the end of the evening.

Caroline turned to Lillie. "Tell you what. After we've made our rounds, I'd love to join you."

Lillie smiled. "I'll be here."

Jim motioned to the door. "Here, or somewhere close to here. We have more guests. Tyler"—he nodded briskly—"I look forward to visiting later as well. When you have time for a serious discussion."

Their hosts stepped away to welcome the next couple.

Caroline allowed Tyler to guide her a few paces farther into the room. "That was both painfully formal and strangely comfortable. Nice people, though."

"Halcyons? Definitely. They've been in the Whitehorse area since February."

"Strange. I've never met them."

Tyler shrugged. Her hand was warm and soft, and he definitely liked the sensation more than as a political necessity. "Not really. Bears don't usually spend much time in public places. And that's part of the reason this event is painfully formal. We know how to be brutes, or we know how to put on the Ritz. There's not much between the two extremes."

They were nearly across the wide expanse of floor, Justin dogging their steps as usual. Small clusters of people stood with drinks in hand, conversing in low tones. A quick glance showed everyone had arrived.

This was about the time things went to hell, at least historically. Sure enough, the next person to catch his eye was not really who he wanted to inflict upon Caroline.

"This will be unpleasant," he warned. "That's Todd

Ainsworth waving at us. Wife is Amanda."

"The enemy," Caroline whispered dramatically. "Dun-dun-dun duhhhhh."

Her smart-ass comment meant he wore a far wider grin than he usually could muster in Ainsworth's presence.

The men shook hands and exchanged greetings, Caroline waiting politely. She smiled at Amanda opposite her. Tyler wasn't shocked to see the other woman jerk her gaze away and ignore Caroline, all attention focused on the men as they spoke.

Caroline's smile faded to be replaced with intense concentration.

Tyler debated breaking in and making introductions, but what would be the point? This was a great opportunity for her to witness the Ainsworth charm firsthand.

It wasn't forever, not nearly as long as it must have felt to her, but the wait was a hell of a lot longer than it would be in normal human society before Todd turned his gaze toward her.

Even then he didn't give Tyler an opportunity to introduce them. Todd kept talking, his gaze examining every inch of Caroline as if she were the arm candy she'd accused Tyler of wanting.

Tyler figured any second her *fuck-it-all* meter should kick in.

And there it was. Caroline shot her hand out. "Nice to meet you."

She stood, hand suspended in midair, waiting for Todd to respond. Tyler figured the only possible thing that could motivate the ass to act out of character would be guilt at confusing the poor human.

Nope. Todd stared at her fingers as if she'd offered him a dead fish.

Caroline glanced at Amanda. Mrs. Ainsworth had pasted on a smile and was looking anywhere but at what was happening right in front of her.

Damn it all. Knowing what he did of Caroline, she was probably ready to stand there like a statue until Todd was forced to deal with her, but Tyler didn't give her a chance.

He caught her hand and tugged it back to his side. "I see the others have all arrived."

Todd mysteriously returned to life. "Yes, they'll call us to dinner in a few minutes. We'll talk later."

Todd and Amanda vanished, the swirl of formal clothing gliding away as if jet-propelled.

Caroline sniffed before turning to Tyler. "That was weird. Do I have cooties or something?"

Tyler slowly led her across the floor toward a second set of doors, ignoring all the other couples murmuring madly together. "Todd Ainsworth at his finest."

"The woman looks like a robot. Amanda isn't nearly as happy as Lillie," Caroline whispered. "Who is a more typical clan leader, Todd or Jim?"

"About half and half? Before you ask, it's not a generational pattern, as far as I know. My father would never have treated my mother that way. Rumour has it Ainsworth makes his woman's life hell."

She glanced around the room, her expression thoughtful as she eyed the ladies clinging to their men. Tyler analyzed them as well, noting which of them were smiling mindlessly like a freaking bunch of Stepford wives.

He'd known the way some of the bears treated their ladies was an issue, but it had never registered this hard before. Not only because a bear gathering like this was a rare situation, but because he seldom had anyone on his arm.

Caroline made him more aware. Brought forward exactly how twisted the situation had become.

Caroline jerked Tyler to a stop, reaching down to fidget with her shoe. She leaned a hand on his chest to keep her balance, but the edge of her fist made contact harder than a casual balance situation would require.

He caught her elbow, both to help her and to stop her from repeating the thump. "What's wrong?"

There could have been steam coming from her ears, but from a distance she probably looked as if she were staring at him in adoration, not one step away from ripping him a new one. "When this evening is over, I am so going to kick your ass for not telling me the things I needed to know. Like that you bears are a fraternity of misogynists."

"I don't hate women," Tyler argued. He definitely didn't hate this one, even though she made his blood pressure rise and fall like a roller coaster. He opened his mouth to say something else, but his chance was lost as they were summoned by a call from across the room. "And I apologized for not preparing you."

She patted his cheek in a loving-like gesture that somehow also promised pain and suffering. "If that was your best shot at apologizing, you need to work on the art of the grovel. Don't worry, I'll give you plenty of time to practice. After we get through the rest of this oh-so-fascinating evening."

Oh, shit. He could hardly wait.

Caroline kept hold of him as they moved toward the dining room. So far she'd said an official hello to four people and she was ready to go home.

Bears? Were crazy. Give her a nice wolf rumble any day. All

this extreme politeness was getting on her nerves, because other than Lillie at the start, everyone was so painfully fake she was ready to gag.

Her sense of humour tweaked again, and part of her wanted to ignore the fancy setting, the upscale hairdo and outfit, and do something outrageous like pull a cartwheel down the middle of the high-gloss parquet flooring.

Of course the outfit she wore meant handsprings were damn near impossible without spilling tits and ass everywhere, and that wasn't quite the what-the-hell image she was going for.

Only the prospect of actual food made the next portion of the evening palatable. Caroline was starving. It was hours past her usual dinnertime, and with the chaos of the day, she just remembered she'd skipped lunch.

Lillie caught her arm, snuggling in close and pulling her from Tyler's grasp. "Come with me until they seat us?"

Tyler smiled indulgently at Lillie, the young woman obviously not considered a threat. "You're stealing my dinner partner."

"Only for a few minutes." Lillie dimpled sweetly. "If that's okay?"

"Of course it's okay." Caroline answered for herself, winking at Tyler in a fit of forgiveness.

He startled upright, blinking hard for a second, then this wonderful smile spread across his face. Anticipation? Hope?

Caroline turned her back and ignored him.

"We really do only have a minute, but come, visit with me." Lillie led her to a corner of the room where an oversized couch filled the recessed space. Even in her formal gown, the woman curled up elegantly, legs under her. "I thought it would be entertaining to host one of the events, but Jim was right.

They're all boring. And stuffy. Except you and Tyler."

Caroline's cheeks warmed at the praise. "Well, I'm glad you like us."

Lillie caught her by the hands. "Will you live in Whitehorse after you get married? I hope so. I'd love to have—"

Caroline shot up a hand to stop Lillie's flood of words, because she couldn't seem to speak through the knot in her own throat. "Married?" she croaked.

Lillie blinked. Then frowned. "Umm, did I make a mistake? I thought that's what Jim told me..."

What was the correct response here? Caroline was caught between a rock and hard place. Neither response that sprang to mind, i.e. *what the fuck?* or *hell, no!* was the right one, not if she was going to knuckle down and help Tyler in spite of himself.

So she didn't answer. Just took her cue from her new friend's earlier enthusiasm and damn near instant bear hug. Caroline cuddled into Lillie's side and looked over the room. "They are a stuffy lot, aren't they? Here I thought wolves were pretentious at times."

"The Takhini pack is funny." Lillie laid her head on Caroline's shoulder. "I heard the lot of them turned to wolves once and had races down Main Street. Someone had to get them out of the dog catchers after that."

Yeah, that would have been Caroline, but Lillie didn't need to know details. "Wolves like dares and bets far too much."

"Bears like bets," Lillie added. "I suppose it's a little like this silly voting thing. It's safer than people getting clawed to bits."

She said it so plainly, not as if the alternative was a bloodthirsty option.

Caroline adjusted position so she could examine her new best friend. "You're a shifter, aren't you?"

"Of course." Lillie rubbed her cheek on Caroline's. "Black bear. Jim wasn't expecting that, since he's a grizzly, but for an arranged marriage, I think things have turned out marvelously."

Caroline's tongue was tied in a knot. Oh, the things she was learning—the curve balls kept coming. "You two do seem to be compatible."

Lillie glanced over the room, sighing contentedly when she spotted her husband. "I adore him. And he's been incredible. And the sex. I mean, bears have that ability to just keep going and going."

Caroline was glad they were in the shadows to hide her flushed cheeks. She might be used to wolves talking all sex, all the time, but this was different. The way she felt about Tyler changed things, and she hadn't had a real chance to find out any details for herself yet.

Lillie's nose wrinkled. "Poor Amanda. I tried to rescue her, but she's trapped with Mr. Stick in the Mud."

Caroline followed the bear's gaze to discover Amanda was indeed, stuck. Clutching her husband's arm and gazing glassy-eyed around her as he controlled yet another conversation. For a second, their eyes met, hers and Amanda's, and the utter hopelessness in them made Caroline's heart ache.

Damn bastard. Tyler hadn't lied when he'd said the man was a tyrant. His wife looked miserable, beyond being bored to tears.

"She's on a tight leash, isn't she?" Caroline asked, staring harder as Amanda's half-jacket shifted position, and what appeared to be a dark shadow became visible on her arm.

Dammit, dammit, dammit.

"We'll try to rescue her again after dinner. We might have a better shot while the men go off and smoke. Or whatever they do in Jim's man-cave."

"That sounds like a good idea—"

The rest was lost under a roar. The doors that had been partially closed slammed open on one side, an enormous ball of fur flying across the room toward the main gathering.

Holy shit, it was a bear. Caroline scrambled upright, sticking to the shadows.

Lillie sighed.

"There goes dinner." She turned to Caroline even as she stripped off her shimmering black dress, totally ignoring her nudity. "You should probably stay here and hide, okay? I need to go help my husband."

"No problem." Caroline reached under her skirt for the knife holster she'd insisted Monsieur Fancy Pants find a way for her to wear. A switchblade against a full-grown bear wasn't much help, but it was better than nothing.

Plus, her sister the vet had taught her a couple of good moves.

Lillie shifted, her bear form smaller than the one who'd stormed across the room, but a hell of a lot bigger than Caroline. Somehow even in her other form she was still Lillie, an adorable tilt to her head as she nudged Caroline gently with her shoulder before racing into the room.

Below her, grown men seemed at first to be backing away from danger. Only a closer inspection revealed they were creating distance between each other to rip off the tracings of sophistication. Clothes were abandoned everywhere in the race to shift.

The bear who'd started the violence had a human form

under his paws. Caroline waited, her heart in her throat, as she recognized a familiar-looking suit being torn to shreds. Only the flying fabric wasn't from the attacking bear doing the damage, it was from Tyler shifting. He roared in anger and flipped his attacker to the floor.

Chaos reigned in the elegant room. A mass of furry bodies swiped razor-sharp claws at each other, howls of pain and snarls of rage filling the air.

The servants had retreated to the edges of the room or vanished altogether, fleeing through smaller doors and closing them firmly behind themselves. Caroline eyed the still-open grand entrance and estimated how long it would take for her to sprint the distance. Calculating if it was worth the risk.

So far the fighting remained focused far from her, but she had no guarantees it would stay there. A couple clasped together in a ball of bloody fur rolled toward her escape route, and Caroline's hopes fell.

A flash of fur appeared to her right, and she swung her knife hand instinctively, jerking the blade back as she recognized the smaller-than-a-bear silver coat.

"Shaun, you idiot. I nearly skewered you."

He grinned briefly, his sharp teeth flashing white, then turned and stood as a sentinel between her and the bears.

Great. If the bruins did decide to come her direction one of her favourite wolves could get hurt. There had to be another solution. She spotted Tyler systematically working his way through a mass of fighters, headed in her direction.

He'd promised to come for her, and he was keeping his word. In the meantime? She wasn't sitting on a tuffet and waiting.

The beautiful dress she wore was about to become an issue, as would the shoes. She kicked her heels off then grabbed the skirt of her dress, wrapping the material around her waist to get the long swath of fabric out of her way.

"Once I make it to a safe spot, you get out of here," she ordered Shaun, returning her knife blade to the holster.

He wagged his tail.

What she had in mind was insanity of a new sort. She put a hand to the decorative brickwork behind her, caught the edge of a protrusion with a toe and made her first move up the wall.

She figured using the light sconce, the bricks and a bit of luck she could make it to the ledge about twenty feet up. High enough no one should be able to get at her.

Caroline reached for a hold when a set of hands closed around her waist, jerking a curse from her lips. She swung a fist, only to have it captured in a huge hand as she was twisted in place, held firmly against Tyler's naked body.

"You can beat me up later. Let's get out of here." A smear of blood on his face made him look like a pirate. He spoke quietly, keeping the attention off them. "I'm going to shift. Climb on my back and hold on as tight as you can."

Good grief, he was serious. The wall of muscle in front of her vanished as he dropped to all fours and simultaneously shifted. Instead of Tyler's muscular chest and gorgeous...everything, there was a massive grizzly bear with a thick coat of fur. He glanced over his shoulder as if to tell her to hurry.

The fighting remained loud and violent, and he didn't have to warn her twice. She crawled onto his back and leaned down, fisting his fur, thighs wrapped around his torso as far as possible. Together, Shaun and Tyler shot forward, headed for the door.

It was a strange sensation, riding a bear. Caroline had ridden horses, but every pace Tyler took involved his torso far more than a horse. As he moved, she moved, the room passing in a blur. To one side, Shaun leapt at an attacker, his teeth sinking into a forepaw and pulling a scream of anger from the bear. Tyler used the distraction to dodge the few bears standing between them and freedom.

Caroline glanced back in time to see Shaun escape through a gap, his smaller body ducking easily around the bears' larger forms. Tyler leapt over a fighting pair, and Caroline gritted her teeth as she clung for dear life, a grunt escaping her as they landed and Tyler increased his pace.

They were out the front doors and into the darkness. Tyler turned them away from the main road, heading into the trees.

Caroline held on, nestling tighter to the warm fur under her. There was nothing to do except wait and trust.

Chapter Eleven

It was the first time Tyler remembered leaving a fight before it was over. He slowed his pace, working to maintain a level surface for Caroline to rest on as he glided silently through the trees.

He'd never left, but then he'd never had someone to protect before either.

When the bear had charged across the room he'd been distracted, checking to make sure Caroline was still in the protected alcove where she and Lillie had settled. The short lapse of attention had been enough he'd found himself under his attacker, his tie the only thing he'd removed in time.

Blast it. He had really hoped they could use diplomacy to end this thing. Instead, people like Ainsworth were calling the shots. From the bits and pieces Tyler had heard during the short visit, Clan Lucerne was being encouraged to be far too aggressive.

Which put him here, in the bush, a shivering human on his back.

They weren't far from Whitehorse, not via the route he could take. He topped the ridge and found them a sheltered spot out of the wind, giving her a moment to crawl off before he shifted.

The moonlight shone on the remains of her fancy dress,

highlighting her shimmering hair. She was a wood nymph in the beams of silvery light.

Caroline folded her arms. He held her to his torso to provide warmth. “You okay?”

“I’m not the one who was being mauled.” She skimmed her hands over him. A light, delicate touch that turned him on far faster than it should.

“Save that for when we’re somewhere warmer.”

Her expression tightened as she otherwise ignored his suggestion. “Where are you hurt?”

Fuck it. He grabbed her hand off his ribs. “Caroline, stop it.”

Her other hand continued to torment him. “You were crazy. I thought he was ripping you apart. *Oh…*”

If she wanted so badly to find something that was wrong, he’d help her. He pressed her fingers lower until her palm covered his erection. “This is the only thing hurting. I doubt you want to do something about it here and now. I stopped to find out where you want to go. The hotel, your apartment? Where?”

She softened in his arms, cuddling in as she shivered. “I’m sorry, I should have known. Not the hotel—it’s too far into Whitehorse for you to make it in your bear, or as a naked man. The apartment is against the tree line. You really plan to carry me the entire way?”

He cradled her to his chest, the flutter of her heartbeat making something inside him quiver. “If I head south we’ll be there in no time. The road had to curve around the mountain. We can go straight down. Look.” He pointed through the trees, and sure enough, the shimmer of city lights answered back.

“That’s closer than I thought.” Her teeth chattered.

Tyler caught her by the chin as he held her against him,

savouring her warmth and the scent of her attraction that she was powerless to hide. “You'll be okay. I'll take you home.”

He should have stepped away, should have moved immediately to shift, but this called to him. The wild part inside him needed a taste, and as she caught his shoulders and lifted her head willingly, he brought their mouths together.

Their last kiss had been violent. Rough, nearly a fight. This was surprisingly soft, shared warmth and passion. Exploring and trying to get closer to each other. He held her, his hands full of her ass, tempted to grind her over his erection but the steady thrill of her hands over his shoulders was enough, for now at least.

They pulled back at the same moment, breathless. Panting. Caroline glanced away and brought her fingers to her lips.

Tyler rubbed his thumb over her swollen bottom lip. “I'm glad nothing happened to you.”

He let her go reluctantly, the cool wind whipping around them bringing a familiar scent. “If you get too cold while we're moving, call out and let me know. I'll stop to warm you up.”

She smiled. “If you stop to warm me, we might never get home.”

The light in her eyes had changed from the denial she'd given him in the lingerie shop. The passion and the fire were back and not directed at turning him away, but burning him up along with her.

He shifted as fast as possible, the solid weight of his bear mind sending up reassurances that together they'd protect her. Care for her. Carry her to safety.

His human couldn't wait to get her home.

The trees went dark with shadows, the moonlight playing peek-a-boo through the tall timbers. Somewhere behind him, a set of footfalls hit the dirt in a rapid rhythm. Her wolf guard, the one he'd scented when they'd stopped.

Good to know the man had made it out of the mess in one piece. Tyler had no desire to start a war with the local wolves. He'd actually been glad of the help in getting Caroline to safety.

Only once they reached the outskirts of town, Tyler was pleased their shadow faded away, heading toward the Takhini pack house instead of staying on their tail.

What he had hopes for needed no chaperone.

He paused, not sure where the best place to shift would be. On his back, Caroline lifted herself upright, her warmth vanishing from where she'd been lying. "More to the right. There's a path that leads to the edge of the yard."

He followed her directions, slipping farther into civilization than he'd usually go in his bear form. It seemed the lights had been deliberately aimed in this section, allowing him to see his way without being spotlighted.

"Stop beside the garden shed."

He slowed, reluctant to allow her to crawl off, but eager to get to the next stage of the game. He shifted as she opened the combination lock and slipped inside the small building.

"How do we get into the apartment?"

She pulled a Rubbermaid tote forward, popping open the lid. "Emergency supplies. Here..." She handed him a dark blue robe. "You'll have to go in bare feet, but at least you won't be arrested for indecent exposure."

He slipped on one sleeve before catching her staring, her cheeks rosy red. "Are you blushing or cold?"

She ignored him and fumbled in the bottom of the tote. "Don't distract me. I need to find the extra key."

He stepped behind her, wrapping his arms around and

pressing their bodies together. “Distract you? How could I do that?”

She had this crazy habit of growling that turned him on. Hard. The wiggle of her hips did nothing to discourage him either.

“Found them.” She lifted a key ring in the air in triumph.

He pressed his lips to her neck as he slid a hand over her belly, loving the way she trembled under his touch. “Congrats. That’s wonderful news.”

She shivered and moaned, laying her head on his shoulder. “God, I want to hit you with something. But I also want you to throw me on the ground and fuck me blind. I’m an idiot.”

He controlled his rush of excitement at her words. “You’re reacting to the danger of the evening and the attraction between us. How about somewhere between the two options?”

“I throw you to the ground?”

He helped her ease the tote back into position, curling his hand around her fingers and the key. “Invite me upstairs. We’ll work out the details as we go.”

For one horrid moment he thought she would refuse, she stood silently for so long, ignoring his caresses.

Then she turned in his arms and smiled. “This might be a huge mistake, but come on.”

Her desire had a flavour. Sex. Addictive sex. The entire way across the lawn to the backdoor entrance of the apartment, Caroline wondered if she’d caught some kind of moon fever.

Silvery light shimmered off his dark hair as he waited for her to punch in the combination to the security door. His hand on her lower back burned, a furnace-like source of heat.

She’d admit it. She’d been scared, but fear had switched far too quickly into resignation. Bears rampaging in a dining hall? *Yawn.* Simply another situation to deal with.

Maybe her life had held one too many unpredictable shifter event after another. Nothing surprised her for long, not anymore. Nothing shocked her. It wasn't a human trait to be so nonchalant about death and dying, but she really couldn't muster anything more at this moment than a pulse of erotic desire.

She was turned on, and that was nearly as appalling as her lack of fear. They'd survived, and now all she could think of was the size of his muscles and the heat radiating from him as they stood nearly skin to skin.

He followed her to her sister's apartment. Allowed her to open the door. There wasn't the same kind of instant up-against-the-wall response from either of them like had happened the last time. Instead, he marched in and looked around carefully.

Her feet were sore, she was cold to the core from being outside in a sliver of satin for over an hour, and she still felt as if she were on fire.

He was a rather potent animal.

Tyler turned back to her, his expression unreadable. "This isn't your apartment. You don't live here."

Strange thing to comment on. She flipped a hand in the air. "My sister's. She's gone north with her partner. I needed a place to stay, and she won't mind."

He stalked closer. "Why do you need a new place to stay?"

"Does it matter?" His eyes flashed, and she hurried to explain, not wanting to lose the edge of passion burning in the air. "I'm not being a smart-ass. I meant that for real. It doesn't matter why, only this is a safe place. I want to see to your injuries."

He scooped her up and carried her protesting body into the back of the apartment. “I have no injuries. Between Justin, your guard and a bit of good luck, I’m unscathed.”

When he ignored the bedroom and took the bathroom door instead, Caroline was disappointed. Until he lowered her to the floor and flipped on the shower. “Strip.”

The dark blue robe she’d loaned him was already coming off. Caroline untied the knot at her waist, swallowing hard at the new expression in his eyes. The one that said she was a bowl of oatmeal at just the right temperature.

Taking off the diamond earrings and necklace gave her a moment to breathe. She fidgeted as she placed them on the bathroom counter, attempting to regain her composure. “I’m glad nothing happened to these. I seem to have ruined the gown.”

“You didn’t ruin anything.” Tyler grasped the neckline and ripped the garment the rest of the way so it gaped open at the front. “I like unwrapping my presents.”

Steam filled the small room, wafting past his thick torso and covering his solid body. He pushed the fabric from her shoulders and observed closely as it puddled to the ground.

A delighted grin erupted as she stood in the new panties and bra he’d bought her—was it only earlier that evening?

Instead of caressing the bits of lace and satin still covering her, his fingers trickled over her thigh and the knife strapped there. “A woman of many talents and surprises. I like this, Caroline Bradley.”

She shivered, this time from his touch, not the cold. He dropped to his knees and took his time undoing the buckle on the sheath. He touched his lips to her skin and branded her, a shot driving from where his mouth landed straight into her core.

Before she found the power to speak, he'd removed her knife, laying it carefully on the counter before turning back to examine her.

"Tell me this is a one-night stand." Caroline cursed the words even as they escaped. If he stopped she'd self-implode, only she didn't want fancy promises given or assumed.

"This is whatever we make it." He caught a finger in the edge of her panties and tugged them lower an inch at a time, his gaze fixed on her sex.

Good answer.

Gazing down at him, she was distracted enough to let this happen. Forget being tough and reacting on impulse to fix things. Forget planning and plotting to do the right thing. She wanted to feel alive and excited, and the man kneeling at her feet was sexy enough to have her panting before he'd done more than caress her skin.

He touched his lips just above her mound, breathing deeply. "This is what you want. What your body wants, what I want to give to you."

Another open-mouthed kiss, this time on her curls, and Caroline caught his head in her hands in an attempt to stay on her feet.

He hummed in approval. "So eager. I am as well, but first things first."

She stifled the whimper wanting to escape when he stood, but he didn't leave her. Simply reached around, and her bra vanished.

"You guys are good at that. Undressing, I mean." Caroline swallowed as he let the material fall to the floor, hands remaining to cradle the sides of her breasts.

"Occupational benefit." He lifted her breasts, his thumbs

teasing her nipples. The tips were already tight peaks, and his caress made them tingle.

She wanted more. Wanted to watch him lean closer and use his mouth. His lips. His tongue. Anything that would increase the pressure building inside her.

What she got was a quick ride through the air into the shower, the heat of the water smarting as it warmed her chilled toes and hands. "Oh, Lordy, that feels good."

Tyler chuckled as he stepped into the tub beside her, his bulk barely fitting into the normal-sized enclosure. "Those are the kind of noises I want to hear when it's me causing them, not a simple shower."

He was a fine, fine looking man. Caroline stepped back to give him room and allow the spray to break over her shoulder onto his chest. The water poured down his torso, rivulets teasing through the trail of hair leading to his cock. His very erect cock.

Tyler outright laughed this time. "You just sighed again. Like what you see?"

She wasn't going to lie. "You make me crazy, Tyler. I shouldn't want you so badly."

"Who says?" Tyler caught her close, water streaming between their torsos. His erection tight to her ass as he turned her and settled her against his chest. "Who says it's wrong for me to want to admire your beautiful body? Like your breasts—damn, tonight when you walked across the room I wanted you to be naked so I could enjoy these." He cupped her, this time able to hold her completely, thumb and forefingers playing lightly with her nipples.

Caroline rested her hands on his hips to keep her balance, her head on his shoulder. "You bears are insane. Do you think anyone got seriously hurt?"

His teeth caught the rim of her ear, and she shuddered. "No more politics. Forget them. Tomorrow will be soon enough. Your guard is safe, so is mine. That's all we need to worry about. Concentrate on us."

"Forget politics, hmm?" She really shouldn't interrupt him when he was caressing her breasts so perfectly. Not when he adjusted position to reach farther down her body, no doubt aiming at her sex. She'd never been very good at making herself shut up, though. "Is this Political Necessity, what we're doing right now?"

He cupped her sex, rubbing lightly. "You're never going to let me forget that comment, are you?"

"Well, it was kind of memorable. *Oh...*"

He'd slipped a finger into her. "I'll have to give you something more memorable to replace it with, then."

The finger went deeper, spreading her, filling her. "Keep going, you're doing grand."

He thrust all the way in, the rest of his hand under her, his thumb centered over her clit. A slow, even rhythm of withdrawing and thrusting made her shake on unsteady legs. Especially when he added a second finger, spreading her wider, his thick digits driving her toward release.

"Oh, Tyler." She dug her nails into his skin and pulsed her hips against his hand, wanting something more to send her over.

His free hand caught a breast and tweaked the nipple, hard, one side then the other. Caroline moaned as her core tightened on his fingers, trying to hold him in place even as he stroked her through her orgasm.

All traces of cold had vanished. She felt as if she was floating, and maybe she was.

Yes, he was carrying her again, out of the shower and into a huge towel, his touch gentle as he dried her.

She was far warmer and more relaxed than a moment before, but she wasn't satisfied. Especially not when he dried himself, his cock bouncing against his belly as he moved.

Caroline reached for him, but he caught her by the wrist. "Uh-uh. No touching until we find a bed. Because the next time I start, I'm not stopping until we're both boneless, and I find lying on bathroom floors highly overrated."

They caught each other's gaze, and Caroline smiled at the honest appreciation he wore. "That's the kind of expression I like to see."

"Enjoy it, you'll be too lightheaded in five minutes to see anything clearly."

"Promises, promises..." She turned and ran for the bedroom, figuring he'd like the pursuit as much as she'd like to be chased.

She made it to the door before he nabbed her. Scooped her up and tossed her toward the bed, throwing himself after her. They landed in a mass of limbs and body parts, rubbing together in a frenzy.

"You're lucky this bed is reinforced for shifter weight," Caroline teased.

"You're lucky this bed is strong enough to take what we're going to do on it." He stretched over her, pinning her to the mattress. Caroline found her wrists caught in an inescapable clasp. He pulled her hands overhead, the position stretching her torso and making her arch her back. Her breasts rose and he licked his lips.

Anticipation made her breathing grow thinner, her torso shaking as he lowered his head to suck her nipple into his mouth.

She pressed against him. "*Yes.*"

He answered with a firmer tug of his lips and a happy hum. He drove her crazy for a while, flicking his tongue lightly over the tip, pulsing his lips closed and drawing harder, before releasing and starting all over again.

And this talented bear? With his free hand he was exploring the tender skin on her hip. Fingers edging in circles closer and closer to her sex.

"I want to touch you," she complained.

"You will." He mumbled the words against her breasts as if he couldn't bear to leave them. "Caroline. Do you want me to use a condom?"

Where exactly could he possibly have such things hidden? And there would be none in her sister's bathroom either, as both Shelley and her partner were shifters.

Lucky for Tyler, she had it covered. "No need. You're a shifter—no disease—and I'm on birth control."

His forehead crashed to her chest for a second as he muttered, "Thank God."

She laughed. "You didn't have a condom, did you? If I'd said we needed one?"

He lifted up on his elbows, searching her face, passion heating her even as he spoke. "I promise I will never hurt you, and I'll always protect you. And that means yes, if you'd said we needed a condom, I would have made you happy but stopped from having sex."

"Good thing one of us is prepared," Caroline teased, lifting a leg and running her calf up the back of his thigh. She rocked her hips, bumping his thick erection against her.

His eyes darkened. "And not hurting you means making sure you're ready."

"I'm ready. I'm ready," she insisted.

He licked his lips. "Oh, you will be, I promise that as well."

A single-minded assault began as he determinedly worked his way down her body. He didn't have to worry, though; she wouldn't protest. Oral sex from a shifter was a form of paradise she'd sworn to never deny herself. They were truly talented with their tongues.

"Oh. My. *Word.*"

He had her pinned with one hand and with no warning had opened her thighs with his broad shoulders, falling on her as if he were starving. Long licks from her core to her clit, a teasing circle then another stroke. Caroline happily widened her legs to give him room to work.

He lifted her to his mouth, lapping intimately, one hand holding her in place. Somehow he got his fingers involved again, pressing against her clit until she gasped for air, teetering on exploding.

He slipped his hand away and covered her clit with his mouth and sucked, and she broke, pleasure enveloping her.

"Tyler, oh *yes.*"

He was over her before the first peak faded, broad cock at her opening. He held her thigh to one side and pressed in, a second pulse of pleasure accompanying his entrance.

She stared at him, his face tense with restraint; pleasure there as well as he sank deeper one rock at a time. She was being stretched so good, his cock teasing aftershocks from her.

When he buried himself all the way, their groins finally meshed, she squeezed her eyes shut to soak in the sensation.

"Caroline, you're incredible." The words whispered beside her ear. He was on his elbows over her, his hips moving slowly as he withdrew his cock then slipped in again. "So tight around me. So wet and perfect. Lift your legs and hold me."

She obeyed instantly, crossing her ankles and groaning as the new angle moved him deeper.

"Yes." He swiveled his hips, and a zing of something extra thrilled up her spine. She must have gasped or groaned or hoorayed *yes*, because his focus narrowed to her and nothing else. "Oh, you like that, do you?"

"Again," she ordered. Panted. Wheezed. The word was barely comprehensible, but he seemed to know what she was begging for. Because he repeated the move. And again, teasing her inside where she never remembered feeling before. Like he'd found the magic button people always talked about, and she never knew she'd been missing.

Sex before this? She'd enjoyed. She'd enjoyed a *lot*. But with every thrust, Tyler erased what had come before and made her see stars. Everywhere.

"Breathe, Caroline," he laughed. "I'm not going anywhere."

"Don't stop," she begged, certain if he wavered this magical event would vanish like rain in the desert.

"Don't worry." He gave another thrust that made her ears tingle. The next one, the top of her head. "This feels too good to stop any time soon."

Lillie's comment about Energizer Bunny Bears echoed in her memory, and Caroline relaxed. Her entire lower body was along for the ride as he worked her over, leaning on one elbow to free a hand.

She was sure he'd go for her breasts, because, hello, consistency in a male was to be appreciated. Then he shocked her by slipping his hand under her head and cradling her neck, lowering his mouth over hers and kissing her tenderly. His tongue explored lazily even as his cock pierced her in two.

Tenderness mixed with incredible passion. A soft kiss pressed to the corner of her mouth as he rocketed his cock into her core, and that extra motion broke her. Her climax hit, washing her with passion as he kissed her one more time then came, his release shaking his torso as he held himself from crushing her.

"Sweet Caroline." The words whispered against her lips, and she smiled, even as the delight shuddering through her made the room go fuzzy.

Chapter Twelve

When his arm strength gave out, he managed to drop to the side and not on top of her. Caroline cuddled in, resting her head on his shoulder, her fingers moving in small circles as she played with his chest hair.

"That was incredible." She exhaled in a long, low rush. "Although, I'm still not sure why it happened."

His bear rolled upward and suggested taking her for a few more rounds so she'd stop with the thinking so much. Tyler kind of agreed with the beast this time. "You need me to explain sexual attraction?"

She leaned up on an elbow, her blonde hair falling in a curtain over her shoulder as her gaze searched him thoroughly. "Oh, I understand sex. I'm still not sure why I wanted it so badly with you."

A myriad of answers waited to be shared, but none of them were as important as clearing the air. He brushed her cheek with his knuckles. "You're more to me than a political necessity."

Some of the softness left her face. "Go on."

Tyler crossed his arms under his head and stared up at the ceiling, trying to put his thoughts into order. "You saw Lillie tonight."

"She's lovely. I hope she didn't get hurt in the fight."

Tyler shook his head. "I saw Jim and her ducking out. She'll be fine, and he's head over heels with her, so you can be sure he'll take good care of her."

"Turned out well for an arranged marriage."

Damn. "I should have guessed you'd have ferreted out secrets even in the short time before the party blew up. Yes, their marriage was arranged, just like my brother Frank's."

She leaned higher, a question in her eyes. "Frank? Really? That must have been successful as well, because I heard he left civilization when she died."

Tyler nodded. "In the clans, arranged marriages are common. We're not like packs who gather together en mass. Usually the clans are spread over a wide area, and chances of finding another bear and falling in love are low."

Her eyes widened, horror filling them. "You're not engaged to someone, are you?"

Shit. He caught her before she could crawl off and take away her warmth. "No, of course not. I wouldn't have taken you to bed if I had another woman. I've been avoiding making a commitment because I was too busy traveling for the family business and, more recently, running the show."

"Evan mentioned you had taken over. I'm sorry, did your father pass away recently?"

"Last year." Tyler paused. "And it wasn't my father who died."

She frowned. "I don't understand."

Tyler forced out the words. "My mother died. My father has been devastated by her loss. He's a shadow of the man he was before."

Caroline sat upright, and in spite of the seriousness of the moment, his gaze involuntarily went to her breasts. She jerked a T-shirt from under the pillow and pulled it over her head while his bear complained bitterly.

"Stop rumbling. We need to talk and eat, and naked isn't a good idea for that," Caroline scolded as she scrambled off the bed and headed to the closet.

"Naked works fine by me, although food would be welcome." He admired her legs and the curve of her ass peeking out from under the tail of her shirt. "Your sister won't have anything for me to wear."

"Her partner might, or you can use the robe again."

"I don't see what's wrong with naked," he grumbled, accepting the pair of sweatpants she thrust at him.

"I'll make eggs and toast. You can squeeze some oranges."

She was gone in a blur of motion. Out the door, leaving behind only the scent of their lovemaking.

Tyler sat on the edge of the bed and wondered what had just happened. He'd been all ready to make a full confession about why he'd been an ass, and she'd cut him off. He thought women liked conversations about emotions.

His bear snickered.

Asshole.

By the time he'd joined her in the kitchen, she had a pan heating on the stove and the carton of eggs open. Toaster loaded with bread. "You have everything under control?"

She snorted. "Always."

He opened the fridge and looked for oranges. "I'm a lousy date. Took you out for dinner and never fed you."

"Look on the bright side, the entertainment was good."

He eyed her as she cracked eggs into the pan, studiously avoiding his gaze. Okay, it wasn't just his imagination. She really was acting weird.

Maybe her blood sugar was low or something. He followed directions as she ordered him around the kitchen, even though he did know how to use both a knife and a hand juicer.

He let her ramble about inconsequential things, answering her generic questions regarding Dzinsen Diamonds. Not until she'd cleaned her plate did he push his own away and lean back in his chair.

"I know we didn't have much time before things blew up, but what are your thoughts on the gathering tonight?"

"Other than the idiot who turned it into a punching match? Todd Ainsworth is an ass. I think he's abusing Amanda."

Dammit. "Chances are, yes, he is. What else?"

She swirled the last inch of orange juice in her glass and stared at the liquid. "Bears are protective of their women. Far more than they need to be, if Lillie's instant response to the attack is any indication."

He paused. "I agree with you that we're protective. It's in our nature."

She blew a raspberry at him. "There you go again, blaming it on your instincts. Why do you shifters do that? Everyone who is not broken wants to protect those they love, whether they're human or shifter. Bears don't have a monopoly on protective reflexes."

"Can I blame the *over*protective part on being a bear?"

"Nope. You can blame that on being an idiot. I know some women need more encouragement, and even coddling, than others, but then again, so do some guys. By cutting off an entire section of your population, you are losing out big-time in harnessing their skills and enthusiasm."

Tyler stared at her. "You got all this out of barely forty-five minutes in the presence of conclave members?"

She held up her hand and flicked off fingers. "The party, the limo ride, the lingerie shop, dinner last night, our little meet-and-greet in the hotel..."

Damn. "So what's the solution?"

Caroline stacked their dirty plates then carried them to the counter. "You need to win this thing, so when you do the territorial fixes, you can smack sense into the guys who need it. Someone like Jim Halcyon—he won't argue if you suggest he and his clan join the twenty-first century."

"No, he won't."

She leaned a hip on the counter. "Todd Ainsworth, on the other hand, should be locked up somewhere for a very long time."

"Locked up?" That was a shocker. "I would have thought you'd suggest something painful, or an even more permanent solution to rid ourselves of the wonder that is Todd."

"I didn't say *where* I'd lock him up, did I? Or who I'd lock him up with."

There was the bloodthirsty woman his bear so appreciated. Tyler took a long slow look, starting at her bare feet and working his way up to her eyes. "I want your help to win this, but I was afraid to let you become more than an assistant."

"You don't have to tell me why—"

"I do." He stood and crowded her, one hand on either side of the counter to trap her in position. "You're pushing me away when I want to explain. I thought I needed to grovel?"

She avoided his eyes. "I changed my mind."

"That's not an answer."

Caroline planted her hands on his chest and attempted to shove him back. "I don't want to know why you were keeping me at arm's length. It's no big deal. The sex thing is fine, and I'll help you at the next gathering, but—"

She wasn't getting it, so he shut her up the only way he could think of. He kissed her. Open mouths together, his tongue stopping hers.

Instead of applying pressure to escape, she was soon sliding her hands around his chest and dragging her nails down his back. They had no difficulties in the physical-compatibility department, that was for certain.

He broke them apart and leaned their foreheads together. "Listen to me. I like you. I want to see where this can go between us, not only for conclave."

Caroline shook her head. "I don't want a new boyfriend."

Tyler hesitated over her word choice. "A *new* boyfriend? You just broke up with someone. That's why you're living in your sister's apartment."

She wiggled uncomfortably.

"I don't get it. If you're not dating someone, then why not make it official and date me? You like me, right?"

"Of course I do. We had sex. I don't fool around with guys I don't care about."

He narrowed his gaze. "Are you trying to escape someone? Was your last boyfriend more like Todd than Jim?"

Her jaw gaped open before she pulled herself together. "Hell, no. Evan is—"

"Evan? As in the leader of the Takhini pack?" Tyler's hackles went up. "What did he do to you? I'll kill him."

She smacked a hand against her forehead. "What is with you Alpha dudes? Stop interrupting and listen to my words. I do not need you doing anything to Evan. I don't need you doing anything in my life. Get it, *my life*. Me, in charge."

Tyler calmed himself. “Sorry, instinctive reaction.”

She narrowed her glare. “You say the word *instinct* one more time, and I swear I will hurt you.”

This time when she shoved him Tyler stepped back, setting her free to pace the living room. “I’m sorry for misunderstanding, but what does that have to do with why you won’t officially go out with me?”

Caroline leaned her head on the window, staring into the darkness of the night. “I’ve been a human in a wolf pack for ages. I’ve done things to make myself important. I’ve worked hard and fought for my position, like any wolf would. And I’m tired of it. I want some time to myself. No shifters to make happy, no rules to follow or worry about breaking. I can’t have that, not with you needing my help, but I can certainly avoid being an official girlfriend and all the extra shit that would bring with it.”

“I feel guilty for dragging you into this, but I still fail to see why being with me isn’t a plus. I’m not more work.”

“Ha.” The derision in her tone rippled across the room like a cold splash of water. “You’re one of the worst types. You don’t think you’re a lot of work, but what you really want is everything. All my attention, all my focus. Admit it. At least acknowledging it would be one step in making a difference in this conversation.”

“You want honesty?” Tyler moved in on her. “I didn’t want to ask you to be my date for real because I was afraid I was too attracted to you. If it’s just business, I could tell myself it’ll be all over in a week. That I don’t have to worry about getting attached, falling in love, and then losing you.”

Caroline’s legs wouldn’t hold her any longer. She collapsed on to the couch and stared at Tyler in shock. “Are you ever leaping to conclusions there, bucko. From a date to falling in love in three easy steps. That's not normal."

He was the one pacing the room now, frustration in his every move. "Maybe not for a human, but I'm a bear."

He continued to stride back and forth, much like her thoughts bounced in her brain. That tropical-island beach was looking better and better all the time.

"So…bears fall in love fast?" And why hadn't she been warned?

Tyler clasped the back of the easy chair, his big hands fisted in the fabric. "We're emotional creatures. Violence, passion, all shades of the spectrum. It makes sense. And as my family demonstrates, losing our life partner is more devastating for us than most."

She shook her head. "Let me get this straight. You're afraid you'll be attracted enough to fall in love, because when I die in some horrible accident in a few years you'll go off the deep end, so you'd better not get involved with me in the first place."

His mouth twisted with resignation. "Not the most logical thing I've ever done."

"I'd say."

He came around the chair and sat beside her, reaching for her hands. She allowed him to take hold, and that's when she noticed she was still wearing his ring.

The sensation of him twisting the ring gently made something twitch inside her stomach, and it wasn't the midnight dinner they'd just eaten.

She cleared her throat. "So. What's changed between now and, oh…four hours ago when you first decided hands-off was a better policy?"

Because she was getting whiplash.

Tyler lifted her fingers to his mouth, his lips tender on her skin. "I changed my mind."

Drat. He'd echoed her words from earlier. She couldn't even snarl at him for being unreasonable. "That quick, huh?"

He nodded, sincerity in his eyes. She blew a stream of air out in the hopes it would clear away some of the cobwebs.

"If we can put the awkwardness behind us, I think we can come to a compromise that suits both of us."

"You're back to sounding like a businessman." Caroline looked him over carefully. In the short time she'd known him, they'd covered a lot of territory. Maybe it was because he was a shifter, and she was so used to spending time with people who were "other" than she was. An internal check put her at the not-mad-at-him and still-interested-in-him stage.

A yawn escaped before she could tug a hand free from his grasp and cover her mouth.

He grinned. "I would take that as an insult, only I'm ready to hit the sack as well. But first, Caroline, I'd like to ask you again. Will you spend the next week with me? Help me politically, but get to know the real me more as well."

She leaned into his side, sleepiness rising as she relaxed. "So we'll date while you're in town?"

"And longer, if that's what we decide. I might not live here in Whitehorse, but I'm not that far away. Not with planes, and phones and the internet."

This was...different. She stared into his face as she considered.

"What's that expression for?" He cuddled her in closer.

"The last relationship I was in, I orchestrated it." She paused. "Come to think of it, I probably set up most of my first dates."

He brushed her hair. "Well, this time you're being pursued. You'll have to tell me how I'm doing."

"Like I have trouble speaking my mind. You'll know how you're doing." She twisted, draping her arms around his neck. "Carry me to bed."

He kissed her cheek. "Does that mean yes?"

"I'll tell you in bed."

Okay, totally wrong of her, since being carried about was the exact opposite of what she'd told him about women being strong and capable. But this was what she wanted, damn it. A tiny moment of being cherished and cared for, in spite of her extreme independence.

Besides, not many guys could haul her around like she weighed nothing, and it had been a hell of a day.

She turned off lights as he made his way back to the bedroom, reaching from side to side and rubbing against him shamelessly at every opportunity. His amusement rose, his expression softening as they approached their destination.

"Which side of the bed do you want?" she asked.

He lowered her to the floor and slipped off her T-shirt, his eyes lighting up. "The left."

Caroline smiled as she pivoted, giving him plenty of time to admire her as she crawled on the bed and settled.

On the left.

He lost the sweatpants in an amazingly short timeframe. The last thing she saw before he flicked off the overhead light was his have-my-wicked-way-with-her grin.

Evan paced by his unlocked door, his phone in his pocket, one eye on the computer. When Shaun or Caroline called, he would be ready if they needed him.

Sending a guard with her had seemed appropriate after hearing fighting had broken out twice within a couple of hours, during what was supposed to be a peaceful vote.

Peaceful, his ass. Bears had no sense of propriety. Fighting in the hall had been bad enough, but out in the street? And not all of them had stayed human, a faux pas which would end up his ball of shit to deal with.

Rumours were already floating through the human population regarding bears being spotted within city limits. The local news station was broadcasting reminders for people to keep their garbage cans locked in garages until pickup day. Which meant so far the sightings were explainable, but if they kept escalating he'd have to take action to keep the secret of shifters from slamming all over the front pages of the national newspapers.

The computer beeped, and he rushed across to check the email.

Only it wasn't the hoped for "we're fine" response he expected. Instead there was a new screen with a blinking line of text. What the hell did Caroline call this? Oh right, instant messaging.

Are you there, Evan?

Oh, *oh, oh*. The mysterious Miles Canyon member Caroline had warned him about. He sat in the chair and rolled into position, making a rare wish he was better at computers. It took a moment to figure out where to click to add his response. *Yes. Who is this?*

Amy. Is everything okay over there?

Interesting. She was concerned about them? *No problems here. How can I help you?*

I'm...worried. Heard a rumour today there's something big planned by the bears in a couple days. The pack is planning to take advantage of the chaos

The pack. *Your pack?*

Yes. Tell Caroline I need to talk

Evan cussed. *She's busy. Will you talk to me?*

Dead silence greeted that suggestion. Not that he'd expected much more. *I can't risk it. I'm sorry. I want to help, but you understand the problem*

Evan could use his shifter power to make her sing like a bird. And he couldn't even promise he wouldn't, because the truth was he'd snatch up whatever advantages he could to protect his pack. *Then tell me like this. What do they have planned? Can I stop it?*

The little curser blinked, then the note *Amy is writing* appeared. Evan waited impatiently for her to finish.

When she finally hit send, he wasn't sure what to make of her message.

Details were really fuzzy. I'll try to get the file I saw and send a copy to your email. It's all I can do

Evan had never been in this situation before. His protective instincts skyrocketed. *Are you in danger, Amy? Because if you get worried about anything, you come on over to the Takhini pack house, or my place. I promise to help you and keep you safe*

The flickering line blinked again. Finally, she responded. *Well, I didn't expect that. Thank you*

He fumbled on the keys, nowhere near as gifted as most people. Heck, he was crap on the computer—Caroline bailed him out every time he crashed the stupid machine. *I mean it. I'm glad for your help, but I don't want anyone hurt, not in the Miles Canyon or the Takhini packs. The goal is to bring us together without trouble*

Caroline told me. I have to go. I'll try to send information as soon as I can

Then she was gone, and Evan sat staring until the instant-message program faded and a screen saver turned on—a series of pictures of the pack on the day he'd rented the local ski hill for a private event.

Wolves flying down the side of a mountain on inner tubes was something every person needed to see at least once in their lives.

"Boss?"

Evan shook himself alert. Shaun stood in the doorway, obviously just shifted from his wolf form as he was stark naked.

"Is everything okay?" Evan asked.

"Bears are crazy." Shaun strode in and leaned over the back of the couch. "Caroline is fine, but there was a fight at the party. Fur flying everywhere. Tyler and I got her out pretty quickly. I escorted them home, but when she took him to her sister's apartment I figured they were good for the night."

"Stupid bears. Wish they'd have picked some other city to host their little jamboree. Guess it can't be helped. What's on your agenda for tomorrow? Can you keep an eye on her again?"

Shaun shook his head. "Caroline's got me flying to grab people from all over hell and back."

Evan frowned. "She didn't tell me."

"She sent me a text earlier today. Suggested if things went ass-up tonight, it might be nice to have a few extra bodies in the area on our side. I figured you'd approved it."

Evan grimaced. Had he lost all control in the past day with his concentration gone? Or hopefully, it was Caroline being her usual hyper-efficient self. "Who does she want you to get?"

"Her sister and Chase, first off."

A doctor/vet who knew about shifters, and her partner, who was a powerful shifter in his own right. "Makes sense. Who else?"

"You know Nadia Lire? The lynx who lives in Chicken?"

Evan whistled. "Shit, why didn't I think of her?"

"Caroline said you'd say that. Her comment was 'this is why you pay me the big bucks, so I think of everything'. Well, actually she told you to *chill out*, but I thought I'd be nice."

"Har-har."

Shaun stood and stretched his arms. "So, you approve?"

"Definitely. Bring in the reinforcements. I'll take over guard duty on Caroline myself."

Shaun gave a salute and headed for the door. "Sleep tight. My mate is waiting to hear all the details. This night is never gonna end."

Evan waved his Beta out then sat back to sort through the new information. Having additional visitors in town who were Takhini supporters would be useful. Once again, Caroline had anticipated beyond the call of duty.

She also seemed to be seriously interested in the big bear dude. Which he'd have no issues with, as long as Tyler was good enough for her.

Evan's skin itched with want for his mate, but he couldn't afford to be less than on his game. He had to put his cravings out of his mind as much as he could, and focus on the pack during the day.

But right now there was no denying the wolf. It was time to hunt.

Evan shifted, nosing the door of his apartment shut, then headed into the darkened city in the hopes of finding a clue that would put him out of his misery.

Somewhere nearby his mate waited, unaware he existed. The need for secrecy stilled his voice as he padded down the streets in the shadows, but inside?

His wolf howled with longing.

Part Three

They have cradled you in custom,
they have primed you with their preaching,
They have soaked you in convention through and through;
They have put you in a showcase; you're a credit to their teaching—
But can't you hear the Wild?—it's calling you.

Let us probe the silent places, let us seek what luck betide us;
Let us journey to a lonely land I know.
There's a whisper on the night-wind,
there's a star agleam to guide us,
And the Wild is calling, calling...let us go.

"The Call of the Wild"—Robert Service

Chapter Thirteen

Waking for the first time in bed with a new lover was always a learning experience. Caroline smiled. It was even weirder when the lover wasn't human.

A furnace of heat at her back combined with the soft tickle of fur gave enough warning that she didn't scream when the first thing she saw when she rolled over was a grizzly bear hogging eighty percent of the bed.

Tyler's eyes were open, and he was watching her.

"Good morning." She ran her fingers through his fur, sitting up to examine him closer. "I never got a chance to admire your bear last night. Let me look before you shift."

He rested his chin on the mattress, plate-sized paws to the side. She lifted one, and it took both hands for her to raise it off the bed.

His rumble of amusement echoed through the room.

"Yeah, yeah. You're a big brute."

He really was, though. Thick fur, muscular legs. She might have once owned a small car the size of his torso. There was a trace of silver in the fur around his muzzle, another lighter dusting on the telltale grizzly bulge on his back.

The wolf shifters she'd spent her life around were on the big side. Northern wolves tended to grow larger than their southern counterparts, but your average bear/wolf side-by-side comparison meant she was sitting next to one of the biggest beasts in the north.

Dating him kind of ensured she'd never freeze to death in the winter.

She straddled his furry back and dug her fingers into the muscles of his neck and shoulders, guessing where the right spots might be on grizzly anatomy.

Tyler melted under her touch, stretching his neck to one side and letting his satisfaction rumble out until there was a steady roar in her ears.

She fought the urge to giggle as she remembered scratching one of the wolves just right and having him go off into doggie-like leg spasms. She wondered if there was a bear equivalent.

After a few minutes, though, he squirmed and she stopped the rubdown. She rested on top of him and soaked in his warmth, the beam of light shining on the bed making her feel lazy this morning. "Just one more minute, then I'll get up."

Under her, fur and bulky muscles shifted to smooth skin and...well, still lots of muscles. She was fully stretched out on top of a very human Tyler, heat of a different sort flashing over her.

"Who said anything about leaving the bed?" He rolled far enough to tip her to the mattress then bundled her into his arms, nuzzling her neck and dropping kisses on her face.

Well, this was sweet. "Okay, I know guys are usually, well, *up* in the morning, but you're, like, way affectionate."

Tyler adjusted position to look into her eyes. "You were nice to my bear. He appreciates that."

"Your bear gave me a lift last night. He was pretty awesome." She laughed. "And it's a good thing I understand shifters, because talking about your shifted self in the third person is kind of weird."

"He's a big part of me—no size jokes—so I like to keep him happy. That keeps me happy." Tyler pulled her on top of himself, arranging her so he could pet her hair out of the way. "Do you have any plans for the day we need to work around?"

She sat up, placing her knees on either side of his body as she rested her weight on her shins. Her lips pulled into a smile as his gaze fell to her chest. "I'm off work for the next week. Whatever we need to do to get conclave in line, that's my focus."

He drew a wavy line up her torso, goose bumps following his touch. "Not the only focus, I hope."

The tip of his finger circled her nipple, and the peak tightened as if well trained.

Concentrating as he played with her breasts wasn't the easiest thing to do. "When's the next bear social event? I'd like to be better prepared this time, please."

"Three nights from now. A music recital at the Nakai Theatre."

"That's...different than I expected." He was doing wicked, wicked things to her with his thumbs. "And everyone will simply show up, as if the fight last night didn't happen?"

"Exactly. See? You understand bears."

Incredible. Take the least comprehensible action and, *voila*, bears. "What if I wanted to get together with a few people before then, can we do that?"

She'd surprised him. Tyler paused in mid-caress, a crease between his eyes. "Get together with who?"

"The ladies, of course. They get to vote, right? Maybe I could meet them all for lunch or something. Invite them out and see where things are at. I never got a chance to talk to that one clan you wanted me to sound out. Nakusp?"

Tyler's face lit up. "You're a genius. Of course, it's perfect. We have to pick a place that's easy to defend, though."

She laughed. "I can get us a discount at the Moonshine Inn."

"I bet you could, but that's probably already considered Harrison territory. How about somewhere a little more neutral?"

A brainwave hit. "I know the perfect spot. Takhini Hot Springs—it's an outdoor pool only fifteen minutes out of town. If anything does happen, it's far enough from city limits to help with damage control, and the pack is part owner. If we set it up for tomorrow, I can guarantee there will be no outside visitors."

He nodded. "Areas for observation, and yet lots of opportunities for private discussion. Sounds like a super idea." When she would have crawled off him to get planning, though, he caught her. "Later. It's still too early to contact anyone. We have plenty of time."

He lifted his fingers to trace her lips, then pressed one digit into her mouth. She licked it obediently, wondering what he had planned. The next trip around her nipple left moisture behind, and now not only his touch but also the cool room air assaulted her.

Her sex tingled madly, and he hadn't gone anywhere near her hot buttons yet. "Oh boy."

"Oh *man*." He grinned. "Let's see what things make you scream in pleasure."

"I'm not much of a screamer." The words slipped out before Caroline realized how much of a challenge they could be considered. "Oops? Just forget I said..."

He sat up, six-pack abdomen flexing under her fingers as he brought their bodies together. Heat radiated off him and wrapped her in desire and anticipation. “Forget what?”

Then he rolled her under him and proceeded to prove that she could, in fact, scream herself hoarse when properly motivated.

Justin stopped by the apartment with a bag of clothes, his alert gaze taking in everything as he stood in the doorway. Caroline was at the desk by the window, sending out email invitations to her gathering the following day.

Tyler pulled his friend into the back room with him. “You want to say something, so you may as well get it out of your system.”

Justin shook his head. “No lectures from me. I might need to say *I told you so* a few times, but nothing happened I’m worried about.”

Tyler pulled on jeans and a thick T-shirt. “You’ve brought me a pretty relaxed outfit here, and yes, I’m ignoring the *I told you so* comment.”

“I rented you a jeep. Figured you might like some time to explore the area with your new friend this morning.” His guard pointedly stared into the living room.

Glory be. “You mean I don’t have to sneak out of town with her to avoid your obsession with protecting us?”

“You’re officially dating?”

It was strange to feel both a thrill and lingering fear at the idea of being formally involved with Caroline—how could two emotions occupy the same mental space? “Yes.”

Justin shrugged. “Then you don’t need a chaperone, and I never said you wouldn’t have a guard. Only you can drive. Just ignore me as I ramble through the trees.”

"You get a thrill out of watching, do you?"

His guard coughed. "Exactly what are you planning on doing during your explore?"

"Never mind."

It didn't need to be said. Justin knew without being told that chances were high Caroline and Tyler would end up testing the jeep's springs at some point, and he didn't mean by going cross-country.

Tyler eyed his friend. "Taking off won't cause troubles in terms of wheeling and dealing for votes?"

Justin shook his head. "If bears go by rote, most of them will sleep in and take it easy this morning. This afternoon everyone will be around Whitehorse. If you and Caroline do some window-shopping, you'll bump into most of the conclave participants on a one-to-one basis. That works better than us arranging formal coffee klatches."

"Agreed."

Justin called out a greeting as he marched into the living room, "Caroline. How did you enjoy the dinner last night?"

She spun her chair, pulling her hair back into a ponytail as she answered. "I've been informed no one died, and people are shocked. Well, people are shocked I even asked the question. Do all bears act like the rabbits in *Watership Down*? Ignore the fact that some of you have dropped off the face of the earth?"

Justin turned, his confusion clear. "Did she just compare us to a bunch of rabbits?"

"Scared and frightened bunnies. Yes." Tyler settled onto the couch.

Caroline blew a raspberry at them. "Hey, you like lemmings better? Or how about hamsters? Little ones, with parachutes, being tossed off the roof of a building."

"I have no idea what you're talking about," Tyler admitted, although her random comments amused him greatly. "Ready for breakfast? And afterward Justin found us a vehicle if you'd like to show me some of the local sights."

She closed the computer and headed for the table. "I vote for Ricky's Grill. And yes, showing you around would be fun. Now who wants to take charge of this?"

She held out a box.

"What is that?" Tyler rose to his feet as he figured out what she had clutched in her fingers. "Oh, the necklace. Just keep it."

Her gaze narrowed and she stepped closer, poking him in the chest with the container. "Hardly."

"No, it's yours. Ready to go?" Tyler frowned as Justin made the strangest motions with his head and brows. "What is your damn problem? Stop twitching like a zombie."

Justin shrugged. "I was trying to warn you a certain female might be pissed off at you. As your friend, I'd ignore your stupidity and be amused by the pain she'll cause, but as your bodyguard I figured I should make sure you have a second's warning. In case you need to be prepared for a physical attack."

Caroline grinned at Justin. "You already had a coffee this morning, didn't you?"

"I'm a sharp cookie in general, but yes. Perhaps you'll take his lack of caffeine into consideration before you flatten him."

"I'm in the room. Stop talking about me like I'm not here." Tyler paused. Something had gone down weird in the last couple minutes. "You are talking about me, correct?"

Caroline grabbed him by the belt buckle and jerked. Well, she attempted to jerk him forward, but he weighed too much for her to make him budge. Instead, his jeans shifted position, and she slipped the box into the gap between the fabric and his abdomen. "You have a good friend there, Tyler. I'll let you off this time. Come on. Let's get you some food and see if your brain wakes up."

Justin headed for the door, checking the hallway. Tyler removed the box from his pants and returned it to his bag. Caroline pulled on a coat and ignored him as if he wasn't even there.

The two of them ended up alone at the table for breakfast as Justin faded unobtrusively into the background. Tyler and Caroline chatted throughout the meal about family and their general experiences of living in the north. By the time they were done eating, he'd figured out what he'd done to piss her off earlier.

She wasn't like any woman he'd ever met before. Most wouldn't have thought twice about accepting the jewelry. In fact, he'd had a few lovers he was pretty sure had angled for nights together more for the trinkets he gave them than to be with him.

Caroline was a breath of fresh air in his life, and his unreasonable fear struck again. That in the midst of the best thing happening to him he would lose himself.

He couldn't afford to have his concentration broken more than it already was, but he'd made her a commitment this was more than simply business.

Six foot four and frightened by his emotions. Hurrah for stupidity. Maybe her comment about rabbits and hamsters made some sense.

Tyler opened the jeep's passenger door for Caroline and watched in bemusement as she crawled all the way across to settle into the driver's seat. "What are you doing?"

She grinned. "Showing you around. Get in."

She expected him to argue, so he did the unexpected and sat, slipping the seat back while she adjusted her chair to reach the pedals. He glanced over his shoulder and noted the pair of daypacks on the seat. "Justin said he left us water bottles and a lunch, so where shall we go?"

Caroline headed out of town and toward the south. "Miles Canyon. There are some great hiking trails we can stretch our legs on for a while, if that's okay with you."

That sounded wonderful. "Lead on."

Every moment left the suit and tie farther behind them, and the opportunity to relax and break away was the last thing he'd expected to experience during this event.

Actually, *Caroline* was the last thing he'd expected during this trip. The thought made him grin.

She parked the jeep under the shade of a towering evergreen, the lowest branches brushing the roof. They both checked the area around them before opening their doors.

Her sense of caution pleased him and made him wonder. "You know to do that?"

She sighed. "You bears might be the biggest game in town right now, Tyler, but you aren't the only things a girl needs to watch out for."

Her comment made the blood rise at the back of his eyes and things turned red. "You've never had troubles with anyone, have you?"

She'd pulled out one backpack already, pressing it into his arms as he stepped to her side. "No, Tyler. I've never been attacked. Well, not deliberately. There was one time that a couple of the pack got mixed up and thought I was the target for a shifter version of Capture the Flag. I had the devil of a time staying out of their path."

He settled the pack in position, shocked she could laugh about it. "You were run down by a bunch of wolves and you're not mad?"

Caroline knelt to tighten her laces. "Who said they caught me?"

Her bright smile shone up at him, and his bear roared to life, sending all kinds of pornworthy images involving her in that position, albeit sans runners, backpack and clothes. He was helpless to stop his cock from reacting.

Some of what he was thinking must have shown on his face. Her gaze dropped over him, lingering for long enough to be a visual caress right where he really didn't need any encouragement.

Then, dammit, she licked her lips, and he was done for. Fully hard and aching, his cock pressed the front of his jeans.

Caroline rose slowly, inching forward as she finished with her body brushing his, her fingers tracing the line of his belt.

"Maybe instead of a hike, we should make this more interesting."

His instant response shot out; half human, half bear, all male. "I'm game."

She slipped her fingers into his pockets, the side of her knuckles skimming the crest of his cock, and her eyes widened. He was mesmerized by her expression, by her lips that were still wet from where she'd moistened them. "You know, I don't mind the idea of being chased."

Shit.

Oh damn.

He swallowed hard in an attempt to stop the ringing in his ears. "Chasing you would be my privilege."

Another soft stroke along his erection sent a shiver of lust all the way to his brain. "Getting caught. That could be fun as well. If you're good enough."

Shit.

Double damn.

"You have some kinky fantasies, baby."

Her expressive face vanished from view as she leaned in close and pressed her lips to his neck. A blast of desire rocked him.

She adjusted her grip, pressing her full palm to his erection. "If you catch me, maybe you'll find out."

"If? I'm a bear." He tucked his fingers under her chin and forced her head up so he could examine her face, wanting to be sure she knew what kind of game she was arranging. He brushed his thumb over her cheek, fighting the urge to pick her up right here and bend her over the back of the jeep. "I'll give you a five-minute head start."

Her eyes sparkled as she stepped back. She whispered as she widened the gap between them. "I'll tell you *no* if I want to stop, but otherwise? Have fun. I plan to."

She blew him a kiss before turning and crossing the empty parking lot, headed for the suspension bridge and the foothills on the other side of the river.

He double-checked the doors were locked then strolled to the bridge, deliberately not watching which direction she headed after leaving the iron contraption.

Below him the Whitehorse River rushed toward the city, the raging rapids a thing of the past since the dam had been built. There was still enough water to create a low rumble of sound, filling his ears with life and excitement. The sun lit the valley, reflecting off rich green limbs and fluttering leaves in stark contrast with the deep blue sky above them. His nostrils filled with the scent of pine and earth...

...and her. Headed across the bridge and into the forest.

Tyler shoved his bear aside. His human needed no encouragement—and the animal part within him was far too excited at the prospect of running his quarry down. He glanced at his watch and gave her another sixty seconds before setting out to retrieve his prize.

Chapter Fourteen

She ran as if being chased by a predator, which she totally was.

The ground underfoot sent up little puffs of dust as her feet hit the hard-packed surface. The land was dry as a bone. Caroline scanned the area and rapidly thought through her options.

It was only a matter of time before he caught her, and she'd like it to be in a private location, now that she'd poked his bear.

Veering away from the main riverside path, Caroline took the high route. It angled sharply toward the mountaintop for a couple of minutes of thigh-burning altitude gain before leveling off and disappearing into the trees. She didn't bother to set him any side trails like she'd done with the wolves any time she'd planned hide-and-seek games before. With only five minutes to get ahead of Tyler, she had no time to waste. It was all or nothing.

The trees fell behind her in a smooth rhythm as she found her stride, the light pack on her back jiggling as she surged forward. Tyler didn't know the area, so his lack of familiarity should slow him enough she could reach her goal. To her right, portions of the river flashed in the sunlight like paparazzi having a heyday.

For a moment she debated the wisdom of the chase. Not

the sexual kink she'd set up—it was the remembrance of the bears fighting last night that made her hesitate. What if she and Tyler were caught unawares by some of his enemies?

Yet how would the other clans know where to find them? It would have taken a bit of talent to follow them from her apartment to the restaurant then off the highway later.

And really, the fact remained. It was either hide in a backroom the entire time he was here for conclave, or trust he could protect them no matter what ended up happening.

The knife she carried was no guarantee of safety either, but she wasn't helpless.

Her ankle rolled, and she snapped to attention, concentrating before she got hurt. Ahead was her target, and she scrambled up the low section of cliff face, easily making it to where the lone pine stood as a sentinel beside the cliff in its sad but enduring glory.

There was nothing left of the majestic tree anymore but its tall skeleton. Nearly fossilized and iron hard, the tree had been around when the original Gold Rushers had barreled through the area, shooting the life-threatening river that had since been tamed. In the day, though, the rapids had claimed more than one life, and this path had offered an alternative route to safety.

Well, not *this* route, the one she was currently taking up the bare limbs of the behemoth. She'd been climbing the tree since she was a girl, a human child with a brand-new daddy who could turn into a wolf. As a little girl with a head full of fairy tales and wonder, the only unbelievable thing was being informed there was no magic she could partake in to make the same kind of transformation.

Her shifter father had hugged her, reassured her, then proceeded to teach her everything he could about living in the wilderness and dealing with the wild creatures shifters could be. His careful teaching had saved her in the end. Made it possible for her to live in the North Country she loved.

Made it possible for her to be playing a game of sexually twisted hide-and-go-seek with another wild creature out of fairy-tale lore.

She was well warmed up by the time she reached the highest branches, muscles invigorated and ready to meet her demands. She glanced back, eyeing the bits and pieces of trail that were visible as it meandered back to the main highway.

A flash of blue shot past.

Tyler.

She pulled herself along the sturdy limb, grabbed the branch in her hands and swung off, rotating until her feet lightly touched the ground, now at the top of the cliff instead of the bottom. A glance over the edge showed Tyler was too close for her to stay in one place, but her climb had given her time to set up a bit of trickery.

Three paths left the clearing she stood in. She raced down the first, cut through a connecting trail and scooted back the second trail to reach her original starting point. One more loop was all she had time for, leaving her scent on all three trails.

Then she ignored the escape routes and instead climbed the rock face behind her. The low wall emptied onto a second platform with a narrow ledge of a path rounding the corner to yet another maze of trails. Leaving her current location was impossible without edging cautiously along the precipice.

There was no way she could outrun him. No way he wouldn't find her. But where she crouched was hidden from view of everyone but a person actually climbing onto the platform, or risking life and limb on the narrowest of trails. The chance of anyone stumbling into their party was slim. With the wind coming directly at her, the fake trails in the woods should catch Tyler's attention first.

She lay on her stomach on the smooth rock surface to admire him as he reached the top of the tree. He'd removed his jacket, and his arms were bare, strong forearms with a dusting of hair on them. His fingers flexed powerfully as he wrapped them around the limbs, pulling himself up before swinging to the ground, knees absorbing the impact.

He rotated to admire the scenery. Her heart skipped. Did he figure she was such easy prey he had enough time to smell the roses and look around? Or did his light-hearted break make her glad?

He was a good man. The longer she spent with him, the clearer his character became. He wasn't very civilized, though. The façade was there. The formal trappings of sophistication, but it was a layer of pretense on top of the real Tyler.

The real Tyler, who appreciated the view in the middle of a hunt.

The man obviously needed more chances to get away from it all and take it easy. She stopped herself from snorting. Kind of like herself—workaholic.

Tyler faced the trees, his gaze darting over the three options. The angle was wrong for her to be able to read his expression, but he moved slowly, deliberate in his approach. No panicked race forward. A considered and rational assessment.

He stepped to the center path and paused, hesitating at the edge of the forest and breathing deep enough his chest rose. Caroline held her own breath for fear he'd hear her.

Only he didn't take the bait. None of the three paths led him astray. He stood for a while taking long sniffs, testing and tasting the air. He eliminated all her fake routes then stepped back into the clearing. His fingers came up to rub his chin, the rough stubble on his unshaved chin making him look like a dangerous beast. Made him handsomer than he had any right to be.

She gasped as he lifted his gaze and looked directly into her eyes.

Shoot.

She couldn't look away. He kept eye contact as he walked to the base of her hiding spot without stumbling even once on the uneven ground. The heat from her earlier exertions had morphed into slow desire as she considered what exactly she'd set up.

He laid a hand on the smooth rock rising to her hiding spot and grinned. "You didn't make that too difficult."

"I'm still out of reach," she teased, sitting upright on the edge of her cliff.

He examined her, the bits he could see. Heat danced on her nerve endings, sensitizing her skin. Growing desire edged toward all the pertinent girl parts that couldn't wait to see what he'd do next.

Tyler stepped back half a foot. "You think it'll take me long to get up there, think again. I'm coming for you."

She scrambled to her feet and retreated to the back of the platform. He was right—there was no way the cliff would stop him for long. She dropped her backpack to the ground, lost her coat. The game was no longer hide-and-seek but inevitable capture.

The sound of him climbing was unmistakable. She turned to eye the wall she leaned on, considering if she could climb any higher. She risked a glance over her shoulder. It was like glancing in a side-view mirror.

Warning. Objects are much closer than they appear.

She ducked to the right, trying for a narrow patch of scrub

that would hold him back, but he'd closed the space between them, his strong fingers curling around her arm and halting her momentum.

He twirled her, jerking her to his body. Air rushed from her lungs in a gasp as he backed her against the rock and crushed her lips beneath his.

Demanding. Aggressive. She planted her hands on his chest and pushed, but she could have been attempting to move a train for all the good it did her. His tongue stabbed into her mouth and she moaned. Wriggled, attempting to break free.

He caught her wrists and slammed her arms to her sides, jerking them behind her back so he could enclose both wrists in one enormous hand. With her arms pulled behind her like that, her chest thrust forward, driving against him.

He never stopped kissing her. Consuming her. His free hand captured her chin and held her exactly where he wanted her.

Over the years, Caroline had enjoyed her share of excellent lovers. Tyler took it to a new level. Took her wild fantasies and made them come true without her saying a word.

He jammed a thigh between her legs and hauled her hips forward, dragging her clit over rock-solid muscles. She was going to come if he so much as blinked too hard.

When he finally let her breathe, she was too busy filling her lungs to do anything else. By the time she'd gotten ready to offer him a few choice words—careful to not say *no*—he shocked the hell out of her. Twirled her in his arms and resettled her on that damn thigh, but this time there was also a beefy palm covering her mouth.

She couldn't complain if she wanted to.

His lips brushed her ear. "If you want me to stop, stomp your foot. Otherwise, enjoy the ride."

The whispered words shook her. Sexual anticipation flooded her system as he rocked her over his leg. Her arms pinned behind her, his other hand dragged her T-shirt up and ripped her bra out of the way so he could fondle her breasts.

Okay, she was officially twisted, but this was too damn hot. She made sure to keep both feet on the ground even as she struggled in his arms. The total inability to go anywhere dragged a hotter-than-I've-ever-been-before-in-my-life groan from her throat.

"Makes you burn, doesn't it? Damn, I'm dying to fuck you. Going to fuck you in a minute. Only first?"

His hand left her breasts and shoved between her legs, fingers slipping under her panties and moving rapidly over her clit. She widened her stance and pulsed her hips, hopelessly lost. Desperate for release.

He jerked her torso against the wall of his chest, fingers still working her clit. The hand covering her mouth slid down to grasp her throat. His grasp remained controlling, yet loose enough she could breathe, her excitement escaping in gasps as he brought her to a climax. Body shaking, shivering in near convulsions as release throbbed through her.

There was no pause. Just rapid motion as he ripped her pants off her hips and his erection bumped her ass. His hand slid between their bodies, adjusting positions, then he was at her core, cock thrusting into her ready sex.

"Oh, *yes*." Caroline arched her back, allowing him to drive deeper on his next thrust. Dirty and wild, his hands controlling her meant there was nowhere she could go to escape. Not that she wanted to. This was what she'd asked for. A keen of excitement escaped, stretching out like a wavering bird cry.

"So. Damn. Good," Tyler growled, a hard thrust accompanying each word. His cock spread her wide as he took her, once again confining her wrists behind her back. He slid a hand along her spine and into her hair, pulling slightly as he brought her head up. The bite of pain made her groan louder.

He slowed for a moment, warm lips at her neck. "You having fun?" he whispered.

"Uh-huh," she moaned. "Your cock is driving me crazy."

"Your fantasy is driving me wild. Ready for more?"

She nodded, her mouth gone dry.

He kissed her shoulder blade—a soft and careful caress. His cock filled her, his groin pressed tight to her ass. The stiff fabric of his jeans and zipper were crushed against her bare skin. All the wicked sensations created an oasis of unanticipated tenderness.

Then he replaced the hand in her hair and shoved her downward until her head was level with her ass. He pulled his hips back, cock clinging to the entrance to her sex.

When he slammed forward, a scream escaped her.

Tyler froze in position.

"*Nooo*, don't stop," Caroline wailed in protest. "That was hot."

He panted, fingers of his left hand running over her bare hip. "You're killing me, baby."

"Fuck me," she whispered.

Another drive pushed the air from her lungs. She gasped for breath as he worked her over, the rapid motions of his hips teasing her back up to the brink in a flash. He pulled her upright again, changing the angle. He hooked his hand under her thigh and lifted. The new position opened her wider, gave him room to play with her clit even as he fucked her.

The combination of wicked, rough, yet so careful motion flipped her final switch.

"Tyler. Yes, oh damn, yes." Caroline squeezed her eyes shut to stop the spinning blackness from taking her under. Her orgasm was so powerful all the blood seemed to have vanished from her brain, centered instead on her sex. On pulsing around his cock and dragging a shout from his lips as well.

The calm, collected diplomat vanished in a rush of passion as he joined her in ecstasy.

They were still vertical, Tyler somehow keeping them upright as their orgasms concluded. His strong hands cradled her, palms warm against her flesh. She took a deep, contented breath and sighed happily.

Caroline opened her eyes just in time to see a flash of silvery fur leaping at them. She threw up an arm and jerked to the side, but it was too late.

Tyler fell away from her, an enormous wolf going for his throat.

Caroline's shout gave Tyler enough warning to release her so she didn't get taken to the ground with him. He hoped she'd catch herself and avoid being hurt, but the dire need to stick his arm into the wolf's way before his throat ended up under the sharp fangs was the most pressing item on his agenda.

While teeth dug into his forearm, he kicked off his shoes. He jerked his jeans down as best he could with one hand, the other occupied with the damn wolf using him as a chew toy. The shift to bear wasn't as agreeable as he'd like it to be. One minute he was having the best sex of his life, the next he was getting attacked. That tended to put a damper on most of life's little pleasures.

Damn having to let her out of his arms when he wanted nothing more than to cuddle her close and make sure what they'd done had been okay with her.

Only he had to save Caroline from the wolf, and the best way for that was to be in bear form.

His T-shirt stretched to the breaking point, seams giving way, jeans falling to the ground and off his lower limbs as he finished the change. Now much larger than his attacker, Tyler shook his arm, tossing the wolf like a rag doll, but the damn beast wouldn't let go.

"Oh no." Caroline's voice rang out strong and confident. "Evan? Is that you?"

Tyler paused in his attempts to shake the wolf burr free, turning to examine Caroline instead.

She'd pulled her clothes to rights, sadly covering the fine ass he'd been admiring as he fucked her. Her cheeks were bright red, and she smelt divine. Well fucked, well satisfied...

His bear gloated.

The wolf on his arm opened his jaws, releasing them from each other. The beast backed away before Tyler could get in a swing and send the stupid thing flying.

Only the furry menace blocked the path to Caroline. Tyler growled his displeasure at the wolf who had his hackles raised, lips pulled back to reveal razor-sharp teeth.

Come between him and his lover? Tyler didn't think so. He lifted a paw in the air to bat the annoyance aside when Caroline darted forward and caught the wolf by the ear.

"Evan Stone. You stop this instant." She raised a hand toward Tyler, palm open, calming him. "It's okay. This is...a friend."

Tyler lowered his paw and sat back warily.

The wolf stopped snarling and whimpered instead as Caroline gave an extra hard twist to the ear she'd captured. "You *idiot.* Shift, and I hope you've got a damn good explanation for your actions."

She released Evan's ear then stepped to Tyler's side, laying a hand on his shoulder. Tyler grinned as the wolf stared, head lowering in frustration.

She'd taken his side, Tyler's. He wanted to gloat—well as much as a bear could gloat. Her fingers in his fur made him wriggle in pleasure, and he nuzzled her.

The wolf shifted back to human, becoming a dark-haired male who glared furiously at him.

Tyler debated stepping forward and biting Evan's arm, just to see how the man felt about human/shifter chewing incidents when the teeth were applied in the opposite direction, but since Caroline had supported him, he didn't need to rub it in.

"What kind of explanation do you need for me to protect you? He was attacking. He was all over you." Evan took a deep breath and jerked to a halt. He dragged a hand through his hair. "Oh shit. You're turned on."

Tyler shifted back to human as Caroline shook her head in disgust. "Dammit, Evan. Jump to conclusions much?"

"Well, what was I supposed to think? Shaun is picking up your special-duty detail team, so I put myself on guard watch. Took me a bit to catch up to the jeep, and when I saw you... Well, it's not your typical place for fucking around." Evan crossed his arms. "I can't win this conversation, can I? No matter what I say I'm going to come off like an interfering idiot."

"Pretty much, yes." Caroline sighed. "Tyler Harrison, I guess you may as well officially meet Evan Stone, head of the Takhini pack."

Tyler held out a hand. "I'm not pleased to meet you."

Evan's grin flashed. "Likewise, asshole."

There was none of the stupid "attempt to squeeze each

other's hands into bloody pulps" Tyler expected. Of course, that was because he took the opportunity of having Evan's hand to jerk the man off his feet. Only when Tyler expected to be able to drive an elbow down on his opponent's back to finish the punishment, Evan surprised him by twisting in midair and wrapping his leg around Tyler's, tumbling them both to the ground.

Nice. Tyler kept the roll going and squashed Evan under him.

"Guys?" Caroline attempted to cut in, but it really wasn't the moment for a distraction. Not when the wolf's grunt of pain was followed immediately by a violent punch to Tyler's kidneys. He retaliated by spinning and catching Evan in a headlock.

It was always enjoyable to have a sparring partner who was fairly evenly matched in skill.

"Guys."

They grappled a little longer before fingers tapped his forearm three times in the universal code to be released. Tyler set Evan free and looked around for Caroline.

She was gone.

"Fuck." Maybe ignoring her hadn't been the smartest move.

Evan chuckled. "That's what I figured. Damn woman is probably pissed off at both of us. You might want to hurry and catch her before she decides you need to grovel for a few days."

They separated and brushed the dirt off. Tyler reached for his jeans then found his shoes. "Think I can make it to the jeep before she leaves me behind for good?"

"With some luck—I'll show you a short cut." Evan handed over the backpack. "Sorry about the interruption."

Tyler grinned. "She's a bit of a wild child, isn't she?"

"More than I imagined." Evan eyed him. "You'll take good

care of her, right? I won't need to track you down and kill you in the future?"

Interesting. How much trouble was the wolf going to be? It was a good opportunity to sound out if Caroline and Evan truly were over, as well as possible alliances. "She's not your concern anymore."

"She's my friend, she's pack, and she'll always be my concern." Evan's pleasant expression vanished.

Tyler nodded. "Good. I hoped you'd say that, because things are moving faster than I thought. Not with me and Caroline—that's just starting, even though the relationship looks promising. No, you will not need to kill me, but I'd appreciate knowing you have my back. There's potential trouble in the next few days. Will Takhini stand with me?"

Evan stared him over, analyzing. Judging.

Then the wolf shrugged. "Damn it all, I want to hate your guts. But if Caroline likes you and trusts you enough to play fucked-up games in the great outdoors, who am I to say otherwise? Takhini has your back."

Tyler adjusted his load. "Thank you."

The wolf flicked a hand down the trail. "Take the steep cut to the right and you half your distance to the bridge. You might want to go get her before you have major begging to do."

The idea of being on his knees in front of Caroline wasn't a hardship to imagine. Not if that meant feasting on her delectable body.

Evan flicked a finger in a mock salute then shifted back to wolf, trotting easily along the narrow ledge, ignoring the mind-boggling cliff to his left.

Strange helpmates Tyler had acquired. A pack of wolves, and one very intriguing human.

Tyler caught up before the bridge, wrapping an arm around her waist and twirling her toward him. She laughed, cupping his face with her palms and moving in for a kiss that made his head spin. She clung to him, legs around his hips, mouths connected as he caressed her back and hips.

When she finally slipped to the ground, he kept hold of her fingers, rubbing his thumb over the back of her hand. “Didn’t want to stick around for the fight?”

Caroline shook her head. “You boys seemed pretty involved in each other. I didn’t want to interrupt a tender moment.”

He laughed as he caught her hand to his lips. “Forget Evan. We’re good. Now back to more important things. Like the fact that bit of sightseeing was fairly spectacular. Thank you.”

Her pupils were wide and dark in her blue eyes. “I found it rather invigorating as well.”

“Any other must-see things in the area?” He caressed the line of skin visible long the edge of her T-shirt neckline. “I’m ready for anything you suggest.”

Her breathing picked up, chest rising and falling rapidly. “All kinds of suggestions come to mind, but first let’s show you an actual sight. You want to see the city from the mountaintop? Great views.”

He tugged her forward, their bodies barely brushing. A soft kiss on her cheek, tender as he could. He spoke against her lips. “That sounds marvelous. This afternoon we have to spend in town, hobnobbing with any bears we come across. And then I’ll take you back to your apartment, and we can work on the plan for tomorrow.”

She smiled, lips curving against his. “My sister will be back by tonight, so we’d better make that your hotel room. Because somehow I think you mean something dirtier than *planning*.”

Tyler tugged her toward the bridge, keeping her hand

trapped in his. "I do my best planning while naked."

Caroline nodded. "That would explain the anticipation in your eyes."

"Deal?"

She grinned. "Oh, you have yourself a deal."

Chapter Fifteen

He held her hand whenever possible.

For the next six hours, as she took him all over the mountainside, ate their picnic lunch and explored town, Tyler listened and made the appropriate responses. His company was lovely and enjoyable, but it was the sweet caress of his thumb over her knuckles at unexpected moments that made Caroline's heart keep up a constant flutter.

Out of the public eye, like when they'd been admiring the city from the high lookout, he'd stood close and wrapped an arm around her. Sat beside her and uncapped her water bottle when it got stuck. Nuzzled his lips against her hair and basically acted swoon-worthy.

Once they hit town he'd become a little more distant, putting on what she was beginning to recognize as his "formal face". She could understand the need—they weren't alone. They weren't in a vacuum, and he had an image to uphold that he'd probably set on fire just being with her. They met bears in the museum, in the bookstore. Everywhere they wandered men in formal suits and ladies in expensive clothing stopped Tyler to chat for a few minutes.

She joined in when necessary, but otherwise watched. Listened. Admired Tyler working magic on his peers. He had a way with them, making each clan feel as if he knew their specific needs and how he could help them move to the next step.

Caroline wondered if appreciating his politicking skills made her twisted.

They were headed back to the Moonshine Inn when she recognized yet another couple walking toward them from the previous evening's gala. Both eyed Tyler's casual jeans with something close to shock.

Shock, maybe even disgust. She swore the gentleman sniffed as he glanced her over, but spoke to Tyler. "Harrison. Enjoying your free day, I see."

"As I hope you are." His outside might not look as shiny as they expected, but Tyler's manners remained impeccable as he bowed slightly to the lady of the pair. "Mrs. Nakusp. Did you receive your invitation for tomorrow from Caroline yet?"

Nakusp. This was one of the important contacts. Caroline ran through names in her head as the woman fluttered her lashes and smiled hesitantly at Caroline. "I did. Thank you. I'm looking forward to it very much."

Lynn, that was it.

"You need anything, Lynn, you be sure to let me know," Caroline offered. "If you don't have a swimsuit with you, I can recommend a wonderful shop here in town."

Tyler squeezed her fingers in warning. Caroline kept her smile to polite levels instead of grinning like a banshee.

"Oh, that would be lovely." Lynn twisted toward her husband. "If you don't mind."

Mr. Nakusp had continued to make a thorough examination of Tyler and Caroline, especially their linked hands. He looked partly repelled, partly intrigued. At Lynn's words, however, he shook himself and faced her, his body and voice softening as he answered. “Of course I don’t mind.”

Caroline gave directions, and the two couples parted, headed in opposite directions.

“You are damn good at that.” Tyler guided her around a crowd gathered outside a coffee shop.

Underestimated again? “I’ve worked in customer service for years, what did you expect?”

He stopped, and she had to pause as well, since he still had her fingers trapped in his. “That wasn’t a negative comment. I’m seriously impressed. You’ve been marvelous all afternoon. Thank you.”

“Mr. Nakusp didn’t seem to know if I was a pet of some kind or not.” Caroline shrugged, deciding to ignore it like everything else she had no control over in the shifter world. She pulled out a set of keys and shook them. “You want to sneak into the hotel the back way?”

Tyler tugged her against him, right there in the street. “I don’t want to sneak anywhere with you. I want to walk right out in the open. Are you not getting that?”

Whoa. “Where did this grumpy attack come from?”

He glared, then stepped away, their hands separating. “Never mind.”

Caroline resisted rolling her eyes. *Oh goodie.* Temperamental mood swings went deep with these bears. It wasn’t worth setting him off again, though, so she took him the long way around and through the main doors.

A squeal of excitement rang from her right, and Caroline looked up in the nick of time to brace herself before being tackled by her sister.

Caroline squeezed Shelley tight before a low growl warned her to check on her boyfriend.

Sure enough, he'd misunderstood and overreacted, probably to protect her.

"Oh, Tyler."

She released Shelley and swung to the side where Shelley's partner had Tyler smashed against the wall. She bet it wasn't often Tyler ended up at a physical disadvantage, not with his considerable size. Only appearances were tricky things in shifters…

Caroline glanced around the lobby quickly, relieved no humans were in sight. "Hi, Chase. This is my new boyfriend, Tyler Harrison. Tyler, that's my sister's beau."

Tyler's eyes were wide as he stared at the massive cougar paw pinning him in position. The rest of Chase remained human, his short blond hair standing in a spiked mess, his expression focused and firm. Only his arm had shifted into the cougar that was one of his animals.

"Caroline." Chase held out his other hand and squeezed her shoulder in greeting. "Your new boyfriend seems stupider than your last. I don't know that he's an upgrade."

"Chase, don't be rude." Shelley stepped in front of Tyler and examined him, tilting her head to the side as she considered. "I think he's cute."

Good grief. Caroline hoped Tyler wasn't about to explode with frustration before she could fix this mess. "People, can we take this somewhere private? With all body parts human and accounted for?"

Chase pulled away and obediently put all his bits and pieces back to fully human. Tyler moved immediately to place an arm around Caroline's shoulders.

She bit her lip and stared at the ceiling, attempting desperately not to start laughing because if she started, she wouldn't be able to stop. "Come on, we can visit in Tyler's suite."

Light conversation carried on around them as they made their way to the upper floor.

The living space of the suite seemed overly full, but that might have been because four Alpha males occupied the close quarters. Justin had been waiting for them, a smirk on his face as he unlocked the door then retreated into the room. Evan sauntered in right before Caroline could shut the door, his satisfied grin making her fingers itch to whack him a good one. Which she wouldn't do in public out of respect, but it didn't make the urge any less tempting.

"You haven't had enough interfering, I take it." She closed the door more firmly than needed.

Evan patted her shoulder as he passed. "Hey, no need to get snippy. I'm not judging or saying anything about outdoor sexual escapades."

Of course, that's the moment everyone else chose to be silent, so Evan's words echoed through the room.

Caroline twisted to examine her companions. Five sets of eyes stared back with various levels of amusement in them. Two bears—Tyler and Justin. Two wolves—Evan and her sister. A crossbreed cougar/wolf in Chase, and her, the lone human. Once again.

Fuck it.

She waved a hand at Justin behind the bar. "I need a margarita. You know how to make one?"

Tyler paced to her side. "We haven't had dinner yet."

Sheesh. "I'll order in Mexican. And it's five o'clock somewhere."

His fingers slipped into hers, and she sighed. His attention was lovely, but her sister's expression, and Evan's, and all the rest of it made her tired. Too many explanations, too many questions.

Her life had become far too complicated.

"Sit down. I'll order dinner then us guys will stay way over here, minding our own business while you say hi to your sister." Evan grabbed the phone. "Justin? Make my margarita a beer."

"You got it."

Shelley patted the couch beside her. "Come on. Ignore them and tell me what's happening. Shaun was amazingly tight-lipped when he picked us up."

Chase snorted as he rose to his feet to make room for Caroline, heading to the bar as per Evan's suggestion. "Tight-lipped? Not bloody likely. The wolf never shut up the entire two-hour helicopter ride from our place to Whitehorse."

"Well, he talked, but he never *said* anything, if you know what I mean." Shelley winked.

"Hang on." Caroline had requested Shaun pick up more than her family. "Where are Shaun and Gem? I'd have thought they'd be here as well, unofficial powwow that we seem to be holding."

Evan pivoted on his bar stool, beer bottle in his hand. "He's still fetching your friend from the north. She couldn't get away until tomorrow. Shaun and Gem decided to spend the night in Chicken so they can help hurry Nadia along."

Okay, that made sense. She nodded.

Evan kept watching her. Tyler was looking her and her sister over, Chase examining them as well. The only one of the guys not staring their way was Justin, and as soon as he finished pouring their drinks, he carried the glasses to them and stood looming like a statue.

Oh brother. "Minding own business, boys?"

A flurry of motion followed her words. Justin retreated behind the bar. The other three swung around on their bar stools so there was nothing but hulking male backs toward them.

Caroline leaned against her sister, providing the physical contact she knew Shelley craved as a wolf. "I'm glad you're here."

"We only left a week ago."

Caroline looked down as Shelley linked their fingers together. "It seems like a whole lot longer, to be honest."

"You've been busy." Shelley leaned in close and whispered. "They can still hear us. You want to go elsewhere to talk?"

Ha. "To not be overheard we'd have to leave the building, and I don't see your partner or Tyler letting that happen. Not with night coming on."

Shelley nodded. "You're right."

Music started out of nowhere. Caroline blinked as Tyler smiled at her then cranked the volume on the music system even higher before going back to the guys' conversation.

"So, the new boyfriend..." Shelley squeezed Caroline's fingers. "He seems nice. Other than the hair trigger in the lobby."

"He's one of the bears in town for the voting."

"What happened with Evan?" Shelley paused, and looked very uncomfortable. "Did he break up with you because of me?"

Caroline jerked upright. "Oh, honey, no. It wasn't that at all—"

Evan was at their side in a flash. "Caroline and I are fine, Shelley. It has nothing to do with you or the pack or..."

Caroline swore she would break an eyeball one day, glaring

at these creatures while they stomped willy-nilly all over her human boundaries. *Damn shifter hearing.* “So much for minding your own business,” she complained.

Evan rose to his feet and shuffled back a step. “Umm, right. Sorry. Go on, I’ll find something to do until dinner arrives.”

It was tough to stay mad at him when he really couldn’t help it, and he meant well. With Shelley giggling beside her, Caroline chose to ignore the guys and focused instead on her sister.

“No, it wasn’t anything you or I did. He got a sniff of his mate.”

Shelley’s mouth hung open for a second. “Holy. Well, that’s awesome. You okay with it?”

“Of course. What kind of question is that?” Caroline shook her head. “As if I’d come between a wolf and his mate.”

Shelley nodded. “That’s what I’d expect to hear you say, even though it’s got to be tough. I love you so hard, sis.”

Caroline paused, concern flooding her. “The situation did make something pop to mind, though. You and Chase…”

Shelley leaned back on the couch. “You’re wondering if we’ll have the same thing happen? One of us sniffs out a fated mate, and the other ends up with our heart ripped in two?”

Whoa. “You’ve obviously given this some thought.”

Shelley smiled. “It would have been stupid not to think about it but, hon, Chase isn’t all wolf—he’s cougar as well. Only wolves have predestined mates, and my wolf is seriously broken. We’ve chosen each other and created our own fate. Nothing is going to rip us apart.”

“Damn right.” It was Chase’s deep growly voice. His back was still to them, the music blaring, and the guys seemed to be deep in conversation, but he’d still responded.

This time Shelley rolled her eyes. “No privacy. Ever. You should move north with us.”

“Once the bear conclave is over, I might move to Siberia.”

“Too many grizzlies in Siberia,” Justin interjected. “You could try Nepal. All they’ve got is sloth bears, and they’re rumoured to be very reclusive.”

Caroline pressed her hands to her forehead. “*Minding your business* seems to have taken a new definition since the last time I looked.”

Shelley squeezed her arm. “Ignore them and catch me up. What’s happening?”

The food arrived about the time Caroline had finished explaining the situation as she saw it. Tyler had joined in the mindless conversation with the guys, but all of them were distracted listening to the ladies. There was no denying it.

Caroline’s concise analysis of the bear situation astonished him. Justin was nodding like a bobblehead, impressed as well.

But in the middle of her explaining to Shelley what was going on, in the middle of the women teasing and reacting to the shifters’ continued interruptions, something poked Tyler.

He found a place at the table next to her. Plates were filled, conversation resumed. Shelley asked about his brother, Frank, and Tyler gave an update. All the while he worried at the puzzle, trying to solve it.

His bear rumbled, confused that he was upset, but this wasn’t a matter for the animal to figure out. Tyler had enjoyed his time with her over the day, even with the moments of frustration, but something about the situation wasn’t right.

They were nearly done the meal when he figured it out. Caroline was wearing a cloak. Her humanness was hidden away under a surface layer that screamed shifter. As if she were speaking a foreign language to make things easier for all of them.

The way she moved was more wolf than human. The way she reacted, like the momentary lowering of her eyes when Evan spoke—respect for an Alpha—followed by her straightening and proving her own strength and value.

She deferred just long enough to offer a kind of give-and-take, never being weak but never unwittingly becoming a challenge either. The impressive display was something most humans lacked and shifters didn't need.

He'd never seen anything like it in his life.

Evan pulled him from his musings as the wolf asked Caroline about the event scheduled for the next day. "You booked off the pool from the public. I double-checked, the staff scheduled for the day are all pack. That will cut down on any humans stopping in, but not eliminate the chances."

Caroline nodded. "The Takhini pool is remote enough to make an excellent setting for the gathering. I'm sorry to have to anticipate trouble, but something could happen."

Evan shrugged. "We need a new coat of paint on the place soon, so don't worry about structural damage."

"I can join you if you'd like," Shelley offered her sister. "Another lady in the mix."

"No." Chase shook his head. "You are not going into a volatile situation where ninety-nine percent of the people around you can shift into bears or wolves. I won't allow it."

Shelley gave him a dirty look. "You won't allow it?"

Chase met her gaze straight on. "You have skills that are needed far more elsewhere. It might make me an asshole, but having you in danger once was enough. If there's fighting, and chances are there will be, you'd do more good having a medical base set up somewhere nearby instead of making me crazy."

When Shelley touched her partner's cheek tenderly, all her anger washed away, Tyler couldn't stop from glancing at Caroline. She was watching her sister, longing on her face for a second before she pulled that cloak back in place and became business as usual.

"I'll organize an RV with medical supplies in the campsite next door." Caroline turned to Evan. "We might want some wolves to help patrol the campground anyway, to keep any human visitors away from potential trouble."

"Deal. I'll talk to the more reliable pack members. The ones who can be trusted to keep their heads." Evan poked Tyler in the arm. "Head's up. My pack won't step in if you guys start fighting, not unless Caroline or anyone other than bears is threatened. It's the best I can do in terms of keeping my territory safe and not overstepping boundaries."

Tyler couldn't believe this was happening. "You guys are really organizing as backup for us?"

Chase sprawled in his chair. "Strange, isn't it? I don't know if it's all wolves or just this pack, but they have some weird attitudes."

"It's a potential fight. Since you didn't send an invitation, we had to arrange one for ourselves." Evan flashed a grin then checked his watch. "It's been fun, kids, but I have things to do. Don't stay up too late."

He was out the door before Tyler could thank him. Or hit him, he wasn't sure which he wanted to do more.

"We're leaving as well." Shelley loaded the empty takeout boxes into the garbage before giving Caroline a farewell hug and joining Chase at the door. "I'll call you tomorrow, okay, Caro?"

"Not too early, I hope." Caroline waved them off. She looked around the room, her lips twisting in resignation. There was only her and Tyler in the room, Justin having vanished into the back of the suite. "Well, that's that, then. I guess I'll see you in the morning."

"Where are you going to sleep?" Tyler leaned on the door. "You don't have a place with Evan, and your sister is back in her apartment."

Her mouth tightened.

Justin stepped from his room, small bag in his hand. "I'm headed to the pack house for the night. Frank invited me to play poker with him and the wolves. Said to bring lots of money."

And there was part of the solution Tyler needed. He opened his wallet and pulled out a roll of bills, pressing them into his friend's palm.

Justin stared at the wad in confusion. "I wasn't hinting for a handout."

Tyler shrugged. "My brother won't accept cash from me, but he'll take it in winnings."

"So you're telling me to lose?"

Tyler nodded.

"Damn it." Justin put the money away. "Fine, you owe me a game. Sometime when I can get sweet revenge and prove I'm a shark."

Justin surprised them both by giving Caroline a hug before heading out, the door clicking behind him. Caroline eyed Tyler as if she'd been left alone in the room with a dangerous beast on the loose.

Which wasn't one hundred percent inaccurate.

He took a slow step forward, closing the space between them until he could touch her arm. "Will you stay the night?"

Her glare softened. “You’re not going to pull an asshole move and order me to stay? That’s what it sounded like you had planned.”

He shook his head. “I was pointing out you didn’t have a place to go in case you wanted to ask to stay. But hoping you’d realize how much I want you to be with me was taking too long.”

Great, she had him talking in circles.

The situation had changed though, after their impromptu meeting with the others. “We spoke earlier about getting together to make plans. We’re done that part, and I still want you around. Please stay?”

Her slow nod made Tyler smile from ear to ear.

She tugged him to the couch with her, curling up at his side and closing her eyes as she leaned against him. “Part of me wants a do-over of this week. Heck, this summer, even.”

“It’s been stressful?”

“Understatement.” She sighed. “Not your fault. Don’t think I’m blaming you or anything.”

Of course she wouldn’t blame him. From what he’d seen, she didn’t let anyone else do anything without her having time to rescue them.

“Come on.” He pulled her into his arms, pleased she rested her head on his chest and allowed him to carry her into his room. “You want to relax in the hot tub for a while?”

She chuckled. “No thanks. Think I’ll stay away from the thing. I’ll just have a quick shower.”

“Why not indulge yourself?” Tyler set her on the edge of the bed, working on her laces until he could remove her hiking shoes. “If you don’t want to go outside, I spotted this awesome soaker tub in the bathroom. Nice and deep.”

"Big enough for two?" Their hands brushed momentarily.

"If you'd like. No pressure." He kept undressing her, attempting to make it as nonsexual as possible in case she wanted time alone.

When she tugged his T-shirt free from his jeans, scraping her nails over his abdomen, he shivered.

They both ended up in the tub that, thankfully, was made for shifter-sized dudes. Her ass rested in his lap. His cock must have been an uncomfortable rock pressed to her ass cheek, but she melted back against him as the water rose to chest level.

It would have been a crime not to fondle the delicate skin within his grasp.

They stayed there, silent for the longest time. Just touching her. Thinking. Trying to listen to what she *wasn't* saying. Remembering what he'd seen of her actions and what he'd seen on her face while talking with her sister, because yes, he'd been staring unashamedly the entire time.

"Caroline?"

"Uh-huh?" Another long exhale, this time accompanied by a small stretch of her back as she pressed her breast more firmly into his hand.

Tyler caressed her nipple with the pad of his thumb. "We never talked about what we did on the trail this morning."

"Did we need to talk? It was hot. I enjoyed it."

The sincerity in her words reassured him, as did the flush on her skin and the softening of her body.

"I had fun as well." He twisted until he could lift her mouth to his, connecting their lips and kissing her deeply. She hummed, a satisfied sound that pleased him as much as her fingers on his chest. When she dug her nails in harder, a growl escaped before he could stop it.

She shivered, her nipple tightening under his palm.

He slowed, lips still moving against hers, but his touch becoming more and more subtle until the tension in her body changed. It seemed she was aroused, but feeling delicate in spite of the cut of her nails into his flesh.

"What do *you* want, Caroline? What do you need? Let me be the one to give to you for a change."

He whispered the words against her temple. This woman who couldn't shift forms had more layers to her than he'd suspected, and something urged him on. Not to wrap her in gauze and protect, but to really listen.

Caroline's breathing picked up.

She cautiously crawled out of his lap and bolted from the bathroom without a word.

Shit.

Tyler followed, holding on to the doorway as he searched her out in the darkened room.

She stood at the window, staring over the mountains. Her blonde hair shone in the streetlights, her spine straight and strong. A thin line of moisture ran down her cheek, and he strode across the room and gathered her in his arms, cradling her against him.

He didn't ask why. Didn't demand a reason. Simply held her and waited, and wondered exactly what he'd entwined himself in.

Because it was true. He was hopelessly entangled. With wanting her to be happy, and to be safe. But most importantly, with wanting her to be herself.

He'd done exactly what he'd figured. He'd gone and fallen in love, at least with the parts of herself she was honest about sharing.

Caroline pulled him toward the bed, wiping her eyes with her fingers. “Sorry.”

“Nothing to be sorry for.” He lay beside her and let her pet him, her gaze burning his skin. Fingertips like miniature blowtorches scalding identifying marks into his soul as she eased over his hip. As she took his cock into her hand and caressed his length.

Harder than he ever remembered, Tyler let her stay in control. He couldn’t stop his hands from crossing the distance between them, though. Massaging her hips, lightly brushing her clit.

When she straddled him then surrounded him in one smooth motion, Tyler nearly swallowed his tongue. His cock was fully sheathed in her body, heat and moisture driving him mad as she undulated with a sinful rhythm meant to break him.

Her eyes, wild.

He couldn’t look away. Didn’t want to. Didn’t want to miss a single second of her bringing him into her core then languidly sliding up until his cock clung to the lips of her sex.

Tyler wet his fingers in his mouth then went back to her clit, circling with a firm touch. Caroline missed a beat, sexual tension rising on her face as her climax drew near.

He increased the tempo of his fingers, tilted his hips and helped her with the final push into orgasm, her eyes closing as she pulsed hard around him.

He kept watching, although to be honest the view went a touch blurry. When she opened her eyes, he caught her cheeks in his hands, ecstasy taking him as he lost control and came.

Chapter Sixteen

Caroline adjusted her bikini, took a deep breath and headed out the door of the change room. Not a super time to develop nerves regarding the wisdom of the ladies' get-together, but there was no denying the fear skittering along her spine. It didn't help that with this much skin on display she had no place for a hidden knife.

Bowling. Why hadn't she suggested bowling as an activity?

A soft whistle caught her attention, and she looked up to discover Tyler scrutinizing her over the low edge of the viewing gallery wall.

Fear vanished in a blazing swoop of lust. The expression on his face was one step away from ravishment, and she liked it far too much. There was also an additional touch—that something extra that had been there when he'd poured her into the tub. The focused attention that had gotten stronger when he'd whispered so carefully, asking what she wanted.

The part that had sounded as if he really wanted to hear the answer.

And the lovemaking that followed? Caroline had hesitantly taken what she wanted, fully expecting at some point he'd resume control like all shifters did in the bedroom. She loved dominance games, as evidenced by the frenzied lust of the morning's chase-and-capture fantasy, but…

He'd actually *made love* to her. Not just sexual pleasure, but a very real, very undeniable emotional connection rocking her as his body set fireworks off.

They'd slept for a while, woken up and done it all over for most of the night. She still wasn't sure what it meant.

Other than there could be no doubt she and Tyler were an item. She might not have shifter senses to smell him on her, but the bite marks on her neck and limbs were hard to hide. Especially in a bikini.

It was time to put the uncertainty of their relationship aside, though. Time to get back into the head of Caroline Bradley who, until recently, was the Alpha bitch of the Takhini wolves. The tough, shifter-savvy woman was the one Tyler needed.

Strolling toward him gave her plenty of time to pull on her armour, to get back into teasing, adding an extra swing to her hips as she moved into position. "Practicing to be a soccer ref?"

His knuckles on the top of the wall were white, he gripped the railing so hard. "You want a sports analogy? I'm looking forward to stripping you out of that outfit with my teeth and scoring as often as you'll let me."

"Isn't that what we did last night?"

Her tease came out far more throaty than she'd intended.

Cars were pulling into the parking lot, and while there had to be wolves watching them from their positions in the trees, the beasts either wouldn't care or, more likely, were hoping for a show.

Ignoring the divider separating their lower bodies, Caroline patted his suit pocket, reassuring herself he still carried her cell phone. Then she walked her fingers up his broad chest. "After we're done the political song and dance today, I think you and I should relax until the next shindig. No other people, no shifters—let's hide for at least twelve hours and not come up for air unless the world explodes."

"The world seems to have a way of doing that around you. Exploding, I mean." He seemed mesmerized by her chest. The huge breath he let out like a balloon losing steam made her lips twitch. He pressed his hand over hers, trapping her fingers over his heart. The pounding registered against her palm. "Alone sounds amazing."

They stared at each other, his eyes shining with more than lust.

"Tell me we'll be okay," Caroline whispered.

"We're going to be great. And you'll be brilliant, as usual."

The compliment slid up and tied her in a big bow. "Pretty words."

"That I mean. You are very talented, Caroline. Smart, insightful. My bear says you kick ass, by the way. I told him to watch it, or the ass you'll be kicking will be his."

So many urges shot through her. She wanted to smile at his attempts to bolster her nerves. Wanted to appreciate his honesty and his out-spoken bear. She wanted reassurances the lust racing through her was normal.

Then again, simply looking him over explained that one far too easily.

It was the note of caring in his voice that made her the most afraid. It seemed he was trying so hard to listen and understand her human side, not taking for granted the influence her chutzpah had granted her in the shifter world over the years.

He was unlocking secrets others who'd known her for years had never suspected she had. Not even her family.

Being stripped bare of all protective layers was a

frightening thing. Far more frightening than knowing she was the only one in the area who couldn't turn furry and sprout claws and razor-sharp teeth.

A lady waved at her from near the change-room door and Caroline sighed. "Time for fun and games."

Tyler jerked a thumb over his shoulder, pointing out the male partner headed his way. "At least you get to soak and relax while you play. I'm in a damn suit and tie."

She leaned in and offered her lips, and he kissed her. Slightly more tongue was involved than was probably considered polite in public, but as if she cared.

She headed to greet her guests. Women joined her on poolside before slipping into the naturally heated waters and sighing happily. Little clusters gathered, ladies talking contentedly as Tyler kept the menfolk occupied and away from the water. The low wall between the pool and picnic tables created two separate oases. There was enough distance between the spaces that at least the illusion of privacy was provided.

Caroline waded through the chest-deep water to where Lillie was waving. She settled onto the seat beside the redhead who leaned back on the low concrete lip behind her.

"I love the idea of a fun activity for us ladies. You're a wonderful person, Caroline. I like you."

Caroline laughed. "I like you as well. But don't get too excited, it's not as if the guys aren't just around the corner."

Lillie played with the water surface, allowing trickles to run off her fingers into the pool. "It's as good as a win in my books. I can't imagine holding an event under these circumstances without some kind of backup. Sorry about the dinner at my place. Once conclave is over, you'll have to come over for a proper meal."

"It wasn't your fault, but thank you. We'd like that."

Automatically including Tyler in her response felt right. And weird.

Lillie sat up and looked around, her voice going lower. "So, while it's relatively quiet, I want to ask you something."

"Go ahead."

Her new friend wiggled her nose. "This might sound strange, but I already know my husband won't win conclave, so I'm trying to figure out who is best to support. Tyler appears the way to go."

Caroline wasn't sure there was a question in there. "He seems pretty amazing to me."

Lillie leaned her mouth next to Caroline's ear. "Does he hurt you?"

Caroline sputtered. "Hello?"

Lillie slid a finger over one of the bruises on Caroline's neck, her gaze meeting Caroline's with an unspoken query.

"Oh, sweetie." Damn it for bad timing in enjoying some rough sex. Caroline took a deep breath and reminded herself she was talking to a shifter. "I can honestly say there isn't a mark on me that I didn't want him to put there. He's got a few love bites as well."

Her face must have been beet red, but Lillie nodded. "Good, that's what I thought, but I had to be sure. So, how can we convince Lynn Nakusp she wants her husband hanging out with Tyler and not that jackass, Todd Ainsworth? Because while I love Jim to pieces, if he ever lays a hand on me—other than in fun—I swear I will slip his balls into a blender on high speed. While they're still attached."

Nice imagery.

Caroline peeked over Lillie's shoulder, searching out a glimpse of Tyler. She caught sight of his head and shoulders, his back to her as he strolled the far corners of the observation area. "I haven't known Tyler long, but I trust him completely. He's a good man. I mean, good bear."

Lillie laughed. "I know what you meant, and I agree. I saw the smile on your face while you were talking to him earlier. You can't keep your eyes off him, either."

Oops? "Really?"

Her friend nodded. "Nothing wrong with that. I can't get enough of my Sugarbear either. But your human/bear comment is a big part of the problem we face. I'm a smart woman." She gestured around the pool at the others gathered together, enjoying the afternoon sunshine. "We all are. We've got jobs and responsibilities in the human world that carry power and influence. It's the damn bear side that makes things difficult at times, especially when someone like Todd takes control."

"He doesn't respect your abilities, does he? I noticed that the other night at your party."

Lillie growled in disgust. "He steamrolls over the human side and reduces our accomplishments to nothing more than we own a vagina. It's not fair. It's no use being a strong individual when at best you're tied to clichés and limitations or at worst, abused. Amanda Ainsworth is proof of that."

Oh hell. Lillie's tirade confirmed what Caroline had feared the most. "She's in danger?"

Lillie gave her *the look*.

Damn. Caroline glanced around the pool. "She's not here yet, is she?"

A snort of disbelief rose from Lillie. "Chances of her showing up are slim to none. He'd never allow her to be somewhere without him monitoring her every move."

Caroline didn't get it. There was something major missing from her considerations.

"If you see the problem clearly, and I had it pretty much called after less than an hour at that first party, why would it be difficult to convince Lynn and the other ladies their only hope is having someone like Tyler elected in the first place?" Caroline made a face. "And I just clued in how stupid and chauvinistic that sounds as well. Why are only the guys getting elected to head conclave?"

"No, you're mistaken." Lillie shook her head as she pressed a hand to her chest. "It's not the guy, I mean, we say that, but really it's the *clan* being elected. If Halcyon won, Jim and I would both have the right to guide changes in the other clans' structure. *If* he let me. Which"—she rolled her eyes—"right there proves that if Ainsworth is elected, no way would Amanda have any clout. It would be all power-hungry-jerk in charge calling the shots."

"Which is why Tyler wasn't as good a representative as a bachelor, right?"

Lillie nodded slowly. "He's a fair man, from what I know of his business practices, but do I want him suggesting changes in my life? I have no reason to trust him. You, on the other hand, I trust."

Never had Caroline imagined her little outing to shed such light on the potential outcomes of conclave. "Thank you for that. It means a lot to me, Lillie."

The redhead nodded, a smile dancing on her lips. "I'm not just going on womanly instinct. I did a search on you. There's quite a file built up when you know where to look."

Caroline laughed. "What do you do in this outside job of yours? Computer hacker?"

Lillie grinned. "Secret service. I'd tell you more, but then I'd have to kill you."

Caroline pulled Lillie toward one of the small groups. "Help me chat for a while. Let's persuade the group they all desperately need to go home and convince their men to vote for Tyler."

"Deal."

It was not Tyler's idea of a good time. Not by any stretch of the imagination.

He lifted the glass in his hand, though, and concentrated on listening to one of the older bears who he respected. The man knew his father, and sharing stories about life in the north made it easier to pass the time.

The entire gathering was an enormous stockpile of coals ready to be fanned into flames. Feminine voices and laughter carried on the air, the gentlemen around him glancing restlessly toward the pool every time it happened, as if itching to go and join their women.

He didn't blame them. He had the same damn reaction every time Caroline's bright laugh hit him. Even from a distance it was like shooting one-hundred-eighty-proof liquor.

Still, looking on the bright side, Ainsworth hadn't shown up, and the couple of clans that had offered support for Clan Harrison were working their magic on the others. The lone resisters seemed to be Lucerne, but they didn't stand much chance of impacting the events other than causing violence.

Another car pulled into the parking lot, and Tyler stepped to the side to watch with interest as the limo driver hurried around to open the door for Amanda Ainsworth.

She glanced toward the pool building, her long coat trailing to the ground as the driver, not Todd, escorted her forward.

Strange.

Tyler made his way toward the front of the deck. By the time he got to a place where he could observe clearly, Caroline had slipped from the water in response to a low-toned feminine request sneaking through the change-room door.

Her lithe form should have been a distraction, but the whispered conversation taking place just inside the doorway was more important than his longing to lick the water droplets from Caroline's skin.

Not being able to hear exactly what was going on was making him crazy.

"Ainsworth didn't show, but Amanda did?" Jim Halcyon was at Tyler's side, tilting his head toward the trees. "We'd better stay alert. I didn't expect him to come—Ainsworth hates the water with a passion—but you can be sure if anything happens to her, you'll never hear the end of it."

"We know exactly who he'd blame."

Jim nodded. "Somehow, it would be your fault. Especially after this afternoon—your appeal is rising fast. It would only take a small nudge to push the entire shooting match into your favour."

That's when Caroline and Amanda strolled from the change room, Caroline in her barely there swimsuit, Amanda covered from neck to toe in a colourful beach robe. The two women made their way around the pool edge.

Caroline called out reassurances to some of the ladies in the water. Tyler moved as close as possible to where Caroline had spoken to him earlier. "Do you need my help?"

Caroline's cheeks were flushed. "Tell her how I got the marks on my skin."

She twisted a hip to showcase a spot where finger-shaped

bruises marred her flesh. He could clearly picture gripping her, riding her hard from behind as they went wild the previous day.

Only the passion faded as Tyler glanced at Amanda, his stomach plummeting. In being free with Caroline had he destroyed his case and lost all opportunity to make things better for the bears in the long run?

Attempting to explain the marks on Caroline in less-than-graphic words wasn't going to work—he was damned no matter what.

The fire in Caroline's eyes caught his attention as he considered what to say. One of her first taunts returned. What he was known for—honesty. She thought the truth would help.

"Caroline and I were playing. Sexual games." He undid his shirt collar and pulled it aside to display one of the more explicit scratches she'd left on him. "We both got overexcited."

Amanda stared at his chest. "You're not in the habit of beating women?"

Caroline slipped her arm through Amanda's. "I told you he's not."

The group of men in attendance had crowded forward, and Tyler motioned for them to step back. "You can watch just as well from across the courtyard. Give the ladies some privacy."

"I've been offered sanctuary by your girlfriend," Amanda piped up. "Do you agree to protect me?"

Oh, Caroline, what have you done? The men forgotten, Tyler moved forward, his gaze meeting Caroline's. He'd trusted her and her instincts to now; he would to the end. "If you require sanctuary, my clan is yours."

"Takhini wolves also offer protection," Caroline spoke loud and clear, obviously to the gathering of men behind him. "And if there's any of the lot of you who think you can mistreat your women, I offer them sanctuary as well, even if I have to personally find them beds and jobs."

One of the clan leaders pushed forward. "See here. This isn't right, going around Ainsworth like this. He should at least be able to stand up for himself." The man shook his finger at Amanda who cowered against Caroline's side. "Asking for sanctuary without reason."

Caroline was between the bear's pointing finger and Amanda at the same moment Tyler stepped to the man's side and laid a restraining hand on his shoulder.

"He forbid her to come," Caroline snapped.

The clan leader nodded righteously. "Then we need to ask him to join us. Allow him to be a part of this."

"You bastard."

Caroline would have hauled back a fist and swung if Amanda hadn't stopped her. The woman patted Caroline's arm reassuringly before stepping into the open. "He didn't want me to come because there's no swimsuit that can cover this..."

The cover-up dropped to the tiles underfoot, and the sound of protesting that had begun amidst the less charitable bears cut off like a cord had been severed.

The marks on Amanda's body were far more brutal than the shadows of lovemaking on Caroline's flesh. For the damage to stay on a shifter, she'd been beaten hard, more than once, and recently.

Caroline grabbed the cover-up and draped it around Amanda's shoulders, turning the woman in her arms and holding her close. "That's enough. They've seen. You have a home with me, because bastards don't deserve a woman like you."

"Thank you." Amanda nudged their cheeks together gently,

then straightened her shoulders. Lillie was there, tucking Amanda against her side and leading her away.

Caroline glared past Tyler, her expression one of total disdain as she took in the clan leaders at his back. "I don't know why you're bothering to complete conclave. If any of you still think Todd Ainsworth is a serious candidate, you've lost your bloody minds. You're voting to decide who can best guide you into the future. Are you really contemplating handing control to a man like that? He doesn't deserve to be in charge of a cage full of rattlesnakes. Not unless he was staked in place and they're dumped on top of him."

A flash of pure passion whipped through Tyler, his bear rattled and roused. It wasn't sexual, but pure sweet admiration plus a desire to grab hold of her fire and never let go.

It might have been insane, but at that moment? Tyler fell completely, and utterly, in love.

Chapter Seventeen

She was on a make-friends-and-influence-people roll. The kind where she didn't give a shit who was standing at the end of it.

Not true.

The women behind her? They were the ones who needed to be standing on their own two feet when the air finally cleared, no matter what.

Tyler moved toward her, leaping the railing in one smooth motion. He smiled for a brief second, before stepping to her side and turning to face the men.

"I stand with her. Clan Harrison will not tolerate the abuse that's been allowed. Not anymore. It's one thing to blame our violence on our bear nature, but instincts go beyond the urge to beat the hell out of someone."

The wind picked up, whipping back her wet hair and raising goose bumps. Or maybe that was an excuse for the reaction she had to the conviction in his voice. Tyler examined his contemporaries, the lot of them shifting uneasily on their feet.

"We've been idiots. Instincts don't just tell me to fight, they tell me to fight for what's right. To be there for the people who I love and care about." Tyler slipped his hand into hers. "Instinct should make us hold back when our bears want to rip another to shreds for stupid reasons like financial or political gain. We're more than our instincts. We're humans as well as bears. Isn't it about time we bloody well started acting like it?"

Her sense of pride was ridiculous—what she felt for Tyler at that moment was way out of proportion. Still, that he'd been listening to what she'd said and put it together without a two-by-four to the head made her beam.

He was a good man, or good bear, indeed. She squeezed his fingers, and the brief glance between them meant so much more than acceptance of her actions and his words. It was an affirmation that together, they were better.

The squeal of tires in the parking lot pulled everyone's attention to the taxi jerking to a stop by the front gate. Fear flared as Todd Ainsworth leapt from the back seat, slamming the door behind him.

Caroline pushed down her panic, darting a glance over her shoulder to where the ladies were slipping from the steamy water, Amanda Ainsworth staring with terror-filled eyes.

Todd Ainsworth left his jacket on the ground of the parking lot, his shirt at the stairs leading to the observation area. Around her and Tyler, clothes fell to the ground as the men prepared to shift.

Caroline regretted the swimsuit thing even more as she had no choice but to back away. Unarmed? No claws? She wasn't a fool. This was no place for her.

Tyler dropped her hand to strip off his jacket and shirt. "I'll deal with him. Find a safe spot."

She snatched up his jacket, slipping it on. "I'll take Amanda—"

"Find a safe spot," Tyler bit out, his voice softening as Ainsworth closed the gap between them. "Please, Caroline. I need to deal with Todd, but I need you to be safe. I can't... God, don't let anything happen to you."

Half the men had shifted, half stood naked in human form listening as Todd crossed the final feet toward them, cursing loudly. It was an eerie sight, bear and man mixed, violence simmering.

Caroline ducked away, not waiting to hear what complaints Todd wanted to make.

The view to the back of the pool was equally frightening. Most of the women had already shifted, making their way toward the assumed safety of the trees. Only their path of retreat was blocked. Dark bodies emerged from the perimeter—more bears.

One of the ladies who had shifted was cuffed in the head by a newcomer, and a roar broke out behind Caroline as the woman's mate barreled along the poolside, racing to protect his partner.

More shifters arrived, snarls ringing through the air. Caroline clutched Tyler's jacket around herself as she fled for the staff room of the pool, the door held open for her by a wide-eyed female wolf lifeguard.

Caroline vanished from his sight down the pool deck, and that was the last glimpse Tyler had time for. He was too busy keeping teeth and claws from ripping off important parts of his anatomy.

Like his head.

Todd Ainsworth snarled a few comments to the crowd about people assuming too much responsibility, taking too much for granted. But when the men didn't leap to take the bait or so much as grumble in response, Ainsworth cut his losses, shifted and attacked.

Tyler shifted, but not fast enough to avoid a paw swipe to his human torso before fur and muscle took hold. Searing pain shot through him and shook his beast, forcing adrenaline into his veins. His vision clouded and rational thought failed.

There were reasons he wasn't supposed to do this, but damn if he could remember what they were. All he could think of was Todd Ainsworth dead in front of him. Preferably in more than one mangled piece.

Tyler lurched forward and snapped, burying his teeth in Ainsworth's shoulder, pushing with his full weight in an attempt to topple his opponent to the ground. Blood flooded his mouth, the taste increasing his anger. His human reasoning was at an all-time low, the bear stepping in and making decisions.

The animal side knew one thing. The shifter dragging his claws down Tyler's chest was a danger to everyone at the pool. Everyone in the conclave. Caroline had been right.

Pain struck again as long claws stabbed viciously into his abdomen, followed by a burst of agony that raked across his stomach and hip as Ainsworth attempted to win his freedom.

Tyler was gone. Only the bear remained, and his claws and teeth went to work.

Five paces from her sanctuary Caroline found herself thwarted as a huge furry body fell over the divider wall into her path. She scrambled back, jerked open the door to the mechanical room and slipped inside.

There was no lock on her side. There was no way out at first glance, either. She searched frantically through the items stored in the small cluttered space, looking for something to use as a weapon.

Nothing. Pull buoys and flutter boards weren't much use.

The back corner held an old filing cabinet, the doors removed, shelves stuffed with water toys. Above the cabinet was a trapdoor—access to the roof?

She shoved the pile of inner tubes over and scrambled to the top of the cabinet, undid the small latches and shoved the door open.

Sunlight greeted her, and fresh air to filter away the chlorine and musty damp in her nostrils. She peeked out, but the roof was clear of everything except some leaves and branches, and one deflated beach ball.

She paused, glancing back into the storage area. The sounds of fighting continued to rage, but she seemed to have a moment of respite. She shoved everything she needed onto the roof, then shut the trapdoor dragging the diving weights she'd found on top to stop anyone from following her.

Underfoot, the rough asphalt lining the roof cut into her soles as she inched toward the roof edge to peer over. Blood and fur were smeared on the deck, groups of bears clustered together making it impossible for her to distinguish the good guys from the bad guys.

Wolf bodies joined the mix as well—and those she recognized after years in the pack. The guards on duty were caught in a corner, more of the Takhini pack coming from the trees to rescue them. The wolves worked in pairs, snapping at heels and darting in and out of reach as they surrounded the pool.

Wheels on gravel sounded, and she tore herself away from the fighting, turning instead to the side of the building that led to the campground.

More vehicles were pulling into the parking lot—a long line of airstream RVs parked in a row at the entrance to the camping area, faces pressed to their windows examining the pool building. How much of the fighting could be seen from the road was impossible to tell from Caroline's vantage point, but she had to stop any tourists from attempting a closer look.

The camper she'd found for Shelley to work out of was parked on the other side of the trees. She jerked her cell phone from the suit pocket and called her sister.

"I need you to run interference. Now, please."

Shelley groaned. "You're damn lucky Chase likes you. Are you okay?"

"Yes. Only, move it, we've got humans exiting their campers." She hung up on Shelley, then hit a preprogrammed message, sending it off to one of her contacts. It only took a second to shove the phone back into her pocket. In a moment of blinding inspiration, she snatched up the basket of pool toys she'd hauled onto the roof. She yanked out the pair of sunglasses sticking from one side of the basket, and perched the oversized lost-and-found item on her nose.

Fingers crossed this worked. Hopefully the glasses and coat made her look mysterious and not like an escaped maniac.

She stood at the edge of the roof as doors swung open and the RVers crawled out. They were, as she expected, a group of older travelers. The type that typically moved from campsite to campsite together as they explored the northern frontier. Caroline had seen her share of RV convoys on the Alaskan Highway since she was girl.

Seen so many campers in the Walmart parking lot she'd lost count.

The retirees stood by their vehicles, staring across the parking lot toward the pool as they talked amongst themselves. One couple headed for the front doors, and Caroline mentally hurried her sister up.

Shelley was just visible through the trees, not close enough to be spotted unless you knew where to look. Caroline had to distract these people. She scooped up a couple of the rubber duckies from the basket at her feet and tossed them in the air. Laughed loudly.

Nothing. The couple kept moving toward the danger zone. So she nabbed the basket and upended it, small yellow birds bouncing everywhere as they hit the concrete outside the front doors.

The gentleman who'd been headed toward the observation area paused, looked at the toys, then upward. He blinked, his eyes widening as he took in her outfit.

Caroline waved and announced in her brightest, reality-show-announcer voice possible. "Hi. I'm sorry, the pool is closed. Isn't there a sign at the highway warning we're filming today?"

"Filming?" The grey-haired woman at her husband's side eyed Caroline. "We didn't see any sign. Sounds as if there's murder going on."

Caroline clapped and smiled broader. "Well done. Yes, a murder mystery. It's a Canadian Broadcast Corporation direct-to-television movie. The director has a marvelous reputation for realism. He's using live animals in this one."

The couple glanced at the edge of the pool house then back up at Caroline. "Is it safe?"

She wrinkled her nose. "Of course it is, they're professionally trained animals. Only I do remind you the pool *is* closed to the public—it's much better for the performers if they're not disturbed during filming. But if you would like to talk to one of our animal trainers, she's right over there."

Caroline pointed back toward their RVs where Shelley had moved into sight, the leash in her hand attached to a collar around Chase's neck.

Her brother-in-law was going to kill her for this. Sometime, somewhere, the big Métis shifter would demand satisfaction for having to pretend to be a domesticated cat.

The deception worked. The couple hurried to join their friends gathering around Shelley.

Caroline called after them. "The campground is open, so go ahead and find spots. Someone will be around to help you in a while, once we're done with this scene."

The gentleman waved a hand without even glancing back, he was so intent to get to Shelley and the giant cougar. Chase sat obediently on his haunches even as he stared at the roof in disgust.

Caroline wiggled her fingers, then darted to the opposite side of the roof to catch up on what had been happening.

Caroline.

The image of her was the only thing that kept Tyler from going completely feral. Her face was in his mind, her voice in his head. The expressive what-the-hell-do-you-think-you're-doing raised eyebrow contrasting with the whispered request for his reassurances.

It was eerie the details his bear remembered about her. Not only expressions and words, but the force surrounding her. The energy and wild impulses that so suited his shifter side.

The peace she exuded in far more rare moments—the part his human hungered for.

The fight became a blur as he let his bear take charge, but pulled his human brain into a kind of side chamber so he could think things through. It was in that place he grasped ripping a chunk from Ainsworth's throat and letting him bleed out on the deck would not be productive in the end.

His bear complained it was unfair, but the realization was true. Change had to come to the bear clans without the winning answer being the old-fashioned urge to eviscerate their enemies.

He'd just figured this out, the no-killing-Ainsworth bit, when the other shifter made a mistake and let his guard down for long enough that if Tyler had chosen, the fight would have been all over.

Humanity, and Caroline's lessons, held his claws and teeth in check. Ainsworth got to live.

Tyler's feet were knocked out from under him as a reward for his benevolence. His beast complained about the indignity of being toppled by someone like Ainsworth, not impressed at all, until Tyler pointed out it was Caroline's idea, and his bear settled down.

Another flash of memory had him smiling. Tyler had to agree with Caroline's summation. His relationship with his shifted side? Was *way* weird.

Then he wasn't thinking about her or the new rules he needed to follow, but protecting his throat from Ainsworth's fangs. Flat on his back wasn't the way to win the fight, but there was nowhere to go. Ainsworth stepped on his lower limbs, knelt on his thighs and pressed a paw to his chest in such a way Tyler couldn't get any leverage.

He warded off a paw swipe that would have blinded him, scrambling his own claws down Ainsworth's throat, but it wasn't the best of circumstances. Tyler didn't want to kill the other shifter anymore, and that knowledge made it difficult to protect himself.

Damn it. Tyler didn't want to lose—not with so much at stake—but winning and not leaving his enemy dead would take more pain to his bear than he'd like.

Caroline stepped to the edge of the roof to examine the situation. Fighting had slowed. In some places, groups had single bears pinned to the ground, and those trapped were giving up the fight and shifting to human. It was easy to tell which were friends, as Takhini wolves had joined in and stood menacing the bears still struggling to escape.

She couldn't spot Tyler anywhere, and that made her concerned he was one of the two still clawing each other wildly near the very edge of the pool. A grizzly and an enormous brown bear, both bleeding profusely as they struggled.

Everywhere she looked, signs of violence marked the ground. Blood, fur. The peaceful haven she'd grown up visiting had turned into a horrid bloodbath.

A single bear lay to one side, motionless.

Caroline's breath caught in her throat, and she hurried down from the roof, using her makeshift ladder to get back into the storage room. She paused only long enough to grab the black hose off the wall, adjusting the nozzle to the tightest setting, then cranking the water to full.

She jerked the door open and raced out, pulling the hose with her toward the pair still fighting.

No more. Maybe they were bears, maybe they fought and killed without thinking, but not here. Not when she could stop them.

The sound of helicopter propellers echoed in the air, but she was too focused on her task to even look up. She opened the water pressure all the way and aimed the tight stream at the brown bear who was preparing to take another swipe at the grizzly he had pinned beneath him.

Out of nowhere, icy-cold water dripped onto his fur. Above him Ainsworth screamed his disapproval.

Tyler stopped struggling while Ainsworth reared and twisted away, his head thrust forward and his angry scream echoing off the walls of the pool house.

Ainsworth dropped to all fours and charged.

In that second Tyler spotted Ainsworth's target. Caroline stood on the deck, the high-pressure hose in her hands aimed straight at the bear who was narrowing the gap between them with frightening speed. Tyler shifted, shouting even as his vocal cords were in midtransition.

"Jump."

How she'd heard or registered his meaning, he didn't know, only she obeyed. Hands free of the hose, her slim body propelled into the air, seeming to hover over the surface of the pool.

Tyler was back in his bear and after Ainsworth before Caroline had time to create a splash. He leapt from behind and wrapped his arms around the other shifter. Squeezed him tight, forcing the air from Ainsworth's lungs. Instead of seizing him like a bear would, though, Tyler had also grabbed on like a man. One arm in a chokehold to the throat.

If he'd been human it would have been easier, the way his elbow bent in his man far more conducive to cutting off an air supply. The bear elbow didn't bend the right way.

But it didn't really matter. Tyler was a lot stronger in his bear than his human, and that was enough. Especially when he took one step to the left, off the pool deck and into the water.

Ainsworth went insane with panic, struggling like a possessed demon. Tyler held tight and took a deep breath. He lifted his lower limbs and wrapped them around his opponent as well, dragging Ainsworth under the water.

Sound cut off. The shrieks and the crying. The strange thumping sound that had begun right around the time

Ainsworth had abandoned their fight to attack Caroline. There was nothing in Tyler's ears but bubbles. His vision remained clear and sharp as he kept Ainsworth trapped. He checked for Caroline, pleased to see her at the opposite side of the pool, her long limbs vanishing as she exited the water.

Good, she was safe.

An extraordinary sense of peace came over him. It must have had something to do with knowing Caroline was all right. That she'd be able to move on after this event was over.

Ainsworth wiggled. Tyler attempted to hang on, his breath of air nearly exhausted as the water grew sparkling bright around them. He couldn't seem to hold his quarry anymore. Tyler fought the urge as long as possible before he could no longer resist. His arms opened, and Ainsworth floated away.

Tyler drifted toward the bottom of the pool. It was rather peaceful down there. No one chewing on him, no one ripping his fur.

A splash disturbed the surface, and slender legs came into view. Pretty legs, followed by a pretty body. His bear figured that human Tyler would like the bits and pieces more, so the animal part took the initiative to shift. Tyler's humanity returned in a rush as Caroline swam down, her blonde hair waving in the water as if she was a beautiful and delicate mermaid. Her eyes blinked, her smile so...Caroline.

Then she caught him by the hair and dragged him to the surface.

Chapter Eighteen

She'd spoken to Nadia before. Had heard about the petite lynx shifter's abilities from Shaun and Gem, but Caroline had never seen anything like the Omega in action.

Right about the time Caroline had leapt into the water, the pack helicopter landed on the roof of the building. By the time she'd swum across the pool width and scrambled back to dry ground, Nadia stood at the lip of the roof, shaking her head sadly. Caroline stared in amazement as the small blonde sat on the edge then jumped down, a massive man following at a short distance.

Fighting between the wolves and bears slowed, the few lingering skirmishes drawing apart and the combatants either sitting peacefully or falling to the ground as Nadia walked the perimeter of the pool.

Omega. A peace-bringer. As the lynx strolled through the war zone, it was as if an overdose of Valium flooded the area. Even Caroline was on the relaxed side, but figured that was more because of her rush of relief the bloodletting was done.

Not seeing Tyler rise from the pool had been her final annoyance, though. Caroline jumped in and dragged him upward, thankful he had the sense to shift, because she doubted his rock of a bear would have been easy to budge.

Tyler blinked as he hit the surface, grabbing the pool edge

with one hand and catching her to him with the other. "Caroline. Watch out. It's dangerous."

She snorted. "You need to catch up, big guy. The fight is over, I brought in the cavalry."

A pair of pretty pink-painted toes stopped beside them as Nadia knelt to say hello. "This is the weirdest pool party I've ever seen a human host."

"I ordered guppies, but they didn't arrive in time. We had to improvise." Caroline wiggled free from Tyler and pushed herself up to sit on the edge. "Thank you for coming."

"No problem. I'm sorry I couldn't make it sooner." Nadia wrinkled her nose. "You'd think these guys would know to contact someone like me before organizing volatile gatherings."

Caroline shrugged. "They're bears. They don't think."

"True."

"Hey, be nice." Tyler was up on the deck, bringing Caroline to her feet and offering a welcoming hand to Nadia. "Maybe it's because your existence is nothing more than a rumour. Good to meet you. Omega?"

"Cross-species. No one is safe from my mind-melds." Nadia blinked appreciatively as she looked Tyler over. "And aren't *you* a lovely looking specimen? If you ever need a personal favour, let me know."

Caroline nudged the blonde out of the way even as she laughed. She'd been warned about Nadia's tendency to flirt. "Stop it, no dallying with my boyfriend."

"Oh, he's taken? Too bad."

Tyler adjusted his grin of delight to a more serious expression in the nick of time before Caroline stomped on his toes. He glanced around the pool. "Dammit, we were terrible."

"You were bears." Nadia patted his chest, her eyes widening

as she spotted the scratches and bite marks marring his skin. "And yes, you were terrible."

Caroline blushed as the particular mark Nadia focused on was one Caroline had caused. "Come on, now that you've got them calmed down, perhaps we can convince them to hire you to hang out for a few more days."

Nadia nodded.

Cleanup took less time than anyone expected. The message Caroline had sent off brought a full emergency-response team—all shifters or humans with shifters in their families. There were medical attendants and RCMP. She'd even alerted her media contacts, and the newspaper was there to interview the campers and a few key well-schooled actors regarding the excitement of "filming in a northern location".

No mention of bloodshed or injuries. Just a typical day in the Yukon.

Typical. Caroline wasn't sure if she should laugh or cry.

Damage Control 101. She was good at it after all these years, sadly. That beach beckoned again. A sun lounge, a fruity drink with a double dose of alcohol...

Except for the women who gathered their things to head back into Whitehorse, each of them stopping to give her a bear hug and offer support.

By the time Shelley had finished examining Tyler's wounds, the pool area was nearly empty, everyone having moved toward the parking lot and their cars. "You were far luckier than you could have been. Just saying."

"I'm a bear. I can take it." Tyler frowned, his annoyance turned on Chase who was staring at Caroline in disgust. "What's your problem?"

Caroline pressed her lips together, trying not to smile.

"Go on, laugh it up. I'll get my revenge." Chase plopped on the bench beside his mate and nuzzled her under the ear. "You were wonderful though."

Caroline pulled Tyler aside before he could make any other demands, handing him the pair of pants she'd found. "You need to come talk to Jim Halcyon and the RCMP rep. They're asking what to do with Ainsworth."

"And you didn't have any proposals?"

Her blood steamed. "I suggested abandoning him on a drifting iceberg, but they didn't take me seriously."

"Let's not inflict him on the Hawaiian shifters, if the ice lasted that long."

Sergeant Major Graham, a black bear she'd learned was affiliated with Clan Halcyon, waited beside a picnic table. Todd Ainsworth was seated on the wooden bench and refused to make eye contact with her.

"Caroline."

"Sergeant Major. Thanks for coming."

He switched his gaze to Tyler. "We have a problem. I'm obviously not going to arrest Ainsworth for anything that occurred at the pool this afternoon related to conclave."

Tyler nodded. "Business meeting."

Caroline snorted. She couldn't help it.

Tyler caught her fingers and squeezed them.

Jim Halcyon spoke from his position on the opposite side of the table. "The issue is whether charges should be brought for spousal abuse."

Todd Ainsworth reared to his feet. "See here—"

"Shut up, Todd." Even the pressure of Tyler's hand on hers couldn't stop Caroline from responding. "This is not your decision."

"Agreed." Graham gestured to the parking lot where Amanda Ainsworth was slipping into the Harrison limo, Justin at her side. "Unfortunately, there is no clear precedent. Amanda said she had no idea what she'd experienced wasn't simply a shifter's lot. All she wants is out."

"Taking Ainsworth from his clan isn't a terrible thing, but caging the bear?" Jim shook his head. "I'm not willing to make that decision."

"If she doesn't press charges, I can't book him through the human courts," Graham explained, his gaze meeting Caroline's with apologies in the depths.

Dammit. "Well, that sucks."

Tyler tugged her to his side and held her tightly. "I have an idea how to deal with this. Can you escort our guest to the Moonshine Inn? If she's willing to stay with us."

Jim spoke up. "Lillie and I would love to have Amanda at our home as well. We have plenty of room."

"As long as the bastard can't get at her ever again." Caroline nodded. "Fine, Tyler, your call. I'll go talk to Amanda and see what she'd like. Because it really should be her choice."

Before she could go, though, Tyler lifted her chin and full-out kissed her. A cop, a billionaire and a bastard observing from a few feet away.

She didn't care one bit they had an audience.

The fear and fire that had sustained her during the fight was washed away with the sweet caring of his touch. A new kind of fire rose as his tongue stroked hers, and small sparks burst into flames like warning beacons shining from mountaintop after mountaintop.

Reality slowly set in—she was in a bikini rubbing rather wantonly against a nearly naked man. She separated them before anything else could rise.

"Trust me," he whispered in her ear.

She walked away, past the staff scrubbing blood from the deck. Past the wolf from the paper taking more "promo" shots who smiled at her.

Caroline walked as she let it sink in.

Trust him? With her life.

His fingers itched to wipe the smirk from Todd Ainsworth's face. "Jim, go find that lynx shifter. Nadia."

Jim nodded and stepped away, leaving Tyler with the RCMP and Ainsworth.

"You have a suggestion how to deal with this?" The sergeant major remained alert even though it was pretty clear any attempt by Todd to run would be squashed in an instant.

"Unfortunately, you're right. For some things we have to work within the human rules, and if Amanda doesn't press charges, you have nothing to go on." Tyler crossed his arms and fixed Ainsworth with a look of death. "So I suggest we do this the shifter way. Following the results of conclave, the new leader will decide his punishment."

"Damn." Graham shook his head in disbelief. "You want me to simply let him go?"

Tyler gestured across the observation area to the little blonde, her protective escort only one step behind as she rapidly closed the distance between them.

"He'll show up when requested by the clans if Nadia stays close by. If you're willing, that is?" Tyler turned the question to the lynx. "We'll need you to stay with Ainsworth for the next few days to make sure he sticks around and behaves himself. Can you do that?"

She nodded, her nose turned up as if Ainsworth smelt funny. "If I have to."

Her guard, a huge brute of a bear even larger than Tyler, dipped his head briefly. "I'll take care of her."

That brought a smile to Nadia's face. "Right. Lovely."

Sergeant Major Graham nodded, backing off. "I'll escort the three of them to a hotel, then wait to hear from conclave."

Tyler didn't pay any further attention to Ainsworth. Instead, he slipped from the observation deck, desperate to rejoin Caroline at the hotel. He wanted to disappear, maybe get a start on those hours of solitude she'd suggested they take.

He found his way blocked, though, by a gathering of his contemporaries. Serious faces on the lot of them as they observed Ainsworth being escorted away by Nadia and company.

"I thought you'd all be long gone," Tyler admitted. "Don't you think we've caused enough trouble here?"

Nakusp stepped forward. "We were about to leave, but none of the ladies would let us go until we'd talked to you."

Oh really. Tyler made sure his jaw wasn't swinging in the wind. The familiar faces he'd seen during the conclave events expanded to include their partners, the ladies' eyes fixed on him. "Is there something I can help you with?"

Shockingly, it was Lynn Nakusp who stepped forward, her hand on her husband's arm. He smiled supportively then waited for her to speak. "We have a say in this event as well, and we're in agreement. Clans Halcyon and Nakusp will withdraw from the next vote, leaving Harrison versus Ainsworth. And right now even the idiots in Lucerne wouldn't vote for Todd."

One of the older leaders standing at attention cleared his

throat. “That would be my clan, and we are idiots, but we’re not fools. You’re a fair man, Harrison. We’ll accept your leadership.”

“Except, and the ladies insist on this.” Nakusp shook his finger at Tyler. “We accept Clan Harrison as long as both sides remain represented. You for the men, and Caroline for the women.”

Oh no, and oh yes. “You want Caroline as part of the deal?”

The lot of them bobbed their heads like a vast display of car-dashboard toys. It was what he’d hoped for, all the long days before when conclave had begun. To take charge and be able to make a difference.

The bears before him had taken a huge step forward in how they operated today, and their courage to move ahead made him proud. Only they had no idea that the arranged relationship they were proposing was not such an easy solution.

He would love to be head of conclave, Caroline at his side, but he couldn’t do it if it wasn’t what Caroline wanted as well.

He looked out over his friends. “Thank you for the awesome privilege you’ve offered, and I promise I will pass on your request to Caroline. But I can’t demand she become a part of this deal, not unless she wants to, because blithely ordering her to join me would make me as big of a tyrant as Ainsworth, simply in another way.”

The bobbing heads stopped, frozen in place.

Lillie Halcyon stepped forward, her smile brightening as she poked him in the chest. “No one said anything about ordering her around. You’ll just have to be at your most persuasive.” She lowered her voice. “Although I think you’ve already got a bit of shoe-in, if you play your cards right. I suspect she might be a touch in love with you already.”

He could only hope.

Chapter Nineteen

She'd been kidnapped. Whirled away to a private suite in a mansion she didn't know existed. It was a bit of heaven on earth, and the frustrations and fears of the past hours melted like chocolate in the sun. Especially as a masseuse worked out another set of knots from Caroline's lower back.

It had never been difficult for her to ferret out information. Over the years working for the hotel, and then for the Takhini pack, she'd prided herself on having all the connections. On knowing people like Nadia who could stop a disaster from happening. On having the resources to arrange the cover-up even now spilling false reports through the media.

Only it appeared everything she'd puzzled out over the years had been one side of the tracks. There was a world of money, power and privilege she'd barely touched the edges of. She'd probably never fully test the extent of their borders.

Lillie and Jim Halcyon were one example. Caroline hadn't known the bear shifters were local to Whitehorse. She was glad to be able to add them to her friend list.

The house she currently luxuriated in was another surprise. Silent servants had drifted out of sight when they arrived. Tyler had guided her up a sprawling staircase to a room the size of her previous apartment.

"When you said you'd like time away, I thought you were

brilliant." Tyler pressed his lips to her temple.

"I have my moments." Caroline made her way to the window. The place was incredible, with enormous log posts and windows big enough to hang-glide out of, all looking over the majestic mountain range. "I feel guilty, though, leaving Amanda behind."

"Wasted energy, guilt." Tyler shook his head. "She needs time to adjust. Don't feel you need to coddle her—she's stronger than you think. Justin will keep her safe, and Lillie promised to stop by."

So.

Caroline turned her back on one gorgeous view to take in the closer gorgeous view. Tyler had pulled on dress pants and a pristine white shirt, and her heart pounded. "A getaway. Just the two of us."

He nodded.

"However shall we pass the time?" Caroline fluttered her lashes, and he smiled.

"I'm sure we can come up with something. First, though, I need to make a few calls before I can unwind."

Drat. "It's not a getaway if you're working," she pointed out.

"I won't be long. In the meantime, you start on the relaxing."

Out of nowhere a woman rolled in a padded massage table, and there were no protests Caroline could make without being a damn liar.

She was laid out on the table in seconds, Tyler squeezing her fingers before leaving the room.

The massage began, and other than the initial rush of *holy cow, we did it* and *holy shit, those bears are scary beasts*, her thoughts drifted into nothing more than *holy moly, this feels wonderful.*

The room had darkened when she finally opened her eyes, the nap that had ambushed her once her massage was done washing away the final bits of nervous stress from her limbs. The low lighting from the wall sconces was enough to guide her to the bed where she found another of the outfits from Boutique Belanger laid out. The shimmering blue gown felt like a caress as she pulled it on, sad to cover the sexy underwear she'd also found there.

The shoes? She had to take a closer look because otherwise she'd have sworn each was carved from a single diamond.

There was a vanity in the corner of the room, a full-length mirror beside it. She wasn't surprised when she discovered a jewelry box waiting for her.

Were the diamonds really blue, or was it the light reflecting from her dress? She clasped the necklace in place, and the earrings, before stepping back to see the final result.

The Caroline she knew had vanished.

Or at least the rough-and-tumble girl who'd clawed her way to the top of the Takhini pack with nothing more than driving need. Gone also was the no-nonsense individual who thrived in the pack chili cook-off and hands-free eating challenges during Spring Thaw festival.

There was a princess in the room wearing her face.

The illusion lasted for all of thirty seconds, because that's as long as Caroline could keep her smile from breaking free. It wasn't a delicate, polite and *how is the weather in the south of France* smile. It was a full out, *hell yeah, this is fucking cool* smile.

Caroline wasn't gone. She'd never be gone, because this was the real her—what you see is what you get. Didn't matter how pretty the packaging.

She paced to the top of the stairs following the scent of food, her stomach reminding her it had been a long time since that morning's bacon and eggs.

She startled him. Tyler stood with one foot on the bottom rung, his hand on the banister as he caught a glimpse of her. The fitted tux and well-groomed hair proved he'd found time to do something other than make his phone calls.

He swallowed hard. "You are astonishingly beautiful."

His compliment sent a thrill through her. "Thank you, kind sir."

Caroline considered the stairs and doing one of those princess-descends-without-looking-at-her-feet deals like in the movies, but decided chances were that in the full-length gown, she'd trip and end up spending the rest of their getaway time in a hospital bed in traction.

So instead, she took a final peek at him, just to last her until she hit the main floor. Then she concentrated on the heels, dress and the rest of her all making it to the bottom in one piece.

His hand slipped over hers on the railing and he lifted it to his lips. "Goddess."

Heat flashed from his lips to her arm and way *way* farther in a sharp jolt. Good-looking duds, but it was his smile that enchanted her the most. Not his polite-greeting version, but one she'd seen in more private moments.

The one that involved eating her up with his eyes and promised he'd be eating her up more intimately later.

"Dinner?" Tyler offered an arm.

She accepted and let him lead her into the dining hall. "I hope we didn't kick anyone from their home."

He seated her before settling at her side. "No. And once

dinner is over, we'll be alone."

Promises of relaxation with a more sexual twist were there in his eyes.

She'd expected soup or some kind of appetizer to arrive, followed by a long list of other courses, all the while she'd slowly grow more impatient for the meal to be over so they could be alone. Because while the trappings of luxury were fun to play with, she was ready for him.

Only everything arrived at one. Servants lowered platters to the table and *poofed* away as if they owned magical vanishing spells.

Caroline lifted a cover, and the rich scent of a cheese sauce seduced her. "I like the casual style of the place."

"To be honest, the only reason I gave you the gown for tonight was I desperately wanted to see you in it." He scooped a serving of vegetables onto her plate, and she smiled. "Once dinner is over we have pyjamas we can trade into."

Caroline laughed. "Flannel?"

Tyler didn't skip a beat. "Of course. We live in the north, what do you expect?" He clicked his tongue as if scolding her.

He poured her wine and lifted his glass in a toast.

He paused for a long time, and Caroline laid a hand on his thigh. "You don't have to have pretty words. We can toast to surviving my bright idea to have a casual get-together with the ladies."

They clicked their goblets together.

"We more than survived. You made an incredible difference in a woman's life. By offering the truth. Thank you for having confidence in me." He cleared his throat. "Thank you for sharing your trust in me."

Caroline took a sip of her wine, staring over the edge of the glass as he fixed his gaze on her. They were totally going to waste the food, she could sense it in her bones. Any moment he would sweep her up in his arms and they'd go satisfy a different kind of hunger.

Which, *okay*.

She lowered her wine glass and placed it carefully beside her plate before facing him.

His rapidly changing expressions were priceless. Lust, confusion, a moment of complete seriousness. "Tyler, is something wrong?"

He blinked then pulled himself together. "I'm trying to plan the best way to tell you something that will produce the least freaking out on your part."

Hmm. "Freaking out is something I like to avoid," Caroline warned, half-seriously.

"I know." Tyler winked. "But there are good bits and bad bits to the conversation."

"*More* than one thing." He was as bad as Evan had been when in a say-nothing-while-talking-your-ear-off mood. Must be something to do with Alpha shifter blood. "How about you order the items from the least oh-my-*Gawd* to the most."

Tyler nodded. "I'm in love with you."

Caroline's heart jolted hard enough she swore the pretty blue outfit over her chest leapt out a foot before returning to its regular position. She gasped for control. "That's the thing on your list *least* likely to freak me out?"

He caught her hands in his. "It's the most important thing there as well. I know it's fast, I know—"

"Holy smoking gun, you ain't kidding."

"I did warn you." Tyler made a face. "Okay, I even outdid my fellow bears this time in terms of falling hard and fast. But,

Caroline"—he cupped her face in his hand—"you're unique. That's why my bear has been shoving me so hard since the first time we met. You understand shifters. You understand power..."

A moment of fear intruded, an icy finger of doubt. The *I love you* bit hadn't been expected—she'd known something was growing between them. She'd felt it as well.

She *didn't* want this to be about admiration for her prowess in shifter-power games.

Tyler didn't let her get a chance to complain, though. He was out of his chair and on his feet, pacing beside the table. He twirled on her. "You understand love."

What kind of statement was that? "I...think I do."

He shook his head. "I saw you with your sister. I know what you did for her, to make sure she could achieve the goals she desired. You might have stepped over a few human boundaries, but you did it out of love. Sacrificial love."

Her throat was tightening. "You've given this a lot of thought, for it being such a short time."

"I'm just getting started. You've done things for the Takhini pack, to help them. Giving of your time, your money, your sanity—you're on a first-name basis with the crew at the RCMP station after hauling the pack out of jail regularly, aren't you?"

Okay, that one kind of made her smile. "They don't mean any harm."

Tyler was down on his knees beside her chair. "Caroline, I have to ask. Why the tears last night? When I asked you what you wanted, why did you cry?"

Oh God.

Caroline stopped. The urge to keep her real self hidden away was so well practiced, she didn't know that she could do this. To make the conversation between them as honest and direct as it needed to be.

Then she remembered the bravery Amanda had shown. How could she do any less? Caroline gathered her courage and let it out.

"No one has asked me what I wanted for a very, very long time." She couldn't keep still anymore, instead allowing her fingers to trace his jaw, the corners of his ear. The fading marks from the fight. "Don't get me wrong, it's not as if I haven't had good things happen in my life, but they're mostly because I've taken. Ordered, demanded, cajoled, teased."

Tyler nodded. He threaded his fingers through hers and kissed her knuckles, his touch soft and caring.

"Caroline, I love you. I love your bravery and what you know about kicking shifter butt. But I love *you* the most. The human who has been living in the shifter world. I've only met traces of her, little bursts. I'd like to spend a long time getting to know her better." He grinned. "Although that sounds about like me talking about my bear in third person. Which really amuses him as well."

Caroline couldn't stop her burst of laughter. "No, I guess you're right. There are kind of two of me in here."

Tyler paused, his smile turning more serious. "I'll ask you again, what do you want? Do you want me in your life? Do you need some time away from shifters altogether? I could fly you to a warm island resort where you can do nothing but take care of Caroline for a couple months. Anything. Whatever it is you really want, I'll give it to you. I'll make it happen."

His voice dropped to a whisper, the words wrapping around her nerve endings and teasing. So many choices, so many options.

And yet...

"I want you to tell me what you want...for us," she answered. Tyler's eyes widened, but Caroline pushed on. "Because while getting away and hiding from the world sounds lovely, it's also wrong."

"It's not wrong to want to be happy," Tyler insisted.

"Oh, Tyler." She shook her head. "I am happy even when I'm giving to others. Maybe...maybe more happy because I'm giving to others. I just wish I didn't *always* have to be the strong one."

He nodded. "I'd like you in my life. I'm a bear—so falling in love will only get stronger with time. So I could grab you a wedding dress and make it a big fancy do for all your pack to attend. And I'd give you a pretty house here in Whitehorse so you could live here when your sister is in town running her medical practice. And when Shelley is gone north, I'd take you to Yellowknife to my house. You could fall in love with my hometown. You could help me make my father smile."

He pulled out a ring case and held it to her. "You could fall in love with me."

Even as his words jolted her heart to a stop, the case brought her back to life. She'd known it was coming. Suspected it, really. There had been no ring with the jewelry he'd laid out for her to wear.

She cracked open the lid, and the light reflecting from the stone nearly blinded her. "Holy shit, Tyler."

She stared at the ring. Glanced back up at him. He held up a finger, asking for a moment.

"Before you answer, I have to tell you the rest of the freak-out list."

The list? *Now?* "You have weird timing, even for a bear."

He sighed. "I know. Item number two. Conclave is over—all

my friendly opponents have withdrawn and I've been promised enough support by the clans to defeat Ainsworth."

Caroline couldn't believe it. "Why didn't you tell me earlier? That's wonderful."

Wait.

She narrowed her gaze. "Why is this on the freak-out list?"

He cleared his throat. "They offered the leadership of conclave to Clan Harrison. Tyler and *Caroline* Harrison."

Dead stop. "Well. That explains why you didn't tell me earlier."

Sorrow and frustration mixed on his face. "How did life get this complicated? I don't want you to feel obligated to marry me to help the bears. But having you at my side would be the most incredible thing. They trust you. They look up to you."

"And the women think I'm pretty awesome as well." Now that the initial *arghhh* moment was past, Caroline saw the solution far more clearly than she'd expected. She poked him firmly. "Hey, they're trying to blackmail me into an arranged marriage. It's not the end of the world."

"It's not fair. I wanted you to make the decision based on your heart, not guilt or anything else."

If the rush of emotions washing through her wasn't love, she didn't know what love was. "You've forgotten one thing, Tyler. You promised me I could make my own decision. That I could pick what I wanted, right?"

He nodded. "Exactly. I meant it, with all my heart. And that's why I didn't tell you at first, because I honestly and completely love you. I want you to want me as much as I want you. Although...if you don't pick me? Fair warning, I plan to woo the hell out of you for the next ten years or so until you give in."

"Nice. Stalker with warning label."

"I promise not to sneak into your room and stare at you while you sleep."

Caroline smiled, then she pressed the ring box back into his palm, folding his fingers over it. "Then, here's my choice."

His face fell. "What—?"

She thrust out her hand. "You have to put it on me. I'm not about to place my engagement ring on my own damn finger. Enough with the making me do everything, right?"

His hands were steady as he slipped the massive stone on. He stood her up and brought her close, fingers firm under her chin to lift her lips to his.

Caroline savoured the kiss. Soaked in his warmth. Passion blossomed in her core as he swayed them together, his body intimately close.

When he let her go for air, she caught him by the suit-jacket lapels and hung on tight. "I would be honoured to marry you, Tyler Harrison."

All the bits and pieces of what she'd done over the years made her who she was. A human with more than a little shifter nature. Maybe that was why falling in love so quickly wasn't impossible.

The shifter-savvy part also knew one more thing. The food would get very cool before they got around to it. She jerked his jacket off his shoulders and latched their mouths together.

Oh yeah.

He picked her up and carried her five paces down the length of the room to a section of the table that had no place settings or food. She was laid out on the surface, naked, faster than she thought possible. "You need to teach me that trick sometime. *Oh...*"

Tyler was between her legs and driving her mad with his tongue. She buried her fingers in his thick hair and enjoyed the ride, the speeding bullet arriving with little enough warning she knocked one of the flower arrangements over as her arms shot out.

One motion later, Tyler leaned over her, his muscular torso right there for her to enjoy mapping with her fingers while he guided his cock deep into her core. After that there wasn't a lot of talking time. Lots of growls and groans, and eventually laughter as Tyler tipped the table over in his enthusiasm and they ended up on the floor, still entwined.

They rolled, Tyler protecting her and bringing her over him. They stared to their right at the upset platters and wine pooling on the carpet. "Well. That's embarrassing."

"You'll have to get it professionally cleaned before the owners get home," Caroline teased.

Tyler brushed a strand of her hair behind her ear. "I don't know. Would you really make me bring in a cleaner?"

What? "Say again?"

Tyler sat up, cradling her in his arms. He gestured around the room. "It's yours, Caroline. If you want anything changed, we'll renovate. But I figured if you didn't say yes, I'd need a place in Whitehorse to woo you from. So I bought it."

"In less than one freaking day you bought me a house? That should have been on the list."

He smiled. "You do know I have a bit of money, right? You won't hold it against me?"

There seemed to be less oxygen in the room than before. "Oh, I-I knew you had money, but I think I need to add a few zeroes to my mental math."

"You can fly with me to Europe when I go. And the South

American trips will be much more pleasurable with you along."

Caroline's head swam with excitement. And then, a flash of an idea. "I feel terrible I don't have a ring for you to wear."

"That's fine, we'll find one later," Tyler assured her.

Caroline shook her head. "Nope, this is important to me. And since it's got to be shifter safe, how about this?" She leaned over and snatched up the ribs that had fallen to the floor. Off the top of the bone she pulled the decorative silver ring.

"You're not serious." Tyler laughed and hid his hands behind his back. Or at least he did until she raised a brow.

He sighed. Brought forward a hand and allowed her to slip it on.

Caroline took advantage of his momentary distraction to escape his lap and race for the stairs. Tyler was up and after her in a flash. Chances of her making it to the top without getting caught were slim to none, kind of like her chances had been of not falling madly in love with the big brute.

If it was her house, she was going to enjoy christening each and every part of it with her fiancé. And there was no time like the present.

Chapter Twenty

It wasn't the wedding she'd thought she would have.

Nahh, she had to be honest—dreaming of weddings had never been a part of her agenda. Other girls might have pored over catalogs and imagined lofty cathedral settings. She'd wondered if she'd ever get married, because matrimony wasn't a deep desire of hers.

Love was what she wanted, far more than the trappings of the occasion.

Although, in a kind of "ode to bear timing", blessed by Caroline's organizational skills and aided by Tyler's money, the trappings had come together in only three days.

As she and Evan finished the long, slow walk to the front of the room, as she pulled away from Evan's unexpected farewell kiss, she turned to discover Tyler stood only inches away from her. Heat poured from him, wrapping around her and protecting her from more than the cold of the world.

He would always ask her what she *really* wanted. With a smile on his face as he waited for her to decide.

Tyler had lost his smile, though, as he examined Evan coolly. "Good friends who don't *ever* kiss from here on. Just so we're clear."

With his usual *laissez-faire*, Evan shrugged. "No problem.

Got it."

Tyler stared him down. Nodded. Then shifted his gaze to meet Caroline's. "You ready?"

He held out his arm, elbow raised high. She pulled herself together once more, and rested her hand on his tuxedo-clad arm. Left Evan standing behind as she and Tyler walked up the short flight to the dais. Left her old life behind.

Emotions of panic had no place in this. What she'd done, she'd done for love. Tyler stood beside her as they repeated the words they'd picked for the ceremony. Simple and short. Vows to cherish each other. To be there for each other.

He was slipping another ring on her finger far sooner than she expected as a buzz began in her ears, the murmur of wolf and human voices rising to fill the hall. People she'd known her entire life all smiling and enjoying her good fortune.

The bears watching? Out of the corner of her eye she saw some pleased expressions, some unreadable. The only face she was completely surprised to see was Ainsworth, three rows back flanked by Nadia and her guard.

The shock was forgotten in a wave of happiness as she spotted Amanda safely in the front row, Justin at her side.

A throat cleared and Caroline's attention snapped back to the woman leading the ceremony. She'd missed something. "What's that?"

The justice of the peace smiled. "Do you have a ring for Tyler?"

"Oh, yes." She reached into her bodice, smirking as Tyler's eyes widened.

He whispered. "You did not..."

Caroline held out her hand, the heavy weight of the diamond cluster he'd already slipped on her ring finger unfamiliar and yet right. Definitely there, making her aware something had changed.

Tyler eyed her warily, but she slipped the shiny silver cooking decoration over his knuckle, keeping her expression serene. “I bought a caseload. So when you break them, you'll have spares.”

Lillie and Jim Halcyon met them at the doors following the service. Lillie hugged Caroline tight, then handed over an envelope. “The final count was a joke. Most of Clan Ainsworth took off the night before the vote.”

Jim lowered his voice and leaned in close. “I heard they're trying their best to distance themselves, and their finances, while we still have him here under surveillance.”

Tyler chuckled evilly. “Well, let's make sure they have enough time to prove their real colours before Caroline and I go check things out. Ainsworth is staying as a guest here in Whitehorse until we're back from our honeymoon, Nadia babysitting him. Once we return we'll accompany him home and start guiding changes.”

It wasn't as bloodthirsty a justice as Caroline would have liked, but it would have to do.

A wedding dinner followed, bears and wolves filling the banquet hall at the Moonshine Inn. There was no fighting. Caroline almost felt not herself, surrounded by shifters and yet no simmering violence to have to put down.

The only destruction caused at the wedding dance was when Evan rushed into the room, all his earlier fooling around vanished. He knocked over a table covered with small desserts, darting out and looking around frantically. Staff rushed to clean it up, as Evan ignored the mess and stomped straight across the dance floor. He tapped on her shoulder, interrupting what was supposed to be her and Tyler's final dance before they snuck away.

"Caroline, I need your help."

Tyler refused to let her go, and she refused to stop dancing, so Evan slipped an arm around both of them and joined in, light on his feet in spite of the panic on his face.

Tyler grumbled softly. "Find someone else to put out your fire. She's mine now."

Caroline shivered at the possessiveness of his words. She definitely liked getting to decide what she wanted. But sometimes what she wanted? Was a big, growly, domineering bear who knew how to listen.

Evan snarled at Tyler, two Alphas refusing to give an inch. Then Tyler laughed and let go of Caroline as he dipped Evan toward the floor, sheer shock twisting the wolf's face.

Tyler snapped him back to vertical, twirled Evan away, and without skipping a beat, slipped his arms around Caroline to finish the dance.

Caroline was going to die.

Evan turned his most beguiling smile on Caroline as he wandered like a puppy at their side. "I opened an email attachment, and suddenly the computer is frozen. I can't get at the bank accounts, so the bill payments have gone to hell. And somehow it transferred to the hotel computer as well and all the bookings for the hotel are fucked up."

Oh dear.

Caroline stared over the short distance separating herself from her husband. They had his private plane arranged to take them for a honeymoon before returning to the work of leading conclave. *Somewhere warm* was all Tyler had told her.

While she felt bad for Evan, the beach was calling. Everyone had to take the steps and learn to do it themselves at sometime, righty?

Caroline patted Evan's cheek. "Don't open email attachments from people you don't know. It's a very simple rule. On the desk, right-hand side, there's a file folder with all the names of the companies the pack and the hotel use on a regular basis. The computer-repair company is there. You'll have to contact them to get things debugged."

Evan let go and stepped back. He straightened his collar, and the calm, cool, in-charge-of-everything Alpha was back. He sent out a warning glance at the pack members who'd started whispering.

A whole lot of wolves suddenly found things to do.

Evan rolled his eyes. "Yeah, I guess I have to learn to live without you. Caroline, Tyler. May the spirits of the north always guide you home."

He gave a quick nod to Tyler, squeezed Caroline's shoulder. Then he was gone, the dynamic wolf who had so much to look forward to. Like finding his mate.

Falling in love...

"You ready to go?" Tyler's lips brushed her ear. She would have stumbled if his arms hadn't been around her.

"Ready. For anything." Including something that had been on her bucket list for a while. "So tell me, Tyler, how big a plane do you own?"

He led her from the floor, waving at well-wishers, laughing as shifters and humans blew soap bubbles into their path in lieu of confetti. Ducking as a few misguided souls used water pistols. "It's big enough. Is this some kind of wolf-humour size-joke I'm not getting?"

She stopped to hug Shelley and Chase, promising to keep in touch. Then she slipped into the limo and waited for her husband to join her.

Tyler had barely settled when she crawled into his lap. While his eyes lit up, his words said otherwise. “Caroline, it’s a really short trip to the airport.”

“Consider this foreplay.” She kissed him into silence and was rather proud that by the time they pulled up next to the plane, his pristine suit was more than a little rumpled.

He guided her into the aircraft, his palm hot against her lower back. “Is it big enough for you?” he asked, still husky with lust.

She left him to explore, a sigh of contentment rushing out as she found what she was hoping for. She hung on to the door and grinned at Tyler.

He was at her side in a flash, staring in at the bedroom. “I should have known. Mile-high club?”

“Once over every continent?”

“*Ohhh*, nice. I love a challenge.” He tumbled her onto the bed and nuzzled the sweet spot under her ear. “I love *you*.”

Sunshine beckoned, a remote paradise without any shifter politics to play. But right now, Caroline had a bear to cuddle.

All was right with her world.

About the Author

Vivian Arend in one word: *Adventurous*. In a sentence: *Willing to try just about anything once*. That wide-eyed attitude has taken her around North America, through parts of Europe, and into Central and South America, often with no running water.

Her optimistic outlook also meant that when challenged to write a book, she gave it a shot, and discovered creating worlds to play in was nearly as addictive as traveling the real one. Now a *New York Times* and *USA Today* bestselling author of both contemporary and paranormal stories, Vivian continues to explore, write and otherwise keep herself well entertained.

Website: http://www.vivianarend.com

Blog: http://www.vivianarend.com/blog

Twitter: http://www.twitter.com/VivianArend

Facebook: http://www.facebook.com/VivianArend

CPSIA information can be obtained at www.ICGtesting.com
Printed in the USA
LVOW06s2353210414

382669LV00003B/289/P